OUT OF BODY,
OUT OF MIND

Ruth Brandon
OUT OF BODY, OUT OF MIND

St. Martin's Press
New York

Library of Congress Cataloging-in-Publication Data

Brandon, Ruth.
        Out of body, out of mind.

        I. Title.
PS3552.R31609   1987   813'.54   87-16363
ISBN 0-312-01076-1

First published in Great Britain by Macmillan London Limited.

First U.S. Edition

10 9 8 7 6 5 4 3 2 1

OUT OF BODY, OUT OF MIND

1

Who would get the Cherfassian Chair?

There had been speculation for some weeks now. Paragraphs appeared from time to time in the papers, giving details of the bequest, and of the trustees' search to find a university that would accept the Chair on satisfactory terms. For although universities, in these straitened times, would accept almost any conditions if the upshot was to be a large sum of money and the establishment of a new chair, many of them did seem to draw the line at Psychic Studies. The Cherfassian Chair was proving unexpectedly hard to place.

Everyone, of course, had heard of Rudolf Cherfassian. Starting, as one might expect of an Armenian, in carpets, he had made not only an additional fortune but also a name with his series of best-selling books on the numinous forces which (according to Cherfassian) control every aspect of our lives. These books, selling in their millions, were never reviewed in the literary periodicals except occasionally in terms of outrage and amused contempt. Cherfassian, holding the thirty-eighth paperback edition in the fifteenth language of his tenth book, had the last laugh.

The spirits, although they brought him fortune, had not blessed him with family accord. After twenty years of marriage he divorced his wife, a devout woman, paying her off with a large slice of the spirits' earnings. She abhorred the provenance but, as he observed at the time, accepted the substance willingly enough. He could not tolerate his only son, who despised both carpets and cheap best-sellers. On his death, therefore, one of the universities of his adopted country was to benefit to the tune of a chair endowed with the entire substantial Cherfassian fortune.

Oxford was not short of endowments and turned the thing down flat. Cambridge, having only recently felt able to swallow sociology as a received discipline, could not bring itself to digest Psychic Studies. Up and down the country, psychology departments considered the proposition, sighed wistfully over the sums involved and emerged from the debate with a clear conscience and a light purse. The Cherfassian Chair of Psychic Studies finally found a home at the University of London. In the nineteenth century this university had been the first to embrace agnosticism and to divorce learning from religion; in the twentieth (so the reasoning went) it should show itself no less open-minded. The Chair was placed. Now all that was needed was a professorial bottom to fill it.

2

Jasper Hodgkin swallowed nervously as he entered the conference room where the Professorial Board was sitting. He was immediately annoyed with himself. For one thing, why should he be nervous? If anyone was a strong candidate for the Chair, surely he was. By training an experimental psychologist, he had the previous year published an article describing ex-

6

perimental work with monkeys which seemed conclusively to indicate some sort of telepathic communication leading to behaviour modification. He hoped soon to extend this work to other species, including human beings. It seemed as if this might be the breakthrough the psychic world had been waiting for – the definitive proof of the existence of mind as an entity apart from the body. As a result of this discovery he was constantly being invited to America to address ashrams on the West Coast and parapsychology seminars throughout the Midwest, and to participate in television programmes examining the limits of thought. He had recently even been invited to take part in *Any Questions*.

Why should such a person feel nervous in front of a load of more or less obscure academics? And why, even if he felt nervous, could he not control the physical signs of this? He glanced casually at the members of the board and settled in the chair they indicated. John Ashwin, at the end of the row to his left, looked down at a sheaf of papers and raised his gaze coldly. Jasper leaned back. Ashwin, the professor of psychology, had never liked him – thought him too bumptious by half even when he was engaged in the perfectly orthodox dissection of monkeys' brains – and now felt amply confirmed in his distrust.

'Telepathy in monkeys?' he was reported to have exclaimed on hearing Jasper's news. 'I always understood that it was supposed to be a function of the highest centres of the brain – supposing it to exist at all, which I have always taken to be the biggest *if* of all. Perhaps it simply confirms my suspicion that Hodgkin is more closely related to the apes than he might have wished one to think.'

'And what do you feel you would bring to this chair, Dr Hodgkin?' Ashwin now blandly asked.

Jasper bit back a number of remarks that occurred to him and launched instead into the expected catalogue: exciting new paths to explore, following the clues, keeping an open mind, the limits of scepticism. He did not mention the reason uppermost in his own mind – namely, that he needed a tenured post. The research councils were unlikely to go on funding him indefinitely. Not only was he becoming too expensive, but they were packed with people like Ashwin; what appealed to ashrams did not appeal to Ashwin.

At the end of his list there was a silence. He felt a weight of hostility spilling over from the other side of the table. Those who were not distrustful were simply envious. To the psychologists he was a traitor, to the parapsychologists an upstart outsider whom they were unfortunately unable to ignore. Padvaiskas, who had been conducting experiments on remote sensing in cats for many years, wanted to know why he had suddenly become interested in this field. Padvaiskas spoke very slowly, as if, like Frankenstein's monster, he was worked by a sort of inefficient clockwork. He had dandruff on his collar. Jasper fingered his cravat and forced himself not to look down at his silk shirt; if he didn't get this job, that would be the last one for some time. And it did not look as if he was going to get this job.

Only Jerry Costigan seemed at all sympathetic. And why not? Costigan, too, had had his successes. He had started out in nuclear physics, had moved via quantum particles to psi, and had published a triumphant paper in *Natural Science* describing his famous series of experiments in remote viewing. Like Jasper, he seemed to have breached the nebulous but formidable frontier between conjecture and fact; for what was fact enough for *Natural Science* was (or should be) fact enough for anyone. He sat at the far end of the table from Ashwin, in a bright cream suit and orange striped silk tie, as remote as he could be from the shabby sports jackets and pipe-puffers of academia.

'Tell us more about your work with monkeys,' Costigan now said encouragingly. Jasper did so, careful to keep his recital as dry as possible.

At the end of this a lady in tweeds who had been introduced as the secretary of the Cherfassian Foundation said, 'You sound as though you are apologising for your work, Dr Hodgkin. The holder of the Cherfassian Chair must be scientific, of course, but there is no need for him or her to be ashamed of the subject. On the contrary.'

It was at this point that Jasper stopped worrying, or even thinking, about the Cherfassian Chair. Whoever was going to get it, he recognised that he was not. Between dislike of the whole business and resentment at the intrusion of scientific standards, he didn't stand a chance. As for his being famous, fame is not necessarily an asset in the academic world. Who was likely to resist the opportunity to put him in his place, given a chance? Not, at any rate, the people on the other side of this particular table.

3

Ever since the interview, therefore, Jasper had been in a bad temper. He was sure he hadn't got the job – 'Not', he explained, 'because I'm not the best, but because I am. They hadn't a single other person there worth anything, academically.'

'So why won't you get it?' asked Becky Ryan, his research assistant.

'Ashwin,' he replied laconically. 'Promised he'd resign if they gave it to me.'

'And isn't there anyone who'd resign if they don't give it to you?'

'In the academic world,' he said gloomily, 'no one cares that much about anyone who isn't themselves. So be warned.' And he returned without enthusiasm to the experiment in hand.

There was nothing here that the lady from the Cherfassian Foundation would have recognised as having anything to do with the paranormal. On the contrary, the whole scene was almost distressingly clinical. Jasper was presently conducting a series of experiments involving sensory deprivation. The subject lay on a bed in a small windowless room, shielded from outside noise and temperature variation. The subject was blindfolded, and white noise played into the room. The person conducting the experiment then attempted to 'send' an image randomly selected from a number of photographs; the 'receiver' meanwhile was encouraged to describe everything that went through his or her mind. Something approximating to the experimenter's image counted as a hit. After the experiment, the subject and experimenter went through the evidence together assessing hits (if any) and misses.

Becky concentrated on the picture of an alp, a postcard someone had sent from Switzerland. Peaks of snow glistened against an aggressively blue sky; at the bottom of the mountain, green fields sloped to a lake. After a while the voice of the subject came haltingly through.

'A man . . . middle height, reddish hair . . . walking along a road . . . seems to be walking a dog . . . I get sunshine, warm sunshine . . .'

'Sounds like Costigan,' Jasper said.

'Doesn't sound like the picture,' Becky said. 'Monkeys may do it, but humans don't. Shall we call it a day?'

'As you like. I'm going out. Can't concentrate on anything.' Jasper walked moodily out of the control cubicle.

Becky watched the door close behind him. She had, she reflected crossly, at least as much to feel gloomy about as Jasper did. Either he would get the job, and leave, or he would not, and would (if the present mood persisted) merely leave the field. And what, thought Becky, thus proving the correctness of Jasper's perception of priorities in academic life, shall I do then?

Everyone needs a helping hand – none more so than young academics struggling to find a foothold on the icy and underfunded slopes of British university life. Jasper Hodgkin had extended such a hand to Becky Ryan early in her career. The world at large had noticed this and assumed, as the world will, that the reason for this was not far to seek. There could be no two reasons why one might wish to take up with Becky. Becky was luscious. Her hour-glass figure and long golden hair could not fail to impress; and with such attributes, what did intellect matter? It was generally assumed that even if Becky was not deficient in this quality (if she were, why seek an academic career?) neither was she especially generously endowed with it. But given her other endowments, what did this matter?

The world, however, in this as in so much else, was wrong. Luscious Becky might be, but Jasper did not incline towards lushness; if anything, it embarrassed him. Becky, as far as he was concerned, had other qualities. She was patient; she was meticulous; she did not perceive herself as being in competition with him,

11

so that her occasional *aperçus* were in no way threatening and might often point the way out of an impasse. Above all she was unquenchably eager to prove the possibilities of psi, and thus ideally suited to conduct those excruciatingly boring experiments whose endless repetition was, it appeared, the only key to success. Boredom did not suit Jasper. He preferred to draw conclusions. When, after the monkey triumph, he decided to try some *Ganzfeld* experiments, Becky proved the ideal partner. They had published some papers together, but the next big breakthrough had so far eluded them.

Becky sighed and switched off the white noise, the video, the tape-recorder and the cubicle heating. She informed the subject that she was coming in to release him and went in to remove the blindfold. No need to go over the findings; there had been no hits today. The subject, a second-year student, left, pocketing his money.

Becky glanced round once again. She was just about to switch off the lights and go when the telephone rang.

'Experimental psychology.'

'I wanted to speak to Dr Jasper Hodgkin,' said a man's voice. 'Is this the right number?'

'It is, but he's just left. Is it important?'

'Possibly,' said the voice coldly. 'Are you his secretary?'

'No,' said Becky equally coldly. 'Do you want to leave a message?'

'Tell him Costigan rang,' said the voice, sounding unabashed, and rang off.

Well, thought Becky. What now? Costigan. That was presumably Jerry Costigan, who (hadn't Jasper said?) had been his friend on the board. Did that mean he'd got the professorship? It was anyway surely

12

something to do with the professorship. Better find Jasper. Costigan hadn't left a number, but that wasn't her worry.

It was a lovely early summer evening. Exam weather: the end of May, when all students not actually immured in the examination hall must spend their time revising, is invariably hot, blue and tempting. The brilliant green of young foliage, daisied lawns and early roses removed the bleakness even from East Midlands University. What a lovely place it must once have been, thought Becky, little hedge-rowed fields, coppices and streams, till it got red-bricked and landscaped. EMU had been built on what was known as a 'greenfield' site, around what was once a pretty little manor house. The heart of England.

Where would Jasper be? Drinking in the beauties of nature? More likely the bar. But he was not there, and had not been there, the regular drinkers assured her. The George and Dragon, then – a dingy pub in the nearby village not much frequented by the university and therefore favoured by Jasper. It was a quarter to six; the place should be open. Becky retrieved her bike from the psychology labs and set off, her dress and hair billowing behind her.

The summer did not penetrate the George and Dragon. Within, it was brown and dark and beer-smelling, benches round three sides of a room in the public bar, musty plush in the saloon. Alone on the musty plush, every limb expressing world-weariness, pale face Byronically in profile, Jasper Hodgkin lan-guished.

He glanced up unenthusiastically as Becky entered. 'To what do I owe this? Coincidence?'

'Clairvoyance.'

'Spare me, just today. Were you looking for me? If so, why? I'm rotten company.'

13

'Who's arguing? Costigan rang. I thought it might be important.'

'So you came racing to find me.' He lay back, apparently unmoved. Excitement was not Jasper's mode. 'Think,' he went on, 'if we were only my monkeys, how convenient telepathy might be on occasions such as this. You would be saved a bike ride. I could preserve my solitude.'

'Unfortunately we're not monkeys, and telepathy didn't seem to be working very well in humans today.'

'How ungrateful I am, aren't I?' said Jasper. 'What did he want? Was he offering me the professorship?'

'Didn't say.'

'Did he leave a number?'

'No.'

'Don't get cross, Becky. I'm sorry. I'm feeling piggish. Have a drink. D'you think Costigan believes in clairvoyance? What was his thing? Remote viewing, wasn't it?'

'I think so. Something like that. Anyway,' said Becky, 'I've got to go.'

'Quite right,' said Jasper. 'You don't want to waste an evening like this in this ghastly place with me.'

'No,' said Becky, 'I don't.' As she cycled off, she began to wonder whether other fields might not interest her more than the unrewarding expanses of parapsychology.

4

Jasper left the George and Dragon soon after Becky, got into his car and drove to the office. Very few people were around. The laboratory staff had gone home; the students were eating. On this balmy evening the experimental psychology labs, housed in what had once been intended as a temporary hut, seemed singularly unattractive. Jasper glanced through his address book. Presumably Costigan had intended him to call back. He had a number against Costigan's name, though whether it was for home or work, or what work Costigan was doing nowadays, he did not know. He dialled it anyway, and got a recorded message giving an alternative number where Costigan might be found. He dialled this; the now familiar voice replied.

'Jerry, this is Jasper Hodgkin. I believe you called?'

'Ah, Jasper,' Costigan drawled. 'Glad you called back. No doubt you'll be anxious to hear about the Cherfassian Chair.'

'Of course.'

'Well, you haven't got it.'

'That doesn't entirely surprise me.' Jasper was never one to be upstaged. 'I heard that Ashwin threatened to resign if they offered me it.'

'That's about it. Some of us thought you should have had it, but there you are.'

'Old feuds die hard. He always was an ungenerous fellow.'

'What will you do now? Go on with . . . *Ganzfeld* work, was it?'

'I suppose so. I'm finding it a bit tedious, I must confess. But that's parascience for you. The more tedious, the more acceptable.'

'That's true,' agreed Costigan, 'and it would have stayed true if you'd got the professorship. So. Look, I may have a proposition for you. Come and see me.'

At twelve next morning, then, Jasper Hodgkin walked briskly past the base of the Telecom Tower and turned into Fitzroy Square, glittering in the midday sun. 'Another wonderful day,' went the conversations all around him on the train, 'what a waste to spend it in London.' Not, however, as far as Jasper was concerned. East Midlands University was enough to sate anyone with the countryside. He glanced at the piece of paper on which he had noted Costigan's address. No. 83. Over the other side.

The elegant houses, once inelegantly decayed, had recently been restored, and the square itself cobbled and pedestrianised. Costigan's office occupied the ground floor of No. 83. Not much sign of university cuts here, Jasper reflected as his feet sank into thick cream pile and his fingers left prints on mirror-polished brass. There was a brass plate on the door: COSTIGAN FUTURES. Not the university – that explained it. What, then? Jasper had no idea what it was that Costigan did. He certainly had been in a university once: nuclear physics is hardly a pursuit for a country gentleman. As for the remote viewing – surely that, too, had been conducted under academic auspices? Nothing could have been more academic than the articles giving accounts of it.

Nothing, however, could be less academic than these present surroundings. An exquisite black receptionist led him to a half-open door through which Costigan could be glimpsed, his feet on the desk, in his shirt sleeves with loosened tie, red hair flaming against the window, smoking a large cigar.

'Jasper,' he said, his soft Irish voice positively burgeoning with welcome. 'Delightful to see you, my dear fellow. Come in. Sit down.' He indicated a large leather armchair, into which Jasper sank while the door clicked discreetly shut behind him.

'Cigar?' said Costigan.

'No thanks.'

There was a silence. Faced with this unnaturally warm welcome, Jasper felt suspicious.

'Goodness,' said Costigan, 'you are laid back. You make me feel quite nervous. God knows the effect you have on poor old Ashwin. Aren't you a teeny bit curious as to why I asked you down here? Do you have any idea what it is I do?'

'Not the slightest,' said Jasper, 'and of course I'm curious. I assume you're going to tell me. Isn't that why you asked me here? I assume', he added, looking around, 'that you're no longer an academic.'

'True.' Costigan drew luxuriously on his cigar.

'Costigan Futures,' mused Jasper. 'It might be cocoa or it might be clairvoyance. Frankly I wouldn't have thought clairvoyance could keep up this style.'

'Ah, but think if you combined the two!' The cigar twirled, describing smoke rings in the air. 'Cocoa *and* clairvoyance. Except that it isn't exactly cocoa.'

'Sounds amazing.'

'Oh, it is. But logical, my dear chap. Just consider it. What's business about? Prediction. Predicting future demand. Anyone who could do that with certainty would make a fortune, whether it's publishing or hats. Isn't that so? Of course it is. Now.

17

Why do chaps like you and I prefer the life of the mind?'

'There are various reasons.'

'Of course. Primarily, because that's what we're good at, so that's what we enjoy. Some people are good at carpentry, some people are good at thinking. That's where we feel comfortable. But not for the money – I'm sure you'll agree about that.'

'It's a reasonable living.'

'So it is, and congenial company. But – I've often thought – it's also a question of laziness. Don't you think? Business is a hassle. It means beating up suppliers and getting things done and delivered – all the time, not the odd research proposal. It's boring. Lucrative perhaps, but boring.'

'Academic company isn't that congenial in my experience,' said Jasper. 'That selection board was enough to make me quit academic life altogether. I felt every single person there except you hated me and wanted to see me down for a different reason. I never felt such a concentration of venom. That frightful woman. That nasty little Ashwin.'

Costigan removed his feet from the desk and leaned forward. 'Look, let's stop beating about the bush.' He ground out the cigar and threw the butt out of the open window behind him. 'I'm frankly no more interested in the nuts and bolts of supply and demand than you are – at least, I assume you aren't. But I am interested in prediction; and over the course of the past few years' work I think I've sorted out some people who are pretty good at it. So I was thinking to myself: how can I use this? After all, I must be able to use it somehow. Now, where does sheer prediction come in handy?'

'The racecourse,' said Jasper, feeling that an answer was expected of him.

18

'Well, that's true enough. That's certainly what Lord Kilbracken found.'

'In *Experiment with Time*?' said Jasper, referring to Dunne's famous book. 'Have you been having prophetic dreams, then?'

Costigan shook his head impatiently. 'I'm not talking about leaving things to chance. Business isn't about chance. No, what I'm talking about is the stock market. Futures. It's obvious. What to buy and what to sell.'

Jasper raised an eyebrow. 'And have you made your million yet?'

Costigan shook his head impatiently. 'That's what I mean. Typical academic attitude. The answer to your question is yes.' He stopped short and looked aggressively at Jasper.

'What I don't see is where I come in.' Jasper uncrossed his legs and crossed them again the other way round. 'I mean, here you are, you and your trained clairvoyants – is that what it is? – predicting away and making millions. But I can't do any of that. I'm merely a theorist, a toiler in the *Ganzfeld*. . . .' His voice petered out languidly.

Costigan said, 'You have a lot to find out about business, Jasper. Business is about confidence. In our field it takes a lot to establish that. I did it with those *Natural Science* articles. They established me as serious. You did it with your monkeys.'

'My monkeys are hardly, what's the word, bankable.'

'Not here, because everybody distrusts strange theories. People think you're a crank, and people don't like trusting cranks with their money. But how many times have you been invited to the States since you published?'

'Lost count,' agreed Jasper. 'They specially like me

19

around Big Sur and Northern California. Southern California, too.'

'That's what I mean. And those people have money.' Costigan waved away Jasper's objection. 'Come out for some lunch and we'll discuss the setting up of Costigan Futures Inc.'

5

'He wants me to go next week,' said Jasper.

He was sitting behind the desk in his office, facing Becky, who was stiffly upright in the office armchair opposite. The scene, he reflected, might have been a parody of the one enacted in Costigan's office the day before, arranged expressly to point up the difference between what he had and what was on offer. Jasper's office was a cubicle, not very satisfactorily sound-proofed, one of a row of identical cubicles ranged along the first floor of the psychology building. Grey vinyl tiles lined the corridor outside and were to be seen protruding round the edges of the kelim rugs with which Jasper had covered the floor. A window looked out on to lawns and covered walkways. The desk was made of some anonymous light wood, and the armchair was one of that uncomfortable variety with curved wooden arms sold in enormous quantities to institutions in the nineteen-fifties and sixties. There were too many books for the bookshelves and too many papers for the desk, whose phone bore the motto: *No outside calls between 8.30 a.m. and 1 p.m.*

'Why the rush?' said Becky. 'I can see it's irresistible, of course.'

'Well, it is rather interesting.'

20

'What does he want you to do exactly?'

'I believe there's quite a variety of different things,' said Jasper evasively. 'First of all I've got to get acquainted with the operation here, of course.'

'Of course.' Becky looked depressed. 'And what about the operation *here*?'

'Sensory deprivation, you mean?'

'That's what I mean, yes.'

'Well, my dear girl—'

'I am not your dear girl.'

'Don't hold it against me.'

'I don't. But do answer my question.'

'Can't you go on with it? You don't really need me at all.'

'But we're just about to put in a new research proposal,' Becky wailed. 'You're the investigator. Remember?'

'Becky, I'm not going to outer space,' said Jasper patiently. 'Only to the USA. And not for ever. There are aeroplanes . . . and letters . . . and telephones. Be realistic.'

'I am,' said Becky grimly. 'The rat deserts the ship and tells the sailors to be realistic. Why does he want you, anyway? Aren't there enough Americans in America? The place is swarming with parapsychologists.'

Jasper looked down and rocked his chair back on its hind legs. 'Well, how can I put it?' Costigan's words echoed in his head, balm to the soul, however much the higher faculties might want to deny such vanity.

'The fact is, Jasper,' Costigan had said, 'you've got glamour. You hit something really new, like the double helix or evolution.'

'Well, Jerry, it's very kind of you to say so, but really—'

'The fact that it's not strictly relevant to Futures

21

business is neither here nor there. It's the right area, and it'll bring in the customers. But I want you soon, before people have begun to forget about you. This sensory deprivation stuff isn't going to draw anyone much.'

'I'm sorry about that—'

'No one wants to know about slog, slog, slog, they just want results – glamour. And if possible, scientifically attested. Not too mad. You've got it all. And you look right – so British. You couldn't be anything else. I bet you wow them in the ashrams.'

Now Jasper faced Becky across the table. 'That's the way it is, love. That's all there is to it. Be honest. You'd do the same thing if you were me.'

'Oh, I expect I would.' Becky got up and went over to the window. 'But it's very depressing. Just look at this place. I only came here because of you, and it's bad enough even when you're here. What's it going to be like when you're gone?'

'I promise you,' said Jasper, 'if I do half what Costigan assures me I shall do, I'll ship you over on the proceeds and you'll be my personal assistant. And if I don't—'

'If you don't?'

'Then I'll be right back here, and all will continue as before.'

6

It was generally assumed by those who gave it a thought – colleagues, acquaintances, people who had designs on Becky and those, fewer in number, who had designs on Jasper – that there was 'something'

22

between the two. More than that no one could have said. Certainly they did not live together. Becky had a very small cottage, thatched and beamed, poky but picturesque, in a nearby village. It was out of the question that Jasper could have been living there with her. For one thing, the place was not large enough to hold them both; it was barely possible for Becky to entertain a dinner guest, let alone a live-in lover. Her bed occupied almost the entire bedroom, leaving a narrow corridor along two sides allowing the occupant or occupants to get in and out. It was a large bed, but nothing exceptional. What was exceptional was the small size of the larger bedroom. (The smaller one had been a cupboard until the previous owner had put in a dormer window.) Lying in bed, Becky could hear the birds scrabbling in the thatch above her head, an extremely loud noise that began very early in the morning. Like so much else in the cottage, this was charming but inconvenient. Occasionally little showers of dust would fall from cracks in the plaster on to the sheets and pillows. Even had their acquaintanceship got this far (which it had not) these surroundings would, as it happened, have spelt death to this particular romance, since Jasper suffered acutely from asthma, and thatch-dust and damp would have sent him into choking spasms. It was a circumstance on which he had commented more than once. 'If ever I suspected you of making passes at me, Becky,' he had mused once over dinner, 'the suspicion flew from my mind as soon as you bought this cottage. I think I should die, literally, if I had to spend a night here.'

'What a fate to contemplate.'

'Mm. "Kiss me, my love, for I am dying of thatch . . ." It's very Pre-Raphaelite, somehow, that, isn't it? What a suitable fate it would have been for someone like William Morris; not much question of it, though,

23

him being so hale and hearty. . . .'

Jasper himself lived in a small modern house near the university, featureless but dust-free. Wherever his considerable personality might have made its mark, it was not in his house. Unexceptionably furnished from Habitat and local junk shops, almost its sole distinguishing feature was the grand piano which occupied most of the living room, leaving space only for an armchair, a reading-lamp and a small table. Jasper spent little time in this house. When he was not travelling he was working. Even his books were not visible, being either in his office at the university or stacked in boxes. The contrast between this austere habitation and its colourful owner, with his dark curls, cravats and (what was it exactly, the subject he did?) Spiritualism (something like that?), was something of which Jasper was as conscious as his neighbours, and which afforded him considerable pleasure. Becky had rarely been to this house, since Jasper did not encourage visitors. Thus, although it offered a spacious setting ideal for romance, none (as far as she was aware) had ever flourished there.

Becky had by now known Jasper for some time. When they first met she had been a nervous psychology student and he had been her supervisor. He would sit in his room, icy in a Cambridge January, insulating the draughts which howled through the window frames by pouring water from teaspoons very slowly down the cracks, where it instantly froze and, layer by layer, built up an impermeable screen. While he did this, they would discuss the outer reaches of psychology, with which he was then interesting himself: functions, conscious and unconscious, of the brain, the ability to train secondary brain circuits to perform functions for which they were not generally used and other such topics.

Becky at twenty was singularly attractive. Her long, light hair was cut in a fringe low over her eyes and fell thickly around her shoulders. She was apple-cheeked and brown-eyed, with a wide, innocent smile and a gurgling laugh. The innocence might conceal a genuinely fresh vision (the opinion of those many who fell in love with her as she earnestly pursued psychology) or the brainlessness of the ur-ingénue (the opinion of most of the rest). Becky, however, was concerned with other things. One evening, after smoking a very great deal of hash, she had experienced an extraordinary . . . well, what was it? Was it a dream, or something more tangible than that? For some hours she had, apparently, left her body, aware of it lying in her room, her friends stretched around her, while *something*, but something undeniably herself, had made extraordinary journeys, flying over forests and through doors, seeing into people's houses; and all the while her bodily self, the one lying there, was describing the details of this journey.

The thing had undoubtedly occurred; her friends could testify to that. But what was it? What was the nature of this thing that had happened to her? It was this that had first drawn her to Jasper, one of the few people genuinely interested in this field of enquiry.

Of course, the attraction had other foundations as well. Jasper fulfilled the romantic ideal in many respects – in looks, conversation (intellectual, but with an endearing relish for the small detail of everyday life), interests (music and parapsychology) and unattainability. For Becky, accustomed to the easy enslavement of any man she happened to fancy, this last was perhaps almost the most important. Everyone, and almost everything about Jasper himself, assured her that it was genuine: the fact being that he was simply uninterested in women. But Becky refused to believe this, or at any rate to believe it in relation to herself. Even should the fact be that he had heretofore slept only with men, why should she not introduce him to new fields of sensuality? A friend of hers had once described a similar endeavour, when she had persuaded a man hitherto exclusively gay to risk her bed. She had done it, she said, by addressing him thus: 'You enjoy masturbation, right? Well, think of this as masturbation, but sort of all round at the same time.' This had apparently succeeded in the friend's case, but Becky, picturing the scene, could not imagine this imagery having an electrifying effect upon Jasper. She could not, however, be sure, never having quite nerved herself to try it.

Even in the cottage, with all its inconveniences, she did not lack lovers. Generally she preferred to confine herself to married men, her reasoning being that she did not wish to get married, or not at the moment; that these men would almost certainly be having affairs whether or not she personally was on the scene; and that the situation was therefore ideal for all participants – for Becky, since there would be no question of being urged to form a permanent attachment when she had no wish to do so; for the man, since the last thing she would do would be to nag him to divorce his wife; and for the wife herself, since Becky presented no serious competition but was merely a ship passing in the night. Besides, if men of an age to be interesting were still unmarried, there had to be some definite drawback to them. As with Jasper.

So the years passed, and from being his nubile but (in that mode) unappreciated supervisee, Becky became Jasper's research assistant and close friend. She was unable to say how far her lack of enthusiasm for

26

marriage or otherwise permanent attachments was due to this friendship; and, although parents and friends muttered darkly, she could not be detached from it. For of one thing there is no doubt in this day and age. A young woman must earn a living, and, the job situation being what it is, should a suitable and interesting living present itself, she must grab it with both hands. At any rate, Becky's interest in Jasper had nourished powers of intellect undreamt of by any of her acquaintances hitherto – enough, indeed, to launch her into an undoubtedly academic career; though as to her field of enquiry, the less said, perhaps, the better.

7

9 East Wind
Venice Beach, LA
30 June

Dear Becky,
Well, here I am finally In Business on my own. Jerry C. flew out with me to introduce me to some people and explain how the set-up works. It's amazing what a difference backdrop makes. You can't imagine how outlandishly flash and brash he seemed in London, especially at the Professorial Board. (What a ludicrous charade – I gather they finally gave it to Openshaw, who has never actually got any results in his life but is a diligent toiler and only too ready to see three sides to any question. I told them I'd set myself a problem, like proving the reality of OOBs, and if

I hadn't got a satisfactory answer within five years, I'd resign and try something else. I bet Openshaw didn't say anything like that and I bet he stays there for twenty years and never discovers an interesting thing.)

But here, it's a curious mixture, everybody is both flash and at the same time so laid back that movement is barely discernible. It's a very different world from the ageing flower-children and mind-rot sufferers one tends to meet at ashrams. There are great lashings of money sloshing around, with no really apparent source – it's just there. You just need to make yourself into the right sort of sponge and soak it up. A great deal of consultancy goes on around here, I believe, and it's all extremely expensive, so up to a point I suppose people take in each other's problems. Then there's a lot of expertise on abstruse and convoluted forms of technology. Well, I suppose what Costigan Futures Inc. does is a form of consultancy. People come to us, they want to make an investment, and naturally they want to know will the market move up or down. So we put them together with one of our people and they get an answer. We deal exclusively with tangible goods, because the clairvoyants have to be able to hold a sample of whatever the proposed investment is, to get a feel for it – silver, gold, coffee, bananas, you name it. We charge a fee plus a percentage of gains, so we stand or fall almost entirely on our success. Jerry's business in London is prospering on that basis, and I think ours will: we have some really good people. Here it's quite usual for people to subscribe to some investment newsletter, anyway, so I think a lot of people around here see us as a cooler, altogether more attuned way of handling investments. They really seem to like it.

Venice is a weird place. It used to be a line of shacks along the beach with a sort of swampy mess of canals behind with a few donkey-engines pumping up a bit of oil. You used to be able to live here really quite cheaply – I remember when I was a student coming to stay with some friends here in the days of incense sticks and wind chimes. Then rows of condominiums got built up along the beach and prices went up, and I suppose things just got too valuable for the swamps to stay, so they built up a great big prestigious place called Marina del Rey just behind, with thousands of flashy boats, and now it's one of the most expensive places you can imagine. Our office is in Marina del Rey, and I'm renting an apartment on the beach in Venice. You just walk out of the living-room window on to the veranda and jump over on to the beach. It's wonderful. I've already had a pair of espadrilles stolen from the veranda. You really must come out – you'd love it. It's a far cry from sensory deprivation at EMU, though a whole lot of that sort of work is going on around here of course. In fact there's a conference next October at Santa Barbara – why don't you come over?

Must get down to the office. I'll write again soon.

Love,

Jasper

This was the first and last letter Becky received from the new managing director of Costigan Futures Inc., LA.

8

For some weeks after receiving this letter, and despite receiving no other, Becky didn't worry too much. Jasper was no doubt busy, and so was she. She had decided, in preparation for the new research proposal, to move from the somewhat fruitless work she had been doing to some new studies of OOBs – out-of-body experiences, the same kind of thing which had originally drawn her to psi. So she was busy designing experiments and finding volunteers. In addition, she had just started an affair with a philosopher upon whom she had had her eye for some time: the departmental Reader, a tall man with a face like an extremely intelligent camel and a nice line in sardonic chat. 'I prefer serial monogamy,' he had explained to her. He was currently on his second wife, but was looking for a third. Becky felt no temptation to become what she felt sure would be merely one more in a line of discarded wives. He had, she reckoned, at least another three in him yet and she did not relish the thought of being referred to as 'my wife', in (no doubt) that very same tone of amused and bitter resignation, as he chatted up his potential No. 4. But he was undoubtedly sexy, which was another matter altogether, although he grumbled ceaselessly about her cottage, in which he could not stand up straight and into whose bedrooms – even the larger one – he could barely insert himself.

'I can see', he moaned as he hit his head for the third time on the way to the bathroom, 'that your future lovers will have to be dwarfs. You're not a dwarf,

Becky – why did a good-sized girl like you think of buying a dog kennel to live in?'

So the weeks passed, until the time came when the new research application had to be thought of. Becky might write the proposal, would clearly have to do so, in fact; but as the official investigator of the project, Jasper would at the very least have to append his signature. It was by now the third week of July, and the closing date for research applications was the fourth of August. Becky had written to East Wind Street and, receiving no reply, had written again. Still no reply. He had given a telephone number; she phoned it, but although she got what she was sure was a ringing tone, there was no answer from his apartment at any hour of the day or night.

Must be away on a trip, thought Becky, and she phoned Costigan Futures in London to ask them for the number of the Los Angeles office. Here she at least made contact. Thousands of miles away the phone was picked up and a soft voice said, 'Costigan Futures, can I help you?'

Becky said, 'I'm calling from England. May I speak to Jasper Hodgkin, please?'

'Oh,' said the voice, 'I'm sorry, Jasper's away on a trip. In fact I believe he should be in London right now. Why don't you call them there?'

Becky began to feel worried. However, it was now ten p.m., time differences between London and Los Angeles being what they are, and no one would be at the Costigan Futures office for another eleven hours.

At nine the next morning, having spent an uncharacteristically restless night, Becky called Costigan Futures once again.

'May I speak to Mr Costigan?'

'I don't know if he's in,' lied the voice at the other end. 'Who's that speaking please?'

'My name is Becky Ryan. I'm a colleague of Jasper Hodgkin, and I've got to get in touch with him rather urgently. I thought Mr Costigan might be able to help.'

'Didn't you call yesterday wanting the Los Angeles number?'

'They say they think he's in London.'

'Hold on,' said the voice. 'I'll try to put you through.'

'Costigan,' said a voice abruptly in Becky's ear.

Becky felt nervous. She was, after all, just a research assistant, and Jerry Costigan was a legendary name. Almost alone among parascientists he was taken seriously by 'real' science – seriously enough, at least, for his work to be published and discussed in a prestigious journal like *Natural Science*. As a particle physicist he had achieved some renown, and as a consequence in the world of psi his name resounded: another real scientist captured for the cause, a recruit to join the ranks of Sir Oliver Lodge, Lord Rayleigh, Professor Hasted, Professor Josephson and the rest. Becky's, on the other hand, did not resound – not yet, as she told herself angrily in moments of uncertainty. Such as this. But it would. It would.

'My name is Becky Ryan.'

'And what can I do for you, Miss Ryan? I understand it was something about Jasper Hodgkin you wanted to know?'

'Jasper. Yes. Well, I wanted to contact him rather urgently, and it's some time since I heard from him.'

'I'm afraid I can't answer for his shortcomings as a correspondent,' Costigan said smoothly.

'So I tried to phone him, at home and at the office. But he hasn't been there, and the Los Angeles office told me they thought he was in London. But I haven't heard from him, and I would have expected to. So I wondered if you could tell where he might be?'

Costigan said cagily, 'I wonder if you could tell me exactly what this is in connection with?'

'A research proposal. He's the investigator, officially at least, and I need his signature.' Halfway through this sentence Becky realised what is was Costigan probably had in mind. 'I am not a postulant girl-friend,' she said angrily, 'and if I were, it wouldn't be any business of yours.'

'My dear Miss Ryan – or is it Mrs Ryan? – nothing could be further from my mind,' lied Costigan cheerfully. 'Sorry if I seemed offensive. The truth is, Jasper has so many fans, I really can't think of another word for them, and some of them are quite mad. I suppose given the nature of our business it's only to be expected, but really, one has to be a little bit careful.'

'Was he here?'

'He was, but only for a day or so. I'm sorry if he didn't get in touch, but things are very busy, and I expect it just slipped his mind. As to where he is now, I'm afraid I can't help you. In the nature of our business we travel about a lot.'

'Oh, dear. I don't quite know what to do. The trouble is, the proposal's got to be in by the end of next week.'

'Ah.' There was a silence, then Costigan said, 'Look, why don't you come down. I might be able to help you.'

9

Although she couldn't quite see what would come of it, Becky agreed to go down to London next morning to Costigan's office. Why not? What, after all, was there to lose but time? And even had she been pressed for time, curiosity would probably have won out. So she caught the 8.23, contemplating with pleasure the next two hours of limbo, fortified against boredom with a detective story and the latest issue of *New Politics*.

Leafing through this, the word 'psi' caught her eye. It was a story by Andrew Taggart, the magazine's chief investigative reporter. Becky was mildly surprised. Taggart usually concerned himself with political affairs, and if there was one sure thing about her field of study it was that it had nothing to do with politics. So it was with a certain interest that she turned to the story.

The interest slackened somewhat when she discovered what it was about. A familiar experience when reading magazines, she found: the stories rarely lived up to the headlines. Then she noticed the name 'Costigan' and read on.

The story turned out to be about that old chestnut, the Pentagon's keen interest in the possibilities of telepathy and psychokinesis, and its willingness to devote large sums of money to the investigation of these effects. Becky was surprised; she thought that had been tried and abandoned years before. Hadn't there been something about secret experiments, failed and unmentioned, during one of the space shots? But apparently the Pentagon was not discouraged. If Taggart's story was to be believed, there was a sudden renewed interest in all this, surrounded by a high degree of secrecy and paranoia. Costigan's name, said Taggart, had been mentioned in this connection; readers of *New Politics* might be interested to know that he had recently gone into business and was reputed to be making large amounts of money – which, considering the nature of the business, was surprising.

Becky found it hard to concentrate on anything else for the remainder of the journey. What if this were true? Was Jasper part of it? Was he somehow caught up in some sort of military work? But even if he were, this surely would not debar him from any contact with the world outside? With questions such as these pounding through her brain, she left the train at Euston and made her way in a panic of curiosity over Euston Road to Fitzroy Square.

She had not considered how the question should be broached, and realised, with her finger on the doorbell, that this might not be the simplest manoeuvre in the world. But she need not have worried. As she entered the room carrying the detritus of the journey – jacket (the cool country morning had become, in the course of the journey, a warm urban one), bag, reading matter – Costigan's gaze fastened at once on the *New Politics* banner.

Almost as soon as she was seated and had accepted a cup of coffee, he said, 'I suppose you've been reading Andrew Taggart's rubbishy piece? What a little mischief-maker he is.'

'Yes. It's a coincidence, really. I don't read *New Politics* that often. On train journeys, mostly.'

'A pure figment of his imagination.' Costigan seemed

unnecessarily agitated, Becky thought.

She said, 'I suppose you'd have to say that even if it was true, wouldn't you?'

'Catch 22. There you are. It won't do my business any good. None at all. I really don't know why he should suddenly pick on me like this.'

He was hardly what she had been expecting. Exactly what that was it would have been hard to say, but this angry, red-haired Irishman in no way fitted her mental picture of a distinguished academic. As if he read her thoughts (and who could say? Perhaps he did), he suddenly pulled himself together and said, 'Sorry about this. I tend to get worked up about things, and it's of no possible interest to you. No, what I wanted to see was whether we couldn't work out some way of you getting your research proposal in. I know how important these things are, and I somehow feel responsible for spiriting Jasper away at no notice and leaving you in the lurch. Now, I'm still officially attached to London University. I wonder . . .' He spent the next hour discussing ways in which he could replace Jasper as her official investigator. 'After all, I know the way these things work. It'll be you doing all the work, that I'm sure of – whether Jasper was there or not, isn't that so? So it's just a matter of form.' When at one point Becky raised the question of whether it might not be simpler just to contact Jasper – surely this must, from time to time, be possible? – Costigan dismissed the idea at once. 'Not worth it, my dear. He's here, there and everywhere, and, I can tell you, he hasn't a moment to call his own just now. Not a second. So let's just leave him be, and I'll make it my business to get something through for you. Leave the proposal with me (you've got another copy, I assume?) and if you don't hear from me within a week, don't hesitate to get in touch and put a bomb under my

36

backside. I shall be here for the next fortnight, at least.'

The meeting was obviously at an end. Clearly thanks were in order, but Becky still felt curiously dissatisfied. It was lunchtime, but Costigan made no suggestion that they should lunch together. As she rose to go, he took a brochure from a pile on his desk and offered it to her. 'In case you should ever feel like using our services!' He smiled, shook her hand and showed her to the door.

10

Spilled out on to the London street, Becky felt overcome by blankness. It was often like this. She really looked forward to going to London for the day. She had been born there and lived there till the age of eighteen, and considered herself a Londoner. But it was no longer her city. She met people only by appointment, and then what? Art galleries, films, concerts – the usual tourist attractions. Or else an expensive afternoon shopping. The alternative was to take the next train and head north: an even more depressing prospect. She felt annoyed with Costigan. Dammit, one must eat, and why not in company? Well, perhaps he had a lunch date.

By this time she had emerged into Tottenham Court Road, lined with furniture stores and odd emporia festooned with Arab writing. What was it to be? If the dash home, turn left. If not, what? Habitat and expensive oddments she did not need? Dillon's, where she could never find the book she wanted? Liberty's and temptation? The South Bank and culture? She felt like none of these. She felt like doing something. But EMU was where she did things these days, and she did not want to go back there either.

She was still carrying her copy of *New Politics*, wrapped round with the Costigan Futures brochure. Suddenly she knew what she would do. Rejecting the smelly, noisy option of street phone booths she walked down to Heal's, where one could phone in cleanliness, and dialled the telephone number which appeared above the list of contents and contributors.

'*New Politics*.'

'I want to speak to Andrew Taggart, please.'

'Hang on and I'll see if he's there. Who shall I say is calling?'

'My name's Becky Ryan. He doesn't know me.'

'Taggart here.'

'Oh, Mr Taggart, I was ringing about your piece in today's issue.'

'About those loonies at the Pentagon?'

'Yes. The thing is, my colleague, Jasper Hodgkin—'

'The monkey telepathy chap?'

'That's right. Well, he's recently gone to work for Costigan, and I'm a bit worried.'

'Worried? Why?'

'Well – it's a bit complicated.'

'Can you come over? Are you in London? Why don't you come to the office?'

Becky glanced at the address. The magazine's offices were in Soho.

'I could be there in about twenty minutes.'

'OK, and we'll go out for a spot of lunch.'

Well, at any rate that was the lunch problem solved. Becky set off for Great James Street feeling much better. Whether anything would come of this she didn't know, but at least she was doing something.

The *New Politics* office occupied the first floor of a

dilapidated house. Inside, however, the place seemed convincing enough. The door opened into a cubbyhole occupied by a pretty Indian girl, who opened another door leading to a large room filled with desks and telephones and subdivided by filing cabinets. She pointed out a desk in a far corner where a pale, bearded figure was sitting. This, presumably, was Taggart. He waved, and Becky made her way across the office.

'Hello,' said Taggart, who on closer inspection turned out to be smallish, scruffily dressed in a crumpled shirt and old jeans, with a rather ragged beard and a cheerful, pale face. He did not look in the least intimidating, as she had somehow assumed he would. No doubt that was part of his technique; who would possibly feel afraid to talk to such a run-down figure? 'You must be the lady who phoned. I'm sorry, I didn't catch your name.'

'Becky Ryan. I don't think I ever told you.'

'It's nice of you to call round. Shall we go and get something to eat? Then we can talk.' He got up and led the way out again. Soon they were ensconced at the back of a shabby vegetarian restaurant. The place was almost empty, it being now a quarter to two, and they were some way from the nearest occupied table. 'OK,' said Taggart. 'You said it was complicated. So tell me all about it.'

Becky explained about Jasper's failure to land the Cherfassian Chair and his subsequent hurried departure for Costigan Futures. 'I wasn't totally surprised. I thought he was in a mood to move on. It was all too much of an anticlimax, just coming back to the daily grind at the lab, and this sounded, oh, all the things he'd want – well, anyone would,' said Becky loyally. 'Lots of money. Interesting. Glamorous. You know. But I did think he'd stay in touch. For one thing we'd known each other such a long time.'

'How long since you heard from him?'

'He wrote on June the thirtieth. Nearly a month now. I know it doesn't sound that long, but it's not like him. He's always so meticulous, and he knew there was this urgent thing to sign – he just doesn't forget things like that. Or people,' she added miserably.

'Were you . . . well, living together, or anything?'

'No. But we were friends and colleagues.'

'If I had a friend and colleague like you, I should soon try and put the whole thing on a less respectable basis.'

'Well . . . Jasper . . . he didn't. He didn't live with anyone.'

The conversation now took another tack, equally predictable. 'You mean to tell me you're really a parapsychologist? Is that the word?'

'Yes. Why not?'

'Oh, just another preconceived idea. You know, one has this idea of people involved in that sort of thing as . . . well, you know.'

'Nuts.'

'Nuts, the very word. But you seem so normal.'

'Well, I lead this normal, boring life, doing repetitive experiments in a normal, boring lab.'

'But how did you get into it?'

Becky explained about her trip out of her body and her meeting with Jasper. 'And now you can tell me a few things. What's behind all this Pentagon stuff? I know they used to be interested, but I thought they'd dropped it. What's Costigan got to do with it all?'

'I don't know, really,' Taggart said thoughtfully. 'When the Cherfassian Chair cropped up, I thought I'd keep an eye on that kind of stuff; it was in the news, in the air, you know the kind of thing. Anyway,

40

I have this contact in Washington, and he knows a whole lot of people. He tips me off about things, and he's often right. So I use a little drip of what he tells me to see if I can't start a hare. It often works – like this, for example.'

'I'm not really telling you anything.'

'Well, it all adds up. Costigan seemed worried, you said.'

'Absolutely beside himself. He said something about it ruining his business.'

'What is his business, exactly?' They unfolded the brochure. It was printed in black on silver, a simple A4 sheet folded in three. The outside said simply, COSTIGAN FUTURES. Inside, the potential investor was invited to take the uncertainty out of stock-market dealing.

'We predict the future of futures. . . . Payment on results . . . All you need to do to join our organisation is pay a small initial joining fee. This entitles you to a session with one of our trained experts. If the advice fails, you pay nothing more. Only if our advice leads to a profitable investment do we charge a small percentage'.

Taggart shook his head. 'Who would do it? There really must be some nuts around. Sorry, and all that, but you know what I mean.'

Becky, too, shook her head. 'I agree it sounds crazy. But crazy things are sometimes true. There may be something in it. Do you know anything about Costigan's work?'

'Not a lot,' Taggart admitted. 'It's not exactly my field.'

'Well, if you did you'd realise that, if anyone could make this sort of thing work, he could.'

'OK, I stand corrected. So let's get back to your

41

friend Jasper. Where exactly did you say his new office was set up?'

'Marina del Rey. It's a part of Los Angeles.'

Taggart considered this. 'Well, that would make sense, wouldn't it? There's an awful lot of military research set-ups just round there. Rand at Santa Monica just along the beach. I'm not sure that there isn't a Rand offshoot in Marina del Rey itself. . . . And the kind of thing you say he was doing. Telepathy. Did you say he'd actually got it to work?'

'He got an awful lot of results that seem completely inexplicable otherwise, and other people did, too, when they set things up as he told them.'

'I seem to remember something. . . .'

'You couldn't possibly have missed it.'

'*You* couldn't,' corrected Taggart gently. 'But even I didn't, it seems. Well, that would be the kind of thing they're interested in, wouldn't it?'

'So what d'you think's happened? Why won't he get in touch?'

Taggart shrugged. 'Search me. Perhaps he can't.'

'You mean he's being held prisoner somewhere or something?'

'I don't mean anything. I don't know. Perhaps he doesn't want to. All right, that's very unlikely, from what you tell me. So perhaps he's under such a tight security clearance that he simply can't speak to anyone, in case it's the KGB. Or perhaps the KGB have actually got him; I've no doubt that if the Yanks are interested, they're interested too. Maybe he's up in a space shuttle somewhere, experimenting. Maybe he's dead. How do I know? Maybe, like Costigan says, he's just so busy rushing about that he hasn't ever got time to see anyone anywhere. People do get like that. It sounds interesting, anyway. Why don't we try and find out?'

This, presumably, was what she had been wanting all along. Now that it was actually put to her, however, Becky felt slightly disloyal. Did she want someone like Andrew Taggart investigating her old friend Jasper? He was hardly sympathetic to the kind of thing they were doing. . . . Well, too late now. She had started the ball, and it would continue to roll without any further help from her. And despite – or because of – Costigan's breeziness, she was worried. There was no doubt about that.

11

As they emerged into the afternoon street, Taggart said suddenly, 'Doing anything this evening?'

'No, why?'

'Oh, just a thought.' He pointed to a flyer stuck on a many-postered hoarding they were passing. IAN EVERITT, it said. AT THE PARIS, PICCA-DILLY, TONIGHT AT 7.30. SPEAK TO OTHER WORLDS.

'Ever heard of him?'

'Of course. But you don't think that what we do is anything to do with . . .' Becky was horrified. Ian Everitt was a medium, making large sums of money introducing members of the public to their long-dead relatives. She had seen him interviewed on the television.

'Science', said Becky firmly, 'is what I do. You may not think so, and I have to admit that since that first time I haven't got anywhere very far. You may think it's nonsense . . .' she finished defensively.

'I didn't say that,' Taggart protested. 'I just can't

see why it fascinates people so much. Say you do get through to Uncle Tom. It's just boring. He was boring alive and most of the time he's even more boring dead.'

'But that's what I'm saying. What I do isn't about getting through to Uncle Tom. Anyway, a lot of people seem to find it interesting enough – like NASA, if what you say is true.'

'Let's not argue about that. Have you ever been to see Everitt?' Taggart asked.

'No.'

'Well, nor've I, and to tell you the truth I'd really like to. It's the phenomenon I find interesting. What I was going to say was, why don't we go along tonight, just to see? There might be a piece in it for me, and I'd rather have company. You never know, you might find it interesting yourself.'

Becky's immediate instinct was to refuse. But then she thought about the alternatives. She was doing nothing tonight; today had been unsatisfactory and worrying. Taggart was good company. So why not, apart from principle? And what was the principle, anyway? Wasn't she always going on about having to be open-minded? In any case, it might be interesting.

'All right,' she said.

The show started at seven-thirty. Becky and Taggart arranged to meet at seven in front of the Paris.

'Do you know the place?' Taggart asked. 'It's the BBC. The place they use when they want a studio audience. Think, we may even get on the telly.'

During the afternoon Becky went and secured two tickets, and at just after seven she and Taggart took their places. The hall was packed, and the audience clearly filled with anticipatory excitement. To judge

44

from the conversations going on around them, many of tonight's audience had seen Everitt before and were expecting great things.

'He knows everything,' said a grey-haired lady in front of them. 'I saw him tell a woman about her husband and her son and her niece, and he got it all right. Not a detail wrong. Perhaps he'll be in touch with your Harry.'

'Harry never was a great one for keeping in touch,' her companion replied gloomily.

Just then the lights dimmed and a spot picked out a man – presumably the floor manager of tonight's show, or one of his assistants – on the stage. 'Now, all you've got to do is act naturally,' he told the audience. 'When we want you to clap, we'll tell you, like this – 'and he waved his arms enthusiastically, like a conductor urging an orchestra to ever greater things. 'Clap!' His efforts were greeted with thunderous applause, and he nodded. 'That's right.' He waved his arms again. More applause. He nodded, and left the stage. The lights went up again, then after a few minutes they dimmed. A hush fell, and Ian Everitt came and took his place on a chair on the stage.

Everitt was a homely looking man, comfortably paunched, balding. He looked round his audience and began to speak.

'Nothing is worse than to lose a loved one. I know – it's happened to me. My wife and son went in a car accident, and I thought I should never recover. But comfort is at hand, ladies and gentlemen. The dead are not dead at all. They live!' At this juncture the floor manager appeared on the corner of the stage and waved his hands. Obediently, the audience applauded. 'They live, yes, they live, and they are in touch with us!' Everitt went on more loudly, as the applause died down. 'And I am here to speak to them for you. This gift of mine is something I have to share with you all. So let us begin.' He stood up and came to the edge of the stage. 'I see a little girl, blonde, the initial is J – Judy, Janet – yes, she's looking for her mummy. "Mummy, I love you," she says. Yes, it's your little girl!' he exclaimed to a lady halfway up the stalls at the side, who had half-risen.

'Jessie!'

'Yes, that's right, about seven – she was seven when she died, wasn't she?'

'Eleven.'

'Eleven, that's right, with light hair. She says to tell you she's very happy—'

'Is her little dog with her?'

'Yes, I see a dog.'

'Penny!'

'"Penny and I spend all the time playing together, and it never rains," she says.'

'Oh, Jessie!'

Everitt went on in this vein for some time. It seemed to Taggart perfectly clear how he did it; he started off in the vaguest possible way, broadened his net and waited for a flicker of response. From then on it was a question of judging whether or not he was on the right track and advancing or retreating accordingly: an art in which he had presumably become very skilled during the twenty-five years he had been making his living in this way. Occasionally there seemed to be instances which could not be explained so easily, when a lot of detail was immediately forthcoming. In the interval Taggart and Becky discussed these interludes. They agreed that the technique was impressive, but on the whole simply a technique; though whether, after all these years, Everitt even realised he was applying it was another question. Possibly he himself, as well as

46

his audience, was taken in by it. 'But there are some bits that simply doesn't explain,' said Becky.

'Depends if he has any helpers, I should think,' said Taggart.

'You mean those are plants?'

'That's one possibility, but it's a bit obvious. No, I mean, if you hang around the foyer beforehand you can hear people talking. Not Everitt, obviously, but someone who knows what to look out for. If you hear something, you make a note and see where the person sits. That kind of thing.'

The bell rang for the next session, and the audience filed back, such of it as had left its seats. The break had been more for the benefit of Everitt, who clearly found the process exhausting. Then the show began again. Becky and Taggart might be entertaining cynical thoughts, but most of the audience were not, to judge from the eagerness with which they received the most banal of messages.

Everitt suddenly said, 'I feel a young man here – name begins with J. Tall, dark hair, quite recently arrived, I think.'

'Must be Jasper,' whispered Taggart. Becky looked up involuntarily, and Everitt's eagle eye spotted her.

'The young lady over there – one, two, three, four, five, sixth row on the left – yes, you, that's right, my dear.'

'Me?' echoed Becky.

'Yes, I have it strongly – a friend of yours, just gone over, J – Jack, Joseph – no, I'm not quite getting it, am I right?'

'Well, I do—' said Becky involuntarily.

'Of course you do! I knew it was you. What does the J stand for?'

'Jasper.'

'Jasper. A good friend, am I right?'

47

'But he's not dead – as far as I know.'

'But you're worried, yes? Haven't heard from him for a time, perhaps. Yes, I thought that was it. Well, my dear, he says don't grieve – he's happier on the other side than he ever thought he could be, and you'll find someone else—'

Becky fainted.

'Close on the girl!' yelled the television director in the gallery. 'Number 4 – that's it. Can we have some audience reaction, Number 2—'

It was in this way that the world, some days later, saw Becky receive the news of Jasper Hodgkin's apparent demise.

12

When Becky came to she did not, for a moment, remember where she was. Then she saw Taggart's pale face with its scrubby surround of dark beard bending solicitously over her, and memory returned. She immediately felt very foolish. 'Let's go,' she said.

'Are you sure you're all right?'

'Yes, perfectly.' Becky felt very impatient now. 'Come on.'

Once outside, Taggart said, 'Feel like a drink?'

Becky did. But once they were seated with their whiskies she shook her head when Taggart tried to question her. 'Do you really believe . . .?'

'Sorry, I just don't want to talk about it.'

'Well, it's certainly all very amazing.' Taggart looked into his drink. Soon Becky said she must be going; she didn't feel like getting home too late.

On the train she sat numbly, not really knowing what she thought. She was as aware as anyone – as Taggart, for instance – of exactly the techniques used by people like Everitt. There was nothing particularly arcane about them. Nevertheless, why . . .? The front of her mind was in perfect working order; but a nagging gloom settled at the back of it, not to be dispelled by reason or logic.

The Everitt show, they had been told, was destined to be broadcast in a week's time. Becky, shamefaced, told nobody about it and hoped that no one of her acquaintance would watch such rubbish. Meanwhile there was plenty to get on with. The research proposal, for a start: she would have to get a copy off to Costigan right away if he was to do anything about it in time. Her interview with him seemed aeons distant, overlaid by more vital scenes. One thing remained clear in her mind, and that was a deep feeling that she distrusted him. But why? On the face of it, it was ridiculous. Surely she didn't, as a result of the absurd Everitt, believe that he had somehow done away with Jasper – or, what she felt was perhaps more probable, that something had happened to Jasper of which Costigan was aware but which he was not revealing? Well, she could scarcely enclose a query with her research proposal; and since her living for next year depended on that proposal, or something similar, landing a grant, she would be a fool to jeopardise it unnecessarily. Not that she could see quite how Costigan could help. Of course, his prestige in the field was high; but what his connection still was with the university was not at all clear. Was he still qualified to act as investigator? Evidently he thought so, for he replied almost by return saying that he had thought of one or two additional possible sources of income for her, and would send the proposal off to them in her name if she was interested. If he heard nothing from her, he would do so.

Becky's next appointment with her marriage-minded philosopher was on the day after the showing of the Everitt programme. She was in an unusual quandary about this relationship. Usually, she found, her men friends were only too relieved to know that the last thing the delightful Becky had in mind was anything permanent. Joe the philosopher, however, did not conform to type in this respect. On the contrary, he seemed to regard the situation as something of a challenge. 'My,' he had said more than once, lying stretched out on the bed, head against one wall, feet almost touching the one opposite, not daring to sit up too suddenly for fear of bursting through the thatch above his head, 'but I should like to have a child with you, Becky. Wouldn't you like that?'

There were few things that Becky wanted less than a child at this particular moment. Nevertheless, to her horror, she could not prevent herself feeling, as Joe said these words, a shameful delight – even a stirring of maternal desire. She was, after all, much attached to Joe; and what greater compliment could a man pay a woman than this? Sternly she said, 'You have a wife and child already. Remember?'

'Three children. I had a wife before this, remember? But that's not the point, my darling Becky. As you know, I incline to serial monogamy. I've never made a secret of it. No, the point is that your affections lie elsewhere.'

'What are you talking about?' Becky was amazed. The conceit of men never ceased to astonish her. 'What d'you want me to do, stop taking the pill at once because you say so? I bet you'd be worried if I did.'

'No doubt I should. No, that wasn't really what I meant. But last night's performance was really most revealing, you know.'

'Last night?' Becky could feel herself blushing and sweating. 'I wouldn't have thought you watched rubbish like that.'

'I wouldn't have thought you believed rubbish like that! Aren't you forever explaining to me how your absurd branch of learning is a science like any other? But now I know better. It's merely a rationalisation of your atavistic yearnings.' Becky bit her lip. Joe went on, 'What's more, it reveals, my dear Beck, the true state of your heart. You're hopelessly attached to your epicene friend.'

'Oh, that's rubbish,' cried Becky, 'and you know it. It's just that I've known him for years and years, and I'm very fond of him. I don't know what came over me. I expect it was the heat.'

'And the shock. You really believe he's dead, don't you?'

'I don't know.' She shifted wretchedly. 'I don't know what I believe. All I know is, it wasn't a set-up.'

'No, it was like all the rest – a fishing expedition, amply aided by the respondent. Unless, of course, it was a set-up. Wasn't that Andrew Taggart you were with? I used to know him a few years ago. I wouldn't put anything past him.'

'Well, that was certainly quite an exhibition,' Taggart's editor said to him. 'Did you set it up, may I ask?'

'The really curious thing about it,' said Taggart, 'is that I didn't.'

'I believe, I believe.' David Cooper, leading light of the unbelieving left, made mock obeisances towards the westering sun, just visible through the grime of the window and the smog outside it. 'Do you believe?

51

Don't tell me. You do. You think the bugger's dead.'

'I . . . well,' said Taggart uncomfortably. 'I wouldn't go that far. I mean, he may be, mayn't he? It's a reasonable possibility. There's this murmur about the Pentagon and the latest thing in military research, and Costigan's name comes up. And at the same time Jasper Hodgkin's just gone to work for Costigan in Los Angeles – Marina del Rey, just down the way from Rand and all those maniacs – and hasn't been heard of since. These things do happen. But I wouldn't go so far as to say I'd actually base a story on that.'

'Oh, good. Good. Glad to hear that. Stony materialism suits you better. Pentagon as in military, not black mass,' said Cooper.

'Nevertheless,' said Taggart, 'I'm convinced there is a story there, and I must say I'm very inclined to try and find out what it is.'

'Go ahead,' said his editor. 'Just keep spiritualism out of it. That's all I ask.'

13

Andrew Taggart, when pursuing a story, always began in the same way: by checking his cross-references. Naturally a chaotic person, this had been dinned into him by years of frustrating experience. Time and again he had spent weeks of effort unravelling a chain of acquaintance only to realise, when he came to enter it into his files for future use, that he already held the key link in the chain – if he had only thought to look it up.

Now, therefore, he picked his way across his study,

avoiding such obstacles as piles of electronics and aviation magazines, kept for current reference, piles of library books, half-read, lying open, face down where he had last left them, piles of other books and miscellaneous folders for which there was no more room on his shelves, and an overnight bag not yet unpacked from an expedition last week, and finally reached his desk, buried under pieces of paper each of which was, in its own way, vitally important. He unearthed his computer from beneath these (an Apple II, rapidly becoming a dinosaur of the computer world but which served his needs well enough) and keyed in the personal file cross-reference program. However, neither Hodgkin nor Costigan turned up anything of interest, or indeed anything at all, other than the piece of gossip retailed from Washington which had formed the tenuous basis for the paragraph which had first led Becky to contact him. Interesting that there had been no reaction from Costigan; not that he would expect confirmation – hardly; but why no angry letter or libel writ? Presumably because he thought discretion was the better part: a reaction which, in Taggart's mind, indicated just one thing – something to hide. He therefore felt confident that there was something there. But what? His files, at any rate, gave no clue. Taggart did not normally move in paranormal circles.

He sat now staring at the green, flickering screen and thinking about recent events. Becky, now there was a strange girl. Attractive – he had always been a tits man. But that was definitely not on the menu at the moment. For one thing, professional involvement precluded personal; he liked to be able to approach a new set of facts with a clear eye, unclouded by irrelevant emotion. For another, she was undoubtedly mad. Taggart was not what parapsychologists liked to call 'open-minded'. In vague discussions with them on infrequent previous occasions, and now again talking to Becky, he had found that this meant (as far as he could see) an infinite readiness to discount those occasions when nothing happened, or when it was too obviously helped to happen, in favour of the odd apparently inexplicable occurrence. Well, if that was what open-mindedness entailed, his mind was definitely shut, and in his view only a readiness to distort reality amounting almost to perversion could give rise to that sort of openness. Becky was a nice girl, one of the nicest he had met for years. But this aspect of her worried him, and Taggart was not a man who found the worrying, the mysterious, the inexplicable, in any way erotic or even attractive – except in so far as it provided meat for his investigations.

No short cuts, then. So back to legwork. Where should he begin? He looked around for a pen with which to jot down the facts immediately to hand. None, however, was to be seen – a normal state of affairs on his desk. He switched off the computer and delved in a drawer, finally turning up a green felt pen. The shop down the road was always out of blue and black. The proprietor explained that the company would only sell its pens in packs containing five each of five colours: blue, black, green, red and purple. By the time Taggart got round to buying a pen, he was invariably out of blue, black and even red. Luckily Taggart was not particular about these things; he even inclined to the lurid.

Hodgkin, he noted down. Colleague of B.R. Works for C. Ostensibly in commodity futures (?) but in fact ?NASA. Ostensibly in or around LA, in fact . . .? Politics? Blackmailing points?

Costigan. Who is he? What is his business?

Becky. Background? Work? Why this mob? What

does she think about H? Will she help unbelieving investigator?

For some time Taggart stared at these notes, then sighed. Better begin. But where?

First, he decided, he needed general background. The dirty side of politics he was used to; the ins and outs of the psi scene, no. So who could tell him? That, at least was obvious. Who but the Cherfassian Professor of Psychic Studies?

The selection board, as so often happens in controversial cases of this kind, had settled upon a compromise candidate who offended nobody largely because he was totally unexceptionable, and therefore interested nobody, either. Openshaw was a Yorkshireman in his early forties, a mathematician interested in chance and probability who had conducted several long and so far unproductive studies but whose open-mindedness impelled him to continue, perhaps indefinitely, along lines which had so far yielded nothing (number prediction was his predilection) but which might yet do so. He was determined to rescue the reputation of mathematicians in this field from the sullying memory of S. G. Soal, the extent and subtlety of whose cheating had baffled so many investigators for so many years.

He was not easy to locate, since he had no department of his own. Finally, however, Taggart traced him to a small office deep in Psychology, at the end of a corridor in an anonymous building opposite Dillon's bookshop. Here, sports-jacketed and pipe-puffing, Openshaw sat exuding respectability and normality along with clouds of choking smoke.

'Only too glad to help,' he boomed in reply to Taggart's thanks. 'I've frankly never got on too well with people like Costigan and Hodgkin. Showy and untrustworthy, if you ask me. They bring the subject a bad name.'

'Can you tell me something about their work?'

'Certainly.' Openshaw puffed his pipe. Nothing like a pipe, thought Taggart, for providing punctuation. This was a colon: the sentence would continue after a longish pause. 'Costigan,' said Openshaw. 'Well, he's Irish. Leprechauns and all that, you know. I sometimes think it has a bad effect on the brain.' He puffed solemnly, as if the work he was doing was as normal as differential equations. 'He's a nuclear physicist, and he was working at CERN on particles when he got interested in the possibilities of prediction. So when his contract was up he came back here and did some experiments on remote viewing. Well, he got some pretty spectacular results, if they're to be believed' – he puffed, a pause for scepticism – 'and got *Natural Science* to publish them. That was the trick. After that, of course, he was made. Every time someone pointed out something a bit dodgy, he could turn round and say, well, if it satisfied them, why not you?'

'But don't they demand all sorts of referees?'

'Oh, certainly they do. The point was, they happened to have an editor at the time who was very concerned about broadening the frontiers, open-mindedness, and quite right, too. So he decided to publish Costigan's article, with an introduction explaining why they had agreed to do it, all sorts of disclaimers. Only thing was, as soon as it appeared Costigan ran off thousands of offprints, without the intro or the disclaimers of course, and used them to get himself started in this business of his.'

'And you disapprove of that?'

'Well, it's not what I should have done,' said Openshaw heavily, 'and the result is, he's made quite sure I shall never have a chance to do so. After that piece of behaviour, the doors clanged shut, and who knows when they'll open again? Still, I suppose everyone must act as he thinks fit.'

'You think he's a bit shady, in other words?'

'Now, I never said that, did I?'

'How about Hodgkin?'

'Ah, well, now, that's more interesting.' Openshaw sat back and puffed expansively. 'I can't say I like his style. You can't be too – how shall I put it? – normal in this job, in my view. Still, you can't deny, he did come up with something. Found that if he got a monkey to do something monkeys don't normally do, like – oh, I forget the exact things, but let's say eat toast and marmalade for breakfast. You get the kind of idea? Well, all of a sudden, according to Hodgkin, reports came from all over the world of monkeys suddenly demanding to eat toast and marmalade for breakfast. Sounds absurd, but it did seem to happen like that. What the papers liked to call telepathy. More a variation of vitalism, really: the vital force, the collective unconscious, whatever you like to call it. Once something enters it, it's passed on to all the other participants, to put it crudely. That's what Hodgkin thinks, anyway.'

'And what do you think?'

Openshaw shrugged. 'There's something there. There's undeniably something there. He's done it more than once. It's a definite effect.'

'That was a couple of years ago, wasn't it? I seem to remember reading something about it.'

'Oh, it certainly caused a stir,' Openshaw agreed, tapping out his pipe now into a large, full ashtray. 'But that's it, really. He hasn't done anything with it, and he hasn't really explained it. In fact, if I remember right, he'd left that work recently and was trying out something quite different, with *Ganzfeld* sensory deprivation, I think it was. But you'll be able to check on that.'

'The last I heard, he's gone into business with Costigan.'

'Oh, well, that's very probable,' said Openshaw, tamping down some new tobacco. 'I believe he was one of the candidates for this chair. It must have been quite a disappointment for him. Have you come across his assistant? Becky Ryan? Nice girl. Clever, too. Hard-working. I frankly don't know why she stays with Hodgkin. He has no sympathy with the way she works. I'd give quite a lot to get her over here, but she won't budge.'

Taggart tactfully did not reply.

14

Taggart returned to the *New Politics* office feeling thoughtful. He was no further on, but at least he no longer felt completely lost amid the mazes of para-psychological politics. Clearly Hodgkin and Costigan were both glamorous stars in this firmament, deeply envied and resented by honest toilers such as Open-shaw. Nothing very amazing there. In the gents', he ran into his editor.

'How you doing? Any further with that story?'

'Getting things sorted out.'

'Anything I can do to help? I'm faintly alarmed by the thought of telepathy in the hands of the military. In the hands of anybody, come to that. What price privacy? One couldn't even keep one's thoughts to oneself.'

'There may be one thing,' said Taggart as they made

their way back to the office. 'I'd very much like to know exactly what it is Costigan's up to; that's to say, the face he presents to the public. If you go to Costigan Futures asking for help with your investments, what happens?'

'Why don't you go and find out? I should have thought that was straightforward enough.'

'Well, it's not. For one thing, Costigan'll be on the look-out for me after that piece. Even if he didn't see the television, he knows me; we've met a couple of times at parties. And another thing, I haven't got any money.'

Cooper sat back and thought for a moment, his feet on the desk. 'What d'you want? Me to find some cash and go, for instance?'

Taggart shook his head. 'No, that wouldn't be any good. It wouldn't be believable. It's got to be convincing. You just aren't the kind of customer that would go to Costigan.'

'I don't expect he's very particular. But I know what you mean.' Cooper was silent for a moment, thinking. Then he said, 'What about Oliver Stallybrass?'

'That's a brilliant idea!' Taggart was delighted. 'Just the kind of thing he'd love – and no worries about cash, either.' He couldn't imagine why he hadn't thought of Stallybrass himself. An occasional contributor to *New Politics*, Oliver Stallybrass had been a contemporary of Cooper's at Oxford, the left-leaning son of a rich Quaker business man. He was now the managing director of the margarine subsidiary of his father's food empire. Although business interested him, and he had no qualms about being rich, he did occasionally hanker after a little disreputable excitement – the kind of thing, in fact, that is part of the life of any journalist. It was agreed that Cooper, who knew him well, would phone Stallybrass.

* * *

59

During the next three weeks the investigation lapsed somewhat. For one thing, it seemed sensible not to risk worrying Costigan until Stallybrass had had a chance to try out Costigan Futures. For another, as Cooper pointed out, there was no proof that anything had happened to Jasper Hodgkin. He might reappear at any moment.

Time passed, however, and he did not reappear. Becky was increasingly convinced that something had happened to him. Taggart, talking to her on the phone, said, 'But why? You can't really take that old fraud Everitt seriously, surely?'

'No, no, it isn't just that, of course. Though I can't get it out of my mind.'

'What else, then?'

'Well, there isn't any word of him, is there? I can't see any reason for that. And then Costigan —'

'What about him?'

'He's funded my new research project.'

'What d'you mean, he's funded it?'

'I mean he's funded it. When Jasper disappeared, it was just the time I had to get a new proposal in. Costigan said he'd handle it for me; that was where I'd been, to discuss it with him, the day I came to see you and we went to Everitt. He said – Costigan – that he was still attached to London University somehow, he didn't explain exactly, and I didn't enquire too closely. So I sent him my proposal, and I thought he'd just forward it on with himself as investigator. That's what we more or less agreed. It's just a formality – it's because I haven't a tenured post, and there has to be somebody tenured in charge of a project; it would be me doing the work. Anyway, I heard the other day that we had the money we'd been asking for, which was great, and then I got the correspondence about it and it turns out it wasn't from the research council or either of the foundations I was applying to. It's from a quite new set-up financed by Costigan Futures.'

'Well, there's nothing to stop him doing that, is there? If he's making the kind of profits he says he is it's probably a tax loss. Take the money and run, I should.'

'Yes, but why should he suddenly do that? I asked him about it – thanked him, of course – and he said he'd only just set the thing up and this seemed exactly the kind of thing he had in mind.'

'There you are. You probably gave him the idea.'

'I don't know,' said Becky thoughtfully. 'Life isn't as easy as that. I think he's got a reason for all this.'

'Oh, yes?'

'Yes, I think he wants to stop me worrying about Jasper. After all, he is – was – my meal ticket, so to speak. What stronger reason could a girl have for wanting to know what's happened to him?'

'I can think of one at least.'

'Well, as you know, that one doesn't apply.'

Taggart was thoughtful after this conversation. He had formed a high opinion of Becky. All right, so in one respect she was barmy; but she had struck him as having sound judgement where people were concerned. She was certainly not hysterical. And what she said undoubtedly made sense.

At this point the phone on his desk buzzed. It was his editor. 'Come and meet Oliver Stallybrass,' he said. 'He's here in my office.'

Stallybrass was seated by the window, a tall, dark man with a smooth, heavy face. He was failing to drink a cup of the dreadful *New Politics* coffee. He looked round as Taggart came in and said, 'Make your fortune with Costigan Futures.'

'What happened?'

Stallybrass waved at some papers lying on the

editor's desk and said, 'I wrote it all down for you, but I can give you a brief résumé. I was telling David. Quite extraordinary. Extraordinary.'

'So what happened?'

'Well.' Stallybrass lay back and raised one eyebrow. Clearly he was going to dine out on this for weeks, even months. 'I approached Costigan Futures, as you may imagine, with a completely blank mind. I mean, I had absolutely no idea what was going to happen. Witches' sabbaths, dancing naked round the maypole, slaughtering a sheep and studying the entrails . . . '

'Goodness, I don't think that's the image, is it?'

'How does one know? Anyway, I rolled up – have you been there? No, well, there's a very sexy receptionist, and then in an inner sanctum sanctorum Costigan himself. Whole place very expensive; there's a great deal of money coming in from somewhere.'

'Prophecy ought to be a very profitable game, if you think about it,' said David Cooper.

'It obviously is, or something is. Anyway, in I went, said I'd heard about him from a friend, had a couple of thousand to spare, always interested in trying out something new. You know the kind of thing.'

Taggart tried to imagine what it might feel like to have a couple of thousand to spare.

'He seemed delighted and explained all about it. He only deals in commodities, because the sensitive, that's the person who does the actual prophesying, has to be able to have the material in hand, literally, to get the feel of what's going to happen to it. You can imagine. I listened open-mouthed. Fellow seemed quite matter-of-fact about it all. You've met him?'

'Once or twice.'

'Seems relatively . . . well, normal, really, doesn't he? Anyway, I said I'd been thinking about investing a bit in coffee. Ideal, he said, a particularly suitable material. Did I want to do the thing soon? At once, I said. Tomorrow. So the upshot was, I was to present myself in Fitzroy Square at ten o'clock armed with some coffee – beans or ground, but presumably not instant. Mustn't be too far removed from the real thing. So I brought a few beans in a bag. Nothing too bulky, you know.'

'Mm.'

'So, ten o'clock, there I was, clutching my coffee, and there was Costigan with this perfectly charming girl wearing a sort of Indian bedspread.'

'Indian is big this year among the folk crowd,' remarked Taggart.

'Yes.' Stallybrass clearly was unused to being interrupted when in full spate. 'Blonde, name of Kate. Either I didn't catch her other name or it wasn't mentioned. Anyway, she was the sensitive. Took my coffee, tucked it down her neckline so that it would be in maximum contact, that was her phrase, then pointed to her car and said, off we go. Red Mini, it was. I don't much like Minis, actually, because there's no room for my legs, but there was no choice; apparently she had to drive and she didn't like driving anyone else's car. So in I got and off we went, Costigan waving us goodbye. Drove out of London, on to the M1, and up we went till we hit Derbyshire, would you believe. Got into the Peak district, this damned Mini, girl drove like an absolute demon. I can't remember when I've been so scared. Wouldn't speak, wouldn't say a word, seemed to be in a sort of coma, and believe me, that doesn't do much for the driving. Anyway. We started to get into the hills, up and down, up and down, round some perfectly terrifying hairpin bends, till suddenly there we were out on this great high hill, wind blowing the car nearly off the road, and she pulls up and gets out. So I got out, too. Jolly glad to, as a matter of fact; I was busting for a pee but somehow there hadn't been the opportunity to say anything about it – too mundane, somehow.

'So there we were, wind blowing through our hair, and all we needed was a white horse galloping up and it would have been an ideal whisky commercial. Then she sort of broke out of her coma and said, "Right, now we can go back", and back we drove to London, a bit less terrifying this time – even stopped for something to eat on the way. Into Fitzroy Square, she brings out the coffee, nice and warm it was, says goodbye and off she goes, leaving me wondering what to do next. So back I went to the office – was about four o'clock by this time – and there's Costigan all agog. "Where did you go?" he said. I told him, and he wanted to know all about the road, so I told him that, too. Hard to believe, this, isn't it? Then he says, "Right, if you invest in coffee now there's going to be a few ups and downs in the immediate future, but before too long it's going to rise, no doubt about that at all. That'll be fifty pounds," he says, "and if you should decide to invest, we take one per cent of any profit. Of course," he says, "there's nothing to stop you pretending you haven't, but that might be a little difficult should you wish to use our services again. It's entirely up to you." So I paid up, and did invest a couple of thousand, as I said.'

'And?'

'Well, bugger me,' said Stallybrass. 'For a couple of weeks it went up and down like a yoyo, just like he said. Then in the last few days news came in that the Brazilian coffee harvest has completely failed this year. A total wipe-out. And coffee has simply gone through the roof.'

There was an awkward silence.

'Of course,' said Cooper, 'it could just be that while you were driving up and down, or after you'd been to see him, he took expert advice on what was likely to be happening to coffee.'

'Could be, of course,' said Stallybrass. 'All I can say is, I wish I had expert advice like that.'

'Well,' said Taggart, 'now you have.'

'Yes,' said Stallybrass, 'and I have to say, in spite of my better self, I'm very much tempted to try and use it again.'

15

When Stallybrass had left, still murmuring about the unknown wonders of the mind, silence reigned for some time in the editor's office.

'Whaddaya know?' said Cooper.

'Made you a friend for life,' said Taggart. 'Thinking of trying it yourself?'

Cooper shook his head gloomily. 'What now?'

Taggart put his feet on the desk and tilted his chair back, thinking. He remained in this position for some time, rocking gently back and forth. Then he returned to earth abruptly and shook his head. 'Can't think of anything else here. Only thing to do is to go to LA, as far as I can see. That's where it's all happening.'

'If anything is.'

'Something is,' said Taggart decisively. He scratched his beard thoughtfully.

Cooper said, 'D'you know, if you wore a Homburg you'd look just like a rabbi. It suddenly struck me. It's the combination of that awful beard and that unnaturally white face.'

'It's a disguise I've used,' said Taggart, 'but

65

unfortunately I'm not operating in Stoke Newington or Bedford Stuyvesant. I don't believe rabbis in California look like that.'

'And who is going to finance you to go to California?'

There was silence again. It was, they both knew, out of the question for *New Politics* to do such a thing. It ran on a shoestring; such pieces as it received from and about foreign parts were the result of contributors happening to be there and finding in *New Politics* a market for opinions unwelcome in the rest of Fleet Street. No *New Politics* budget would cover getting to Los Angeles, let alone living there.

'You're going to have to sell the idea to someone,' said Cooper.

'They'll want an exclusive.'

'Can't help that. We might be able to work something out. Anyway, there's sure to be lots of titbits for us. Unless you can think of a better way.'

'No.'

'Who d'you think?'

Taggart shrugged. 'I'll try the *Review*.'

The news editor of the *Sunday Review* was an old friend of Taggart's. They had worked together briefly at the BBC and then taken different routes into Fleet Street, both having found the apparatus of television too cumbersome for the kind of muck-raking they most enjoyed. Alan Congdon, the *Review* man, having acquired a wife, was faced, when the first baby arrived, with the classic dilemma: job or family? He could not, his wife assured him, hope to retain both – not when the job involved him spending roughly one night in ten at home, or, if he was by some strange chance based at home, about six hours out of twenty-four there, and no hope of knowing at any time

66

exactly which six. She, too (she pointed out forceful-
ly), had once had a job – hoped to have one again, one
day; that was how they had met, remember? And since
he was a reasonable fellow, fond of his wife and mildly
curious about his offspring, he had capitulated and
taken a desk job. The hours were not shorter, but at
least they were predictable, and he lived at home. He
was still, after ten years, married.

When Taggart stuck his head round the office door,
he was speaking on two phones simultaneously, and
nodded towards an armchair. Twenty minutes later he
had finally disposed of both calls and their consequ-
ences and informed his secretary that he was taking no
more for the next half-hour. Then he turned to
Taggart.

'Sorry to keep you waiting. Nice to see you. What
brings you here?'

'Got a story.'

'Still plugging away, eh? You still shacked up with
that big blonde?'

'Which one?' Taggart, small, dark and scruffy, was
irresistibly drawn to large blondes and, to the surprise
of all who knew him, had a considerable success rate
with them. Some put this down to their inability to
resist trying to mother him: trim his beard, wash his
socks, tidy his house and so on. Others, more
accurately, diagnosed yet another example of the
remarkable efficacy of genuine enthusiasm. He was
not, after all, inconsiderable, nor was he boring – both
familiar qualities among spouses. He was merely
inelegant.

Congdon shook his head. 'Still not settled down?'

Taggart said with genuine regret, 'Never seems to
work out that way, somehow. Nothing I should like
better.'

'It would cramp your style.'

'Maybe. Let me tell you about this one.' Taggart quickly unfolded the events of the past few weeks. 'There's quite a story there. I feel it in my bones.'

'And David Cooper can't afford the tag, that it? Well, I don't see why not. In fact I don't see why you don't just move over to us anyhow. What about it?'

Taggart shook his head. 'Don't like the politics here.'

'You could still write stuff for *New Politics*. And think of the money.'

'What would I do with it?'

'You must be the only man in the world who would ask that.' Congdon shrugged. 'OK, I'll let the accounts office know about the trip. But strictly exclusive to us, OK?'

'Of course.'

As Taggart got up to leave, Congdon said, 'By the way, d'you know anyone out there?'

'I expect I can raise a few phone numbers.'

'Well, here's one.' Congdon took out a battered book, riffled through the pages and scribbled on a piece of paper which he handed over. The paper said 'Prue Heisenborn' and gave a telephone number and an address in Santa Barbara. 'Old friend of mine. Works at the university there. Give her my love.'

16

Travelling courtesy of the *Sunday Review* was a different thing from scrimping along trying to save money for *New Politics*, Taggart reflected as he sat back in the taxi which was taking him from the airport to a hotel Congdon had recommended in Santa

Monica. Not that a scheduled seat on a scheduled flight was any less unpleasant in itself than a charter seat on a bucket-shop hop, although the feeling of relative certainty was nice. In fact, Taggart had had the misfortune to be seated immediately in front of a small and hyperactive child, something of a penance on a thirteen-hour flight. Still, here he was, credit cards at the ready and a certain feeling of expansiveness discernible through the jet lag.

Taggart had never been to Los Angeles. For him it was midnight, but here it was mid-afternoon. Taggart stared confusedly out at a city apparently constructed out of pastel-coloured cardboard. The temperature was in the nineties, and there was a haze of smog. He knew he was in the right place by the palm trees – those incredibly tall, spindly palm trees which he had seen on a thousand television shows. They induced a sense of instant romance. Hollywood! And indeed there it was; he followed the cabby's pointing finger and saw the writing on the hill: H L YWO D, in letters twelve feet high, some of them slightly askew now, but that was only as it ought to be; the great days of the cinema were past.

The cabby dropped him at his hotel. He checked into his room, had a shower and wondered what to do next. He felt tired, but it seemed somehow indecent to go to bed in the middle of the afternoon, even if it was someone else's afternoon.

He studied his map of LA. Venice Beach, where Jasper Hodgkin had his apartment, was just south of Santa Monica. He could probably walk it. He could do with a walk, after that frightful flight. It was still hot outside, but less unbearable now. He put on his lightest clothes – a once white T-shirt and some filthy jeans – then locked his room carefully and went downstairs.

'Could I walk to Venice Beach from here?'

The woman behind the reception desk stared at him. She was middle-aged, her shell-pink hair perfectly matching her non-crease trouser suit. 'Walk?' she repeated in apparent stupefaction. 'To Venice?'

'Well, it didn't look very far on the map.'

'Oh, it's not far. . . . Look,' she said kindly, as one might address a child, 'you haven't been here before, right? Well, this is no place to walk. Believe me. There are some very funny people on the streets. You'd probably get picked up by the cops. Listen, why don't you let me call you a cab?' She picked up the phone.

'Denis? There's someone here wants to go to Venice. What did you say the address was?' she hissed at Taggart.

'Oh, one minute—' He pulled a crumpled sheet of paper out of his back pocket. On it, among other items of useful information, Hodgkin's address was written. It was almost but not quite obliterated by the crease where the paper had been folded. 'Nine East Wind – does that sound right?'

The pink lady shrugged and said to the phone, 'East Wind . . . OK . . . I'll tell him.' She put the instrument down and said, 'He'll be here in a minute.' Then she turned back to her movie magazine.

A few minutes later the hotel door opened and a small, dark man came in. The pink lady raised her head, said, 'Hi!' and nodded towards Taggart who said, 'Taxi?'

'That's right,' said the man, and led the way out to where his cab, a large pink Chrysler, was waiting. For a moment Taggart wondered whether he was being abducted by a branch of the white slave trade, but he was reassured by the sight of the meter and the impenetrable wall of bullet-proof glass set between him and the driver. With such protection, this had to

70

be a bona-fide cab. He stared out of the window as they drove, but the streets were a blur. In a very short time they drew to a halt.

East Wind Street turned out to run parallel to the into the microphone set behind his seat. 'That'll be fifteen.'

Well, thought Taggart, fingering the map in his other back pocket, I shall certainly walk back.

East Wind Street turned out to run parallel to the beach. At one end it led into a sort of shopping arcade, where large numbers of people seemed to be loitering. Those were probably the suspicious characters the pink lady had been referring to. Taggart turned firmly in the other direction, where a narrow sidewalk ran between the beach and the traffic, which consisted mainly of bicycles, all travelling quite silently at about eighty miles an hour. Intimidated, Taggart kept well towards the beach. A strong breeze was blowing, and eddies of sand rippled along the tarmac, giving the place a curiously homely feel. Somehow something as natural as sand blowing by the seaside felt out of place is Los Angeles, and it gave Taggart an unreal sense of being on holiday. He passed some small private houses set behind high fences, no doubt inhabited by millionaires. Then, a little further along, the sidewalk left the seafront, which was now entirely taken up by condominium buildings three or four storeys high. On the beach, children played and joggers made their lugubrious way up and down the firm sand by the water. Taggart followed the street away from the sand and began to look at the numbers on the condominiums. Jasper, if his letter to Becky was to be believed, lived, or had once lived, at No. 9.

He soon found his target. Nine East Wind was constructed of concrete and wood, more or less indistinguishable from the buildings on either side of it. On the street side it was almost windowless, showing only a few portholes which looked as though they were probably bathroom ventilation. Who would want windows on to the street when they lived on the beach? Taggart went in the door and found himself in a lobby containing a bank of mailboxes, each with its doorbell and entryphone. The name-card at 1B said HODGKIN. Taggart rang the bell, not really expecting anything to happen. Sure enough, nothing did. He tried again. Nothing again.

He turned to the other mailboxes. Not surprisingly, he didn't recognise any of the names. At random he rang one which read STAVISKY. 3C. A male voice answered. 'Who is this?'

'I'm sorry to disturb you,' said Taggart into the little grille. 'I'm trying to find Jasper Hodgkin.'

'Who?'

'Hodgkin. He's an Englishman. Lives in this building at number 1B.'

'I think I know the one you mean,' said the voice. 'Tall guy, dark, that the one?'

'That sounds like him,' said Taggart, who had managed to locate some agency photographs.

'Well, I haven't seen him in some time. Must have gone away.'

'That's a shame,' said Taggart. 'I've come over from England specially to see him.'

'Oh.' Stavisky sounded as though he was getting rather bored with this conversation.

'Is there a caretaker or anything? Someone who might know whether he was coming back here?'

'You mean a janitor? Well, there's the leasing company. They're up in Marina del Rey. But they'll be closed now till tomorrow.'

'Could you give me their address?'

'Sure. The Beach Apartment Company. I don't

have the address right here, but it'll be in the phone book. Marina del Rey.'

'Thanks,' said Taggart, noting this down on his filthy scrap of paper.

'You're welcome.' Stavisky rang off abruptly.

Taggart turned back into East Wind Street and squeezed between a couple of buildings on to the beach. All the condominium buildings were very similar. Each apartment had at least one big picture window opening on to a wooden deck; the larger ones presumably had two. Many of these wooden verandas were cluttered with tables, towels, papers, the usual detritus of daily life. Taggart soon located Hodgkin's. There were four such windows on the ground floor of No. 9, and each had different blinds or curtains, so these were presumably four different apartments. Two had their windows open and figures moving back and forth between the veranda and the room within. Two had shut windows. Of these, one was at the left-hand far end, so it must be either 1A or 1D. The other occupied the right-hand middle position. This must be 1B. It didn't look particularly deserted or gloomy, not unless one was predisposed to read hindsighted emotions into inanimate objects. It merely looked shut. Taggart wondered whether he should climb on to the veranda and try the window. He glanced around. The family parties were thinning out now – time for supper, perhaps. And if anyone saw him, he would simply explain that he was a friend of Jasper's and trying to get in touch.

Only a low rail of three slats stood between the veranda and the beach. It was the work of a moment to jump up and scale it. If anyone saw him they weren't bothered, or else they made it their business not to interfere in what didn't concern them. Who needed to get mixed up in unnecessary unpleasantness? The windows were of thick glass, framed in strong metal. Taggart tried them. As he expected, they were locked tight. He peered in. There were no curtains at the windows, but he couldn't make out very much. White carpet on the floor, a couple of chairs, a dead plant. No one had watered that for some time. It was brown and withered.

He jumped back on to the beach and glanced at his watch. Seven o'clock. Nothing much more he could do tonight. Besides, jet lag was starting to catch up with him. Suddenly, he felt very tired. No taxis were in sight, and he had no idea how to find one. He began the long walk back to Santa Monica.

17

By the time Taggart reached his hotel he was so tired that he was barely conscious. Contrary to the pink lady's dire prophecies, nobody had set on him during his walk, although he had received more than one strange look. Nevertheless, the experience had been unnerving enough to make him realise that his first action next morning must be to rent a car. Once, as he had padded exhaustedly along a sidewalk, a car had pulled up and his stomach had jumped into his mouth, but it turned out merely to be a police car.

'Just where you makin' for, sir?' enquired a large Irish officer, who bulged in a number of strange places, whether with flesh or firearms Taggart found it hard to discern.

'My hotel,' explained Taggart, mentioning its name. 'It's in Santa Monica.'

'Yeah, I know it. You walkin' there?' asked the officer, genuinely amazed.

'It's not so very far,' said Taggart defensively. He hoped that, if the policemen were so concerned, they might offer him a lift.

'You're British, right?' said the officer. This obviously explained everything. 'Well, take care.' He wound the window back up, and to Taggart's regret the car drove off.

He was so tired that, in spite of the time difference, he did not wake up next morning until seven o'clock.

He had breakfast at a small restaurant along the street. His fellow-breakfasters were mostly girls whose finish achieved a degree of gloss which made them seem almost inhuman, certainly not of the same species as Taggart. He was in a way relieved at this, as they were almost all tall blondes, a combination which in less forbidding circumstances he would have found hopelessly distracting.

Having achieved a relatively unperturbed breakfast, he returned to his room and looked up Beach Apartments of Marina del Rey. A polite girl answered the phone and confirmed that 1B, No. 9 East Wind, was leased to Mr Jasper Hodgkin. He had taken it for a year, so the lease still had some months to run. As far as she knew there was no problem about it. The rent was paid regularly – yes, still being paid. She would certainly know if it wasn't. It was paid through the bank.

Taggart explained that he was worried about Hodgkin, and that he had come over from England especially to see him. He had not been heard of for some weeks. Would it be possible to get inside the apartment to see if any clue to the mystery could be found? Did Beach Apartments perhaps have a spare

75

key he could borrow, or could they send someone round to accompany him, perhaps? But the polite girl was politely adamant. It was against their policy. If a person leased an apartment, then that was his apartment; so long as the rent was paid, there was nothing more to be said. Sorry she couldn't help. Have a nice day.

No luck there. He hadn't really expected anything else. Still, it was hard to think what to do next. Call Costigan Futures, he supposed. They might have something to say. He looked them up and dialled the number. Another polite girl answered. 'Costigan Futures. May we help you?'

'I'm looking for Jasper Hodgkin. Is he there, please?'

'I'm afraid Dr Hodgkin hasn't been here in some while,' said the girl. 'He's away on business.'

'Have you any idea where I might be able to contact him?'

'I believe he's in Britain at the moment.'

'Well, he isn't, you see,' said Taggart. 'I've just come from there, and to tell you the truth his friends are beginning to get worried about him. At the London office they refer us to you, and you refer us to them, and meanwhile there's no sign of him.' For the moment it seemed more convenient to be a friend of Hodgkin's than a snooping hack. It inspired more trust. No need to put the wind up people unnecessarily.

'Oh,' said the girl. She seemed at a loss. Perhaps she really didn't know what was up. Perhaps she really believed Hodgkin was in London. Come to that, perhaps he was. One couldn't prove the contrary. It just seemed unlikely.

'Is he in hiding or something?' asked Taggart.

'Not that I know of,' said the girl. 'Look, who is this?'

'I told you, I'm a friend of his from England. My name's Andrew Taggart. We seriously are rather worried. What makes you think he's in England? Do you know he's there?'

'Well, no, not really, I suppose. It's just . . . now, what made me think so? Perhaps – yes, I think Dr Costigan said so. So naturally I believed him.'

'I suppose you would. Did he actually say so in so many words?'

'I don't really remember. Perhaps not. But that was what I understood. You see, he never was here all of the time. He has his research to do as well.'

'What into?'

'Well, you know. You're a friend of his, aren't you? Telepathy.'

'Yes, of course,' Taggart said. 'Look, I was wondering if there might be some clue in his apartment. Do you happen to have a key?'

'Why, no, I'm afraid I don't,' said the girl. She failed to add that, even if she did, she wouldn't give it to Taggart, but there was no need. Her tone of voice said it for her. 'If you're so very worried you'd better go to the police,' she added. And put the phone down.

Well, thanks, thought Taggart. He wondered if he had been wise to make that call. If something funny was going on, then people might be better unalerted. Costigan knew his name, and knew he wasn't a friend of Hodgkin's – or at any rate, knew that he wasn't only a friend of Hodgkin's. Better get on with it fast.

Get on with what? The girl had said go to the police. Why not? There were, of course, reasons why not, the chief of which was that it went against the grain.

Taggart regarded the police as his natural enemies. They represented authority, and he was against authority in whatever form it presented itself. Nevertheless, they might know something. Or they might be able to get into that apartment. But which police? Call them and ask. They ought to know. He looked them up in the phone book. Police Department. There was a precinct office in Santa Monica. He consulted his map and found it was just round the corner from the hotel. All right. He would go and see them.

Taggart felt uncharacteristically nervous as he climbed the steps which led into the precinct station. He couldn't remember when he had last been inside a police station. Never inside an American one, certainly – and American cops didn't have a good reputation. It wasn't just that one didn't want to draw unnecessary attention to oneself; there was also the question of whether one would ever come out alive. He tightened his belt a notch. One doesn't want one's pants falling down on one in a situation like this.

Inside, all was disappointingly normal. The usual glossy girl, this time wearing a uniform, was at the front desk. Taggart told her his story. She referred him to a sergeant, a large black man, who took him to a small cubicle of an office in a big, noisy room and sat him down. Just like a newspaper office, Taggart reflected. Same sort of job, really, just on the other side of the fence.

'So you're worried,' said the sergeant.

'Well, yes, officer, I am. That's why I'm here.'

'And what am I supposed to do? We're real busy around here.' He gesticulated at the teeming madhouse outside the cubicle. 'Your friend's decided to take a vacation and he's told everyone he's in the other place. How about that? Isn't a guy allowed to take a vacation?'

'Of course, but it's been rather a long vacation,' Taggart said politely.

'So? You're worried. What do you think might have happened? Give me a for instance.'

'I don't know. He might be dead, I suppose,' said Taggart, thinking of Ian Everitt.

'OK, let's call the morgue,' said the sergeant. 'What's he look like? How old is he?'

'Thirty-seven.' Taggart felt smugly efficient. Lucky he had thought to get this information from Becky. 'Tall, about six feet. Slim. Thick dark hair, wavy.'

'OK.' The sergeant picked up his phone and dialled. 'Hi, Jake, that you? Got a description for you. Male, thirty-seven, six feet, slim, dark wavy hair. Got anyone like that in at the moment? Sure.' He stared impassively across at Taggart while he waited for the information. 'Yeah? OK. We'll be along.' He put the phone down. 'Well, apparently they do have a body there that fits that description. Care to come along and see?'

18

Sitting in the police car as it drove soberly through the sunlit streets, Taggart reflected, not for the first time, that his was a strange life. What was he, the respectable son of respectable suburban parents, doing here? On his way to a Californian morgue to identify the body of someone, it now struck him, he had never met? Somehow, with Becky having talked so much about Hodgkin, and the whole thing at the front of his mind for so many weeks, he felt he knew him. Still, he had seen photographs. Might as well have a look.

Something else he had never seen, he now realised, was a dead body. Funny, that, considering he spent so much of his time writing and thinking about the most efficient methods of producing, or preventing the production of, multitudes of them. Well, there's a first time for everything. He wondered whether people who spent as much or more time considering the same questions but from the other side – the war-games boys, for instance – were equally unacquainted with the real thing. Probably. The whole point was they weren't bothered about individual corpses, just large heaps of them thousands of miles away.

The car slowed in front of an unexceptional two-storey building. The sergeant had not addressed a word to him since they left the police station. He seemed preoccupied with other things. For him this was merely a diversion. He turned the car into a parking lot behind the building and got out. 'OK. Let's go find your friend,' he remarked, and led the way towards the building. Taggart thought he had better refrain from confessing to the absence of any first-hand contact with this particular friend.

They entered a cool, tiled corridor. The sergeant nodded at someone inside a pigeon-hole at the entrance and flashed a card. The place smelled of disinfectant and formaldehyde, reminding Taggart of his school labs. They went down some steps and through a door into a tiled room which struck cold even to one used to the icy air-conditioning which rendered all Los Angeles interiors arctic. Taggart wondered how the natives survived. Did they keep a store of winter woollies hidden in the office drawer to protect them against the chill?

A corpulent middle-aged man with a fringe of grey hair, dressed in white overalls, came forward to meet them. The sergeant said, 'Hi, Jake. This is Mr

80

Taggart from England. He'd like to know if this stiff you've got is an old friend of his.'

Without saying a word, the fat man turned towards a wall lined with large square drawers – the kind of thing Taggart had seen in family vaults on the infrequent occasions when friends persuaded him to spend a day in the country looking at churches. Still without a word, he pulled out one of the drawers and, removing a sheet, gestured towards the contents. 'The face isn't too good,' he said.

That, Taggart thought, preventing himself with the greatest difficulty from turning away and retching feebly in a corner, was the understatement of the century. The face was neither good nor bad. It simply didn't exist. It was a battered pulp. About all that could be made out was that its owner had been slim and had had thick, wavy dark hair.

'That him?' said the sergeant.

'Can't really tell,' said Taggart thickly. 'It's possible.'

'No, it isn't easy.' The sergeant turned to the fat man. 'Any clothes or anything?'

'Sure.' He closed the drawer carefully, raising the sheet to cover the face, then left the room for a moment and returned with a transparent plastic bag. In this, neatly folded, were a pair of cream cotton trousers, a cream silk shirt, short-sleeved, and a Liberty-printed cravat.

'No documents?'

'No.'

'How long's he been here?'

The fat man consulted a label on the drawer. 'Over a month now. Came in July twelve.'

'Can I look?' The sergeant held out a hand for the label and checked it over quickly. Then he turned to Taggart. 'That figure?'

'We last heard from him on June the thirtieth. That was the date on the letter, anyhow.'

'OK.' The sergeant held out the plastic bag of clothing. 'Recognise any of that?'

Taggart shook his head. 'It might be his, but I can't be sure. It's the kind of thing he used to wear,' he said, recalling photographs he had been shown by Becky. 'But I didn't know him that well.'

'Know anyone that did? Might be able to identify the stuff?'

'His colleagues might.'

'He work in the city?'

'Costigan Futures, Marina del Rey. If it's him.'

'OK, let's go round there. Mind if I take this?' The fat man waved assent. The sergeant picked up the bag of clothing and led the way out.

Marina del Rey sparkled with newness. In the marina itself brightly painted boats jostled each other in moorings so crowded it was impossible to imagine how they ever got in or out. Taggart, gradually recovering from the horrid sight of the body in the morgue, registered them as a blur of expensive colour. The sergeant was apparently unmoved. He had seen that sort of thing often enough before, and was making few concessions to civilian queasiness.

They parked the car and made for the Costigan Futures office, which was situated in a three-storey professional building behind the marina. Most of the other occupants seemed to be dentists, though there was one astrologer and one company called Data Research Inc., which might have been anything or nothing. They entered the building and rang the Costigan Futures bell. A girl's voice said through the intercom, 'Who is this?' The sergeant nodded at Taggart.

'This is Andrew Taggart,' he said into the grille. 'I

82

called yesterday about Jasper Hodgkin.'

'He's not here,' said the voice impatiently. 'I told you.'

'That's what we've come about,' said Taggart.

'We?'

'Miss,' said the sergeant into the intercom grille. 'This is Sergeant Shilling. LA Police Department. We've got some clothes we'd like you to identify if you can. May we come in, please.'

'Police,' said the voice, sounding nervous. 'OK, when you hear the buzz, push the door. It's the one on your right.'

The office, when they entered it, was in great contrast to the somewhat dark and dingy hallway where they had been conducting this conversation. It was gleaming white; cascades of greenery filled every available niche and spread insidiously across the walls and floor. Beside a desk, a dark, pretty girl wearing a red cotton jumpsuit stood nervously awaiting them. 'Well,' she said, 'I guess you'd better sit down and explain what all this is about.'

They sank into black leather armchairs, and the girl and the sergeant turned expectantly to Taggart.

'I explained on the phone,' he began awkwardly. 'We're worried about Jasper Hodgkin. He seems to have disappeared. Everyone says he's somewhere else, and he never is there. I'm a journalist – friend of some colleagues of his – and I came out here to check what's happened.' He looked at the girl, who seemed unperturbed by this changed story.

'Well, he's not here,' she said.

'No, and he's not in England, either. So I thought maybe I'd better contact the police—'

'Why come here to contact the police?' enquired the girl. 'Wasn't that rather a complicated way to do it? Don't you have police over there?' She seemed jumpy

83

now, though perhaps that was natural enough.

'Yes, we do, of course.' Taggart felt that this was not the moment to explain why he would hesitate to contact the British police about a matter of this sort. His name was not exactly an Open Sesame in that direction, many of his most notorious pieces having been exposures of police malpractice and partiality. Luckily his name hadn't rung any bells in Los Angeles. 'But here's where he lives. Lived,' he corrected himself.

'Lived?' The girl sounded at once horrified and nonplussed. Whatever the clairvoyant abilities of the Costigan Futures staff, they clearly hadn't prepared her for this particular turn of events.

It was now Sergeant Shilling's turn to speak. 'Miss,' he said, bringing out his plastic bag, 'I wonder if you can identify any of these clothes?' He took out the pants, shirt and cravat and laid them on the desk. The girl stared, and turned a little pale.

'Why, yes,' she said, pointing to the cravat. 'That's Jasper's. He always used to wear it, said a friend had given it to him—'

'You sure of that?'

'I couldn't mistake it.' Indeed the cravat was very distinctive, an art-nouveau design in purples, greens and dusty pink printed on crêpe de Chine.

'In that case,' said Shilling expressionlessly, 'I'm sorry to have to tell you that your friend seems to be dead.' The girl leaned back in her seat. Under her tan she had turned very pale. She gulped a couple of times.

'I'm sorry. I think I'm going to pass out.'

'Put your head between your knees,' advised Sergeant Shilling. 'Thanks for the ID.' He was not an emotional man.

'What now?' muttered the girl.

'We'll be back in touch if we need you.' Shilling turned to Taggart. 'Know where he lived?'

'Yes.'

'OK.' The black man nodded towards the door. 'Let's go.'

19

As they walked down the stairs to the street, Taggart was turning over in his mind various ways of asking Shilling whether he could come with him to the apartment. It was not a suggestion he would have dared make to a member of Her Majesty's Police, but the presence of journalists here seemed to be altogether more taken for granted. Nevertheless he felt slightly nervous, and had opened his mouth a couple of times without any sound coming out when Shilling solved the problem by saying, 'I'd like you to come with me, if you don't mind.'

The last phrase was clearly a formality, but Taggart chose to reply to it. 'No, I don't mind,' he said, omitting to add that this was precisely what he wanted to do. 'Why? What's up?'

'That's what I'm hoping you're going to tell me,' said Shilling. 'You come to my office out of nowhere and lead me to a corpse. Now I want to find out some more about it. I'm a naturally curious fellow.'

'But look here,' said Taggart, who was by now beginning to feel uncomfortable. 'It's nothing to do with me.'

Shilling held the car door open for him. 'Then how come we're both standing here?'

'I told you.' Taggart was aware of a plaintive note in his voice that he could have wished away. 'We hadn't heard from him, we were worried, I came to find out if anything had happened. I'm a journalist. It's the kind of thing I do. Anyway.' he added defensively, 'when did you say the body was found?'

'July twelve.'

'Well, I was in England all through July.'

'Who says you weren't?' Shilling negotiated a traffic light and stopped outside the Beach Apartment Company's office. 'Listen, buddy. A body in the morgue, no name, nobody interested, that's just fine. I'm busy, I've got other things to do. Then all of a sudden someone comes by asking questions, the body gets a name, and people want to know the answers to some questions. Like how did he get into that morgue?'

'That's just what I'd like to know myself.'

'OK, then you'll know just how I feel. You're my lead, Mr Taggart, and I'd like to have you right by me just for the moment.'

Faced with a member of the Police Department, the Beach Apartment Company's scruples about the privacy of their leaseholders crumbled away. It was not long before Shilling was opening the door of 1B, 9 East Wind Street.

What had he expected? Not, Taggart realised when he saw it, what he now saw. The body, according to the morgue's label, had been found under the board-walk near Venice Beach. Given the characters he had noticed hanging about in that vicinity – as unpleasant a crew as he had ever seen (Taggart had realised the previous evening why few people walk the Los Angeles streets at night) – he had assumed that Hodgkin was the victim of a mugging. Nipped down the road for a bottle of wine or a packet of butter and never made it back to the apartment. In that case the place should have looked something like the *Mary*

Celeste: television still on, half-eaten sandwiches on a plate, dirty plates on the table and in the dishwasher, mouldy food in the kitchen.

But nothing of the sort. Under its layer of dust the place was as ordered as a newly cleaned hotel room. The fridge was empty. The dishwasher was filled with clean crockery. The television stood dark in its corner, the computer terminal silent on its table.

Shilling looked around him and said, 'Wa-al!' He, too, was surprised by this almost impersonal orderliness. 'You been here before?'

'This is the first time I've ever been to Los Angeles,' said Taggart firmly.

'Welcome to Venice Beach. Don't touch anything; I'm going to call the fingerprint guys.' Shilling moved to the phone, and Taggart gazed around him.

The apartment consisted of two rooms: the big living room, of which one wall was the picture window giving on to a wooden deck over the beach, and a bedroom at the back ventilated by a small window high up in the wall looking out, if one could reach to see, on to the street. There was also a bathroom, between the bedroom and living room. There was no separate kitchen. The level at the back of the living room was raised; a counter separated it from the body of the room, and against the back wall were stove, dishwasher and fridge. The place was carpeted in shaggy cream pile and dotted with dead plants.

Shilling finished his call and began to prowl round the apartment. Taggart went to the bookshelves. There were a few books, mostly recent novels and psychology. On the desk were some typewritten sheets. Taggart turned them over gingerly. It looked like a paper on the monkey work. The phone, too, was on the desk, but no noticeable book of numbers anywhere around. Must have had it on him, and it had been taken together with the rest of his papers. Then Taggart realised that this was a phone with a memory, since it had a small VDU and was attached to a microcomputer. Using his shirt tail – this was no moment to start leaving his own fingerprints all over the place – he pressed the MEMORY button and then the number buttons in turn. A series of numbers appeared on the VDU. He quickly noted them down. Shilling appeared in the doorway, and Taggart wandered over to the window. Through the thin blind which obscured vision from outside he could see a tall, cadaverous-looking man wandering along the beach. 'What now?' he asked.

'Wait for the fingerprint boys.'

'Do I have to wait?'

'Sure do. They'll want your fingerprints, for a start.'

They waited in silence. Taggart picked a novel from the bookshelf and started to read it, while Shilling paced around. He opened the window and went on to the deck. Just below him, on the beach, a blonde was keeping up her tan. 'Don't you wish you were down there,' he said wistfully to Taggart.

'On the beach? Certainly not.'

Shilling looked surprised. It had evidently never struck him that anyone might not like the beach. 'Why not?'

'Too hot. And I don't like sand. Can't stand it between my toes and crunching in my teeth.'

Silence fell again, until the doorbell signalled the fingerprint department. This consisted of a single officer, who busied himself first of all taking Taggart's prints, then Shilling's, for reference, and finally got down to dusting likely surfaces in the apartment.

'You can go now,' said Shilling. 'I'd like to keep your passport, but the fact is I just don't have the grounds. If you weren't here you weren't here.' He looked regretfully at this document, which contained the date of Taggart's entry into the United States stamped firmly across his visa and which confirmed that he had made no other visits across the Atlantic during the year, and handed it reluctantly over.

The fingerprint man said, 'This is the strangest thing I ever saw.'

'Oh, yeah?'

'Obviously I haven't been over it all yet,' he conceded. 'But so far I've done the kitchen and the bathroom. And there isn't a thing. Not a thing. Someone has been over this place and wiped it clean.'

20

By the time he got back to the hotel, Taggart was in a daze. Too much had happened, and his body had no idea whether it was night or day. He had no way of knowing what Shilling was going to do next, and didn't really care. Shilling had noted his address and told him not to move without letting him know. Of course this was no real barrier, but it meant that if he disregarded this instruction he automatically attracted suspicion. Despite, or perhaps because of this, he felt curiously uninvolved, as if he were hovering in some world at one remove from this one in which such strange things were happening. He put this down largely to jet lag, and certainly after a sleep and something to eat he felt somewhat recovered. What now? he thought, as he sat in a dark coffee-shop which advertised BREAKFAST SERVED ALL DAY. A stack of hot-cakes with maple syrup was a definite improvement on no hot-cakes, but it was no substitute for action. But what action? Idly he brought out his diary and leafed through it. He found this often brought forgotten names and facts to his attention. Sure enough, the trick worked. HEISENBORN, he read. The name was followed by what looked like a telephone number. Heisenborn. Heisenborn. He didn't know anyone of that name. Then he remembered. That was Alan Congdon's old friend. What was her name? Prue, that was it. Lived in Santa Barbara. Well, he could just do with someone to talk these strange things over with. He went straight back to his hotel room to telephone.

The phone on the other end of the line rang for some time. Taggart glanced at his watch. Three o'clock – probably out at work. He was just about to hang up when someone answered. 'Hello?' said a breathy and decidedly British voice.

'Is that Prue Heisenborn?'

'Speaking. Who is this?'

Taggart explained who he was and how he had her number.

'Hodgkin,' she said. 'He came to speak near here. I nearly went. Have you got anywhere?'

'In a way.'

'Well, come over and tell us about it. Fred'll be back soon. Come to dinner, why don't you? Are you doing anything this evening? Have you got a car?'

'I can rent one.'

'It'll take you about two hours.'

Drifting north along the freeway listening to the radio, Taggart felt more than ever unreal, as though he were caught up in one of the numberless films he had seen featuring this very shot. In between tunes he learned that today's high would be eighty-nine, low sixty-three, and that smog in the LA area was bad. He felt smugly pleased to be leaving for fresher air. Prue had told him to bring swimming trunks. He couldn't remember when he last felt more like a swim.

The Heisenborns didn't live in Santa Barbara itself, but a little way out in the hills behind the town. Turn off the freeway at exit Santa Barbara North – here it was; he pulled off to check his instructions. Driving briefly through the town he was struck by the contrast with the tacky cardboard that was LA. Here not a blade of grass was out of place by so much as a millimetre, nor was anyone dressed in anything less than the latest designer leisurewear. In contrast to the shining dollies of Los Angeles, the line in Santa Barbara seemed to be naturalness, but so perfectly detailed as to be unattainable without large expenditures of time and money. Taggart, genuinely a natural product, felt that he would have no place in a town like this. It was with some relief that he took his sweaty jeans and grubby T-shirt out of town and into the hills. About twenty minutes' drive, Prue had said. Finally, after a lot of twisting and turning and wrong directions, he found himself at the end of a dirt track facing a mailbox that read HEISENBORN. Here at last. He drove slowly onwards, and soon the house came into view: a pretty frame building that needed repainting, shaded in front by a large live oak. No one was in sight, but as he got out of the car a tall, thin woman wearing a bikini came round the side of the house.

'Hi,' she said. 'I'm Prue. You must be Andrew Taggart, right? Come round. We're by the pool.'

He noticed with relief that the Santa Barbara aura of perfect finish did not extend out here. It was not just a question of the house. Prue herself exhibited definite signs of wear and tear – at least three wrinkles round the eyes and quite a few grey hairs. Also, she was too thin. If she had not been so utterly the antithesis of the healthy blondes he generally fancied, he would have made a pass at her out of sheer relief.

Round the corner of the house, screened by large oleanders, a swimming pool sparkled in the late afternoon sun. Beside it a large, grey-haired man sat drinking a long drink.

'Hi,' he said. 'Have a swim. Then have a drink. Then you can tell us all about it.'

Splashing gratefully in the pool, Taggart reflected that there was apparently no end to the unreality of life. Despite its many attractions – sun, blondes – he was not sure that he would like to live in California. He was not sure he could take it. Hoxton was grimy, and the climate left something to be desired, as did the sartorial finish of the inhabitants, but there was a certain welcome predictability about the place.

Sitting in the sun a few minutes later, clutching an Old-Fashioned, he began to describe the events of the past few weeks and, more specifically, the past day. Fred and Prue listened with gratifyingly open mouths. When at last he had finished and sat back to drain his drink, there was a silence for some while.

Then Fred said, 'Well, sounds to me like you got your story. Famous Parapsychologist Slain. You'd better file it quick – it's sure to get out soon enough. You'll probably find it's all over the *LA Times* tomorrow.'

Taggart shook his head. 'I don't think we're anywhere near the real story yet.'

'Why not?' said Prue. 'Sounds straightforward enough to me. He went out and got mugged and rolled. Happens all the time in Venice, or so the papers say.'

'I don't think it's that simple.'

'Why not?' asked Prue again.

Why not indeed? Taggart wondered. He tried to identify the reasons why he felt so strongly that Hodgkin's demise was part of some more complicated pattern. 'The fingerprints for a start,' he pointed out. 'Or rather, no fingerprints. It wasn't a chance mugging, or a chance anything. It was a professional job.'

'Why would anybody do a thing like that?' mused Fred.

'Easy,' said Prue. 'Whatever happened, happened in the apartment. Or the murderer often went there. He wanted to make sure there wasn't anything there that might lead to him, so he cleaned the whole place up.'

'Yes, and there's something else,' said Taggart. What was it? A question that had been flickering in and out of his mind all day . . . yes. 'Costigan Futures,' he said.

'What about them?' asked Fred lazily. 'Better get dressed before the mosquitoes come out,' he added.

'It's obvious,' said Taggart. 'If Hodgkin just disappeared, why didn't they say so? Why weren't they worried? Why didn't they report it instead of telling anyone that asked that he was in the other place?'

'They might genuinely have thought that,' said Fred, 'if he was the sort of guy that was never in the office much.'

'But not for weeks and weeks. And what was he doing there anyway?'

'Helping to get it going,' said Prue. 'He's a big name round here. People are into the occult, all that kind of thing. They really like it. Fate, karma. You don't have to take responsibility. It's all part of being laid back. People don't like asking why things happen; all they want is to accept them when they do. Prophecy's big business.'

'Especially when it works,' added Fred.

'It worked once,' said Taggart defensively. 'Anything can work once.'

'You can see you haven't been here long,' said Prue. 'So what do you propose to do next?'

'I got these phone numbers,' said Taggart. 'From the memory of the phone in Hodgkin's apartment. I thought I'd phone them up and see who they are.'

21

They sat in the dusk on the paved area outside the kitchen, waiting for the barbecue to heat up. Fred and Prue were holding more Old-Fashioneds. Taggart, who generally drank very little, was watching them, awestruck. The awe increased when he saw the size of the steak Prue brought out of the fridge. She noticed the expression on his face and laughed.

'I got the biggest one I could to confirm your prejudices about America. I always do it when British friends visit.'

'It works. I'm impressed.' The words covered not only the size of the steak but the pool, the oleanders, the scrub-scented evening and the capacity of the natives for absorbing enormous quantities of hard liquor without any apparent effect. 'I find it hard to imagine what it can be like to just live here,' he said.

'It takes a surprisingly short time to get used to it,' said Prue. 'By Californian standards this place is pretty run-down, actually. It was Fred's father's – that's how we come to have it. He's a second-generation Californian. Take a long look. It's a rare breed.'

Heisenborn sat stolidly drinking. 'When are you thinking of making those calls?' he enquired.

'I wondered . . . is there any way you can find out who a number belongs to, without calling it?'

'Not that I know of. Is there in Britain?'

'No, but you never know. Well, then.' Taggart glanced at his watch. Six-thirty. 'Depends whether they're private or office numbers really.'

'Try them,' said Fred. 'I'm fascinated. Wait there.' He went into the house and emerged with a phone which he presented to Taggart. 'Another marvel of modern technology. Do you have those back there?'

'We do, but I don't.' Taggart tried to envisage a cordless phone in Hoxton. 'My place isn't big enough for it to be worthwhile,' he explained.

He got out the list of numbers and began to work through it. There were six altogether. Before he began to call, Taggart decided what his line was to be. The best thing, he concluded, was to be an old friend in search of Hodgkin who had been given this number previously by their mutual friend as that of someone he could call should he happen to be in the area. He was now in search of Hodgkin. Could they help?

That was for the private numbers. Any office numbers would identify themselves and also be unlikely to answer at this hour.

The first number was a Philadelphia one. It turned out to belong to an old family friend who had not heard from Jasper for some months and was worried. One was in New York, and its recorded message informed him that it was a publisher's office; presumably Hodgkin had been planning to publish a book. Taggart noted this down for further enquiry. Of the remaining four, two were in Los Angeles and one in

95

San Francisco. These, it emerged, were all old friends living in the area who had helped Hodgkin settle when he first arrived but had heard nothing of him recently, now they came to think of it. They had assumed he was travelling or busy. The last was a Washington, DC, number. Taggart dialled it, not really expecting a reply, since he assumed it was probably some government office. But the phone at the other end was picked up almost immediately.

'Heirs of Washington Foundation,' said a brisk female voice. 'Can I help you?'

'Oh,' said Taggart, unprepared. 'Er, can you tell me – um – exactly what you do?'

'This is the Heirs of Washington,' repeated the woman testily. 'Who is this, please?'

On the spur of the moment Taggart decided against identifying either himself or his request. 'Thank you very much,' he replied, and hung up.

'Who was that?' asked Heisenborn.

Taggart put the phone down gingerly. 'Something calling itself the Heirs of Washington Foundation. Ever heard of it?'

'Heirs of Washington!' Heisenborn put his drink down so hard that it spilled over his hand. 'Damn,' he said, shaking off drops of whisky.

'Why, have you ever heard of it?'

'Yes.' He was thoughtful now. 'I have.'

At this point they were interrupted by Prue, who had decided that the barbecue was hot enough and came bustling out to deal with the steak. For some time they were occupied with laying it out to grill in the optimum position, and surrounding it with peppers and corn cobs. Things started to sizzle appetisingly.

Taggart said, 'So what is it?'

'Turn that steak,' shouted Prue from inside, 'unless

you want it burned to a cinder.'

'She means cooked,' Fred explained, turning the meat obediently. 'I hope you like raw meat.'

'Well . . .' Taggart was uncertain. He rarely ate steak, and had little confidence in his teeth, weakened by years of digestive biscuits and toffees chewed to keep himself going through long night stints. But he could not very well decline a tourist attraction bought especially for his benefit.

'The Heirs of Washington,' Fred went on ruminatively. 'I'm surprised you haven't come across them, if you're interested in politics.'

'The name seems vaguely familiar,' Taggart admitted. 'But I can't place it. There are so many organisations with names like that.'

'They try not to keep too high a profile. It's a privately funded organisation run by a man named Cal Baker. He's an oil millionaire from somewhere in the Bible Belt. Fundamentalist and very right-wing.'

'But what on earth would Jasper Hodgkin have to do with a set-up like that?'

Fred shrugged his shoulders. 'That's one for you, I guess. What are his politics?'

'No idea. What do this lot do?'

'Fund lobbyists for their pet causes. I don't know in any detail. But it should be easy enough to find out.'

Prue now came out with plates and cans of beer, and Fred was occupied for some time in cutting the steak into three enormous pieces and handing out corn and peppers. Taggart braced himself and began to chew. The steak was not as hard going as he had feared. Even so, he felt some unnerving creaks in his gums.

'Tell you what,' said Heisenborn. 'You got anything planned for tomorrow?'

'No. Why?'

'Then why don't you stay over here – we can find a
bed for you easy enough – and come in with me in the
morning. We'll see what we can find out about the
Heirs of Washington.'

22

Next day at breakfast, Fred Heisenborn, who was
already drinking his coffee when Taggart appeared,
handed him a folded copy of the *Los Angeles Times* as
he sat down. He pointed to a small paragraph halfway
down an inside page. BODY IDENTIFIED, said the
headline uninformatively. The piece itself was almost
as non-committal. A body which had been in the
possession of the police for some time, it said, was
yesterday identified as belonging to Jasper Hodgkin, a
British parapsychologist. Hodgkin had recently come
over to work in Los Angeles. It was thought he had
been mugged and his body dumped in Venice Beach,
near where he lived.

'Nothing else,' said Heisenborn. 'I suppose it'll get
picked up. Coffee?'

'Yes, please.'

'I told you about this institute where I work, didn't
I?' said Fred, pouring coffee.

'You mentioned it.'

'It's a hangover from the sixties, really. Endowed by
very rich men salvaging their liberal consciences.
Atoning to the shades of their parents who were
garment workers on the Lower East Side and probably
members of the IWW and friends of Emma Goldman.
The capitalist system got them out of all that but they
still managed to retain a vestige of intelligence—'

'Still managed to see the Russians as people, though possibly misguided,' put in Prue. 'Comes of being second – or third – generation Americans, if you ask me. It's amazing how much of the trouble here is caused by recent East European immigrants slavering for vengeance.'

'At any rate,' said Heisenborn. 'We're sort of equivalent to Rand. They plan the war, we plan the peace. They're much more in demand, naturally. But we have our uses, and as you can imagine we have to be well informed about what's going on. In NASA, among other places.'

'Of course.'

'So I thought you might like to come and meet someone who knows a bit about that end of things.'

They drove into town in Heisenborn's car, a very small open-topped MG. The aromatic scent of the hills rose up around them as they made their way dustily down into Santa Barbara. Taggart felt somewhat bemused. How long had he been in California? Two days? As usual when visiting the States, he felt intensely foreign. He could understand what the people were saying, but that was about all. How they were thinking behind all those words remained a mystery to him.

They drove out of town on the coast road and pulled off into a smooth-lawned enclave containing a low, glass-walled building surrounded by lush trees. Along walkways crossing the lawn, and bordering the cliff from the foot of which the sound of surf could be heard, figures whizzed by on skateboards, skirting obstacles in their path with an expertise which, however, was not reassuring for the obstacles nor conducive to sustained thought.

Taggart said, 'My God, I thought joggers were dangerous enough.'

'Come inside to my office. We'll be safe there.'

He led the way to a door marked DIRECTOR, waved to a pretty girl the other side of it and went on through another inner door. He motioned Taggart to a chair, picked up the phone, dialled and said, 'That you, Tex? I've got Andrew Taggart here. Will you come to us or shall we come to you? OK, we'll wait.' He put the phone down. 'He'll be along right now. I think Tex may be able to tell you something about the Heirs of Washington.'

The door opened, and a model specimen of young American manhood burst in, filling the office (which was not large in the first place) both with his body, which was long and broad, and with the aura of extreme, almost excessive physical fitness he carried with him. He was blond and crew-cut, and wore a sweat-shirt, jeans and the regulation even tan. Taggart glanced down at his own small but well-defined paunch and felt a blaze of European pleasure at the cultivation of things other than the body. He tried to define these, but failed; it would not be accurate to say that the mind was his chief preoccupation, nor that he specifically preferred to be unfit, though that did give him a certain pleasure in company such as this. He smiled pleasantly at Tex and resisted the temptation to worry a blackhead he could feel under his beard. There is such a thing as carrying passive resistance too far.

'Andrew, this is Tex McKendrick,' Heisenborn was saying. 'Tex, this is Andrew Taggart. Tex', he explained, 'is our secret weapon. You've got to admit, nobody would take him for a parlour pink. All those guys at places like NASA know where he works but they can't really believe it.'

'Specially when they know where I come from,' said Tex cheerfully, folding himself neatly into a chair.

'And where's that?' asked Taggart politely.

'Texas. Amarillo in the Panhandle. Ever been there? They live on making nuclear weapons. No, I'm serious. Home of the Pantex factory. Yes, sir. Great thing about Texans, they don't have no imagination. No, sir. All they care about is solid things like gelt. Yup, Texans know where it's at. So I can approach this whole phenomenon with entire objectivity. I am a student of manners.' He smiled his open, all-American smile.

'What Andrew here wants to know is if you're a student of the Heirs of Washington in particular,' said Heisenborn.

'The Heirs.' Tex looked surprised, and then glanced narrowly at Taggart. 'Why them?'

Taggart considered for a moment. 'Fred's heard all this. But I think I'd better tell you the whole story,' he said. 'It's about as clear as mud anyway.' And he launched into his tale, beginning with the rumour linking Costigan's name with NASA in some undefined way which had first brought Becky to see him, and ending with the list of telephone numbers.

Tex listened to this recital with great interest but with a surprising (to Taggart) lack of amazement or derision. 'Well, that ties in,' he said at the end.

'What with?' asked Heisenborn.

'Some stuff I was hearing about Baker. Do you know anything at all about the Heirs of Washington?' he asked Taggart.

'Not a thing.'

'OK. Well, they're a right-wing pressure group, funded by an oil billionaire from Oklahoma, name of Baker. Cal Baker.'

'Fred told me that much.'

'Right. Well, they've been going for some years, usual sort of stuff. Lobbying, funding a research outfit

101

which publishes their stuff in a sort of academic disguise, running a television channel: they've got a big networked religious show with I don't know how many millions of eager subscribers.' Tex's face was impassive, but his drawl as he mentioned these activities became so pronounced that it was hard to believe he would ever reach the end of a word, let alone a sentence. This was evidently a mark of derision. 'Anyhow. Li'l Cal, he's a religious fellow, and he was real fond of his mommy. She died about three years ago, and he was in despair – until . . . he discovered spiritualism. Yes, sir. Livin' proof of the world beyond the grave.'

'Ah.'

'Yup, you kin probably guess the rest. All Mr Baker wants now – aside from a world free of communism, naturally – is more and more scientific proof of the world beyond the grave.'

'Which is where Costigan comes in.'

'Probably. You know how it is. Everyone wants backing, and nothing gets round the world quicker than word of who is giving out money in your particular field of interest. But it goes a little further than that, naturally. Everything the Heirs do has to go that little bit further.'

'How d'you mean?'

Tex took a breath and looked out of the window to the lawns where the skateboarders whizzed and twirled. 'Well, these are just rumours, of course. Hell, how could they be anything else? But the word is that the Heirs are funding a totally new departure in the fight against the Red Menace and that it isn't totally unconnected with li'l Cal's big interest.'

'But what I heard was that it was NASA,' said Taggart.

'Could be. Could be there's more than one project.

102

Could be they're collaborating. In Southern California, could be just anythin' at all,' Tex drawled cheerfully. 'Southern California,' he went on dreamily, 'war-games centre of the universe. The place lives on two things: silicon chips and defence contracts. Used to be agribusiness as well, but pollution and diseases of one sort and another are taking care of that. It is also, as I imagine you must have noticed, tops in credulity. Anything new and crazy, Southern California can't wait to try it. And those guys at the Pentagon don't take too much persuading. Hell, half of them come from Southern California, too!'

'But the number I called was in Washington.'

'They've got an office there, sure. But they've got one here, too. Hell, they've got offices all over the place.'

'So what now?' Heisenborn sighed.

'Depends what Andrew here wants to do,' said Tex. 'But speaking for myself, I'd really enjoy a chance to take a closer look at the Heirs of Washington.'

'Sounds great,' Taggart assented.

'OK,' said Tex. 'It's a deal. Just give me a little while and I'll try to find out what's going on over there.'

23

After this meeting, Taggart decided to return home, at least for the present. It would be some time before Tex had anything to report on the Heirs of Washington, and other matters were pressing. Tex would contact him when he was ready. Meanwhile, Prue had decided that she was going to sample Costigan Futures Inc.

'Who knows?' she said. 'It may be interesting. It may even work.'

Before he left, Taggart called Sergeant Shilling. 'I'm going home,' he said.

'Stay there,' said Shilling. 'You're nothing but trouble. I had enough to do without this. I keep getting called by clairvoyants who want to tell me just what happened to your friend.'

So Taggart returned to London satisfied that he had left affairs nicely on the boil. He did not, however, relish the thought of his return, since the first thing he would have to do was to ring Becky. Still, he thought as he picked up the phone reluctantly, there's no way out. It'll be even worse if I don't tell her. He debated sending her the *Los Angeles Times* cutting through the post, but rejected the thought. There are some things you can't do.

It was as bad as he feared. Becky's eagerness when she heard his voice was transformed into shocked misery by what he had to say. Despite Jasper's silence, despite Ian Everitt, she had not really believed he was dead. Now she couldn't escape it. When Taggart described the cravat the Costigan Futures girl had identified, she burst into tears.

'I gave him that for his last birthday!' she sobbed.

'I'm terribly sorry,' said Taggart awkwardly.

'Oh, it's not your fault. It's better to know, at least. What do they think happened?'

'No idea.' Now was not the moment to start going into complex possibilities.

'Why did he ever go there?'

There was no answer to this.

'So what will you do now? Drop it, now we know what happened?'

'No, there's still quite a story there for me. Anyway, I'm not sure what did happen.' He explained his doubts and added that he was on to something, but he did not specify what it was. Out of sheer paranoid habit, Taggart never discussed anything important on the phone. Becky made him promise that he would keep her in touch with any developments, and also that he would tell her more when they met face to face.

Next day he noticed that there were some paragraphs in the British papers about Jasper's sudden death in Los Angeles. *The Guardian* ran a piece on his work and its potential, now possibly never to be realised:

> In cases of this sort, where a piece of work is obviously so far from its conclusion, one can only hope that there will be individuals committed and talented enough to carry it through. The commitment will undoubtedly be there. But Jasper Hodgkin's special combination of scientific persistence and poetic imagination will be sadly missed.

The piece was not signed. Taggart wondered who had written it. Not Openshaw – of that he was sure.

On the first of September, about a week after his return, he found a message on his desk at *New Politics*. Could he contact Joseph Horne? A telephone number was appended which turned out to be that of the Shaftesbury Theatre. Mr Horne was not there at the moment, but would be in after lunch as that day was a matinee. Perhaps Mr Taggart would call back then?

The Shaftesbury Theatre: the name rang some sort of bell. Horne, thought Taggart. Horne – not an actor, as far as he could recall. The Shaftesbury did not advertise in *New Politics*, but he found it in a copy of the previous day's *Standard*. Joseph Horne the Wonderworker, on for a limited season. Of course, the magician: Taggart had seen him once or twice on television, but knew little more about him. He had no idea why the Wonderworker should wish to contact Andrew Taggart. Still, there was one way to find out: ask him. The Shaftesbury was a short walk from the *New Politics* offices. He would go to the evening show and visit Horne afterwards backstage.

Somewhat to Taggart's surprise, the theatre was crowded. Very popular with coach trips, the box office assured him. He was able to get a seat by the gangway about halfway down the stalls. To the accompaniment of a thousand sweet-wrappers being discreetly unfurled, the curtain rose.

The programme notes promised a tantalising show. Horne was shown by his photograph to be a dark man with high cheekbones, satanic eyebrows and a somewhat thirties hairline moustache. He had been obsessed with magic since he was five, the programme said, and had begun performing in public at the tender age of nine. He had taken a degree in psychology, and the programme quoted his psychology professor as affirming that he had 'developed a striking and unique method of communication', whatever that might be. Taggart, feeling cynical and superior, glanced behind him to take note of any suspicious-looking persons who might be lurking around the theatre checking on interesting details among the audience. He even felt surreptitiously under his seat for hidden bugs. None appeared to be there, but one could never tell.

The programme photograph was of a rather imposing man. Horne, however, as revealed in the spotlight, was small and slight. But technique has little to do with stature. Horne took immediate command of his audience. He began with an informal chat in which, among other things, he teased them about looking out for spies in the theatre and searching for bugs under

106

their seats. Taggart shifted guiltily.

Horne then went on to assure his audience that ESP was nothing extraordinary; it was a faculty shared by very large numbers of people. He would give them some examples of this. He was now going to think of two simple geometrical shapes, and they must try to guess what these were. He was now projecting them on his mental screen. 'Now, ladies and gentlemen, I am asking you to open your own mental screen to these images.' There was a silence while the theatre concentrated. Horne talked with a slight Lancashire accent; its homeliness somehow increased his credibility. In spite of himself, Taggart thought of geometric shapes: a circle inside a square. Horne broke the silence. 'Now, then. I was thinking of a square inside a circle. Who got my message?' About a quarter of the audience raised their hands. 'But before that,' Horne went on, 'before I fixed on it, I thought of a circle in a square. Did any of you get that?' A further good sprinkling of hands were raised. Taggart, who did not raise his, estimated that about a third of the audience had caught Horne's thought.

Horne embarked upon another feat of communication. He was going to think of a number between one and fifty. Both the digits would be odd, and the same digit would not be repeated. Thus, eleven was out, but fifteen, for instance, would be all right. 'I'm going to think of it now,' he said, 'and once again I'm asking you all to open your minds to my thought.' He shut his eyes, apparently concentrating deeply. After a couple of minutes he opened them again. 'All right, ladies and gentlemen. I was thinking of the number thirty-seven. Thirty-seven. Did any of you get that?' There were gasps from the audience. A forest of hands waved in the air. Horne the Wonderworker smiled. 'I almost fixed on thirty-five,' he admitted. 'I suppose quite a few of you got that instead?' More hands were raised. Taggart was bemused with the rest of them. He had thought of thirty-seven.

The show went on. One of the acts consisted of Horne asking the audience to write down a short thought or message on a slip of paper – something personal that he would be unlikely to guess. Taggart wrote the title of a book he was currently reading, a Dick Francis thriller: SLAY RIDE. While the audience were writing, Horne moved about the theatre, up and down the aisles, distributing paper slips, pencils, envelopes. He then ran up the gangway, carrying a tray containing envelopes. The folded messages had all been passed down to those sitting by the gangways, including Taggart. Horne handed Taggart an envelope, into which the messages were placed; then he darted on. Finally all the messages were collected up and placed on the tray at the front of the stage.

Horne now proceeded with a thought-reading act. Various members of the audience agreed that they had a daughter who had recently scalded herself, had a crack in the kitchen door or had lost a chequebook. Then Horne suddenly said, 'I'm getting a name. I think it's a name, or a title . . . begins S L A – does this mean anything to somebody?'

Taggart felt his skin prickle. He was in two minds what to do. Should he sit tight? Somewhere behind him someone seemed to be standing up. But Horne was looking straight at him now, as if he could read his mind. Taggart slowly rose.

Horne said, 'I'm getting two words. Is that right?'

'Yes.'

'And the first word has four letters, right?'

'Yes.'

'It's coming now. The first word's SLAY. I think it's SLAY.'

'Yes,' Taggart admitted.

'Hold on now. The second word has four letters. SLAY KILL – no, that's not it. It's a ride. That's it, isn't it? SLAY RIDE.'

Taggart nodded and sat down. He felt very strange.

24

After his unnerving experience during the show, Taggart was undecided about his next move. How could he possibly face Joseph Horne now? At least on the telephone he could remain anonymous. But the magician, depending on what he had to say, would be sure to suggest a meeting. There was really no excuse. And if he didn't face up to the situation now, it was (he had to admit) that much less likely that he would face up to it later. He would simply let the thing, whatever it was, slide – which might not, but might, be a matter for regret. Anyway, he had already left a note at the stage door saying he would be coming round after the show. If he failed to turn up, that would be plain discourtesy.

Reluctantly, then, he forced himself round to the back of the theatre and found himself knocking on Horne's dressing-room door. He felt thoroughly discomposed, in anything but the right mood to conduct an interview.

From inside the room, Horne called, 'Come in!'

Taggart went in. Horne, sitting in his shirt sleeves in front of his mirror, cleaning make-up off his face, said, 'Mr Taggart, I presume?' and turned round. He looked very unimposing. When he saw who his visitor was, he first looked disbelieving and then said, 'It is Mr Taggart, is it?'

'That's me.'

109

Horne burst out laughing. 'Well, well. I hope you enjoyed the show!'

'I found it fascinating.'

'Took you for a bit of a ride, eh?' The magician turned back to his mirror and, still chortling, went on removing make-up. 'Do sit down.' He waved towards a chair at the side of the room, finished with his make-up, dried his face, slipped on a sweater and turned to face his guest. 'Sorry about that. Look, I usually go and get a bite to eat after the show. Why don't you come with me?' They walked out of the theatre, Horne bidding the stage doorman a cheerful goodbye. It was just on ten o'clock. They walked up Greek Street and turned in at a small German restaurant. It was evidently a place Horne came to every night, or most nights at least. He led the way to what seemed to be his regular table and rapidly ordered a meal. 'Same for you?'

'I'll just have some soup, thanks.' Taggart was not particularly hungry, and if he had been, foreign food of this sort was not what he would have chosen. Horne was tucking into a dish of goose with red cabbage that looked, to Taggart's jaundiced eye, thoroughly untrustworthy.

'Delicious,' said the magician, holding out a loaded forkful. 'Try some?'

'No thanks.'

Horne smiled and went on eating. He had particularly expressive eyebrows. They were the reason why the programme photograph was so striking. They were rarely still, conveying nuances of expression otherwise undetectable in his face, which, like the rest of his body, seemed to be under unnaturally strict control. The Lancashire accent was less marked now than it had been on stage: possibly a device for conveying homely trustworthiness. At last he pushed

110

his plate away, wiped his mouth and sat back. 'That's better.' He surveyed Taggart quizzically. 'Well, Mr Taggart, it's very kind of you to respond so promptly to my message.'

'Very kind of you to get in touch with me.'

'Maybe it was. But it's not an opportunity I should have cared to miss.' The magician sat back and lit a cigarette. 'Smoke?' Taggart shook his head.

Taking a deep puff, Horne said, 'Well, d'you think I'm psychic?'

'I assume you're not, though how you do all those things I haven't the faintest idea.'

'And what d'you think about psi? The whole racket?'

'Until very recently,' said Taggart, 'I'd never thought about it at all.'

'Then you are almost unique,' said Horne. 'The entire population's addicted to it. Horoscopes, predictions . . . they can't get enough of it.' He sounded almost angry.

'You make quite a good thing out of that yourself, wouldn't you say?' Taggart observed mildly.

'Oh, absolutely. I can't deny it.' Horne leaned forward. 'You know, everything I do is a trick. Every single thing. Anyone could learn how to do what I do, if they applied themselves and if I told them how – which I'm not about to. But will people believe that? No!' he answered himself. 'And why not? Because they don't want to believe it, that's why not. So I let them believe what they want. It's good for business. But I can tell you this. If you meet anyone that tells you they've got psychic powers, then they're lying. Don't believe it, because it isn't true.'

'Is that why you wanted to see me? To tell me that?'

'Well,' said Horne, 'it's relevant to your current area of interest, isn't it?'

'And how, simply as a matter of interest, do you know about that?'

'Don't be so suspicious, Mr Taggart,' said the magician, signalling for coffee. 'Not because I'm psychic, I assure you. For one thing, you published something about our old friend Jerry Costigan. Had you forgotten?'

'Oh, that.'

'That's right. That. And I wouldn't really need ESP', said Horne pointedly, 'to deduce from your answer that you're also interested in other aspects of the subject. Am I right?'

'Well . . .'

'I know I'm right. And that's why I got in touch with you. It's a small world, the psychic world,' said Horne quickly, as Taggart seemed about to protest. 'Everyone knows everyone, and if something's up, then everyone knows that, too.'

'But you're not a psychic, you just said.'

'Ah, but I'm part of it,' said Horne. 'Just as much as if I'd set up as a spirit medium or as a disciple of the late Dr Rhine. As far as they're concerned, I'm in business as a sceptic. And of course, as far as most of my public's concerned, I am psychic. I told you. The people who come to my shows are the same ones who pack out the halls for that sham Everitt. Incidentally, weren't you in the audience for his last television spectacular? I thought so. I never forget a face.'

'So what does your information tell you I'm doing?'

'Got you really worried, haven't I? said Horne. 'Brandy?'

'No, thanks.'

'Mind if I do?'

'Go ahead.'

When his brandy came, Horne said, 'It's all perfectly simple, really. I was talking to that nice girl

112

Becky Ryan. Met her at a conference.'

'So why couldn't you say so in the first place?'

Horne grinned. 'Habit, I suppose. Partly that. But I do like to see how people react. That's my business, after all.'

'You know Becky?'

'Known her for years. An honest seeker after truth, Becky. Not many of those in this game. She doesn't approve of me, of course. Thinks I'm a hardened old cynic. Which I am.'

'How about her friend Hodgkin? Was he an earnest seeker, too?'

'Was?' interjected Horne. 'Has something really happened to him, then?'

'He seems to have disappeared.' Taggart did not enlarge on this, and, somewhat to his surprise, Horne did not pursue it. He had, it seemed, other preoccupations in this area.

'Jasper Hodgkin,' he mused now. 'No, he's altogether more complicated, if you ask me. Clever fellow, and very imaginative. Sees the chance to make his name as one of the world's great theorists, and can't resist it. Who could?'

'When you say he's imaginative, do you mean he's a fraud?'

'No. No, that isn't it. Too easy to catch him out if he was. He noticed certain effects, and when they were pointed out, other people claimed to notice them, too. Can't say I've ever been able to make it work myself, but there we are. What he doesn't do is explain the cause of his effects. There they are; it's enough that he's noticed them. Doesn't seem very scientific to me. I always thought science was about explanations.'

'Seems to be enough for NASA, or Rand, or somebody.'

'Ah, well, that's another matter. They haven't been

around in this particular business as long as I have. But Jerry Costigan, now – that's a different matter.'

'He's a fraud?'

'Well, of course. Surely that had struck you? Still, if people want to be taken in by these things, that's their affair. That's how I make a living myself, after all. It's a business, like any other. No, it's how Costigan managed to get himself into a position to set it up in the first place that interests me.'

'How d'you mean?'

'Well, it's not very complicated. What does Costigan have that enables him to set himself up not just as some crazy charlatan catering for the astrology trade but as a serious scientific business man? Just one thing,' said Horne firmly. 'He published his stuff in *Natural Science*, and it was refereed, and they wouldn't have accepted it if it was all a set-up, would they?'

'Well, I wouldn't have thought they would.'

'But supposing they did?'

'Have you got proof of that?'

'I may be able to put you in the way of getting it,' said Horne, 'if you're interested.'

25

Some days after this conversation had taken place, Taggart received a bulky envelope in the post. It contained an offprint of Costigan's article in *Natural Science*, the one that had done so much to establish his reputation in both the normal and the paranormal worlds.

The article was entitled A STUDY OF REMOTE VIEWING. Its author, Dr Costigan, was described as

Reader in Particle Physics at the University of London. The experiments it recounted were simple. They had been conducted with a team of two 'senders' and three 'receivers', selected over a long period for their apparent facility in this area. The 'senders' had been given a list of ten possible locations within a ten-mile radius of the site of the experiment (a laboratory Costigan sometimes used at Sussex University, which, he explained, he had chosen on account of the extremely varied and distinctive nature of possible locations available within the chosen radius). The 'receivers' had stayed at the laboratory under carefully monitored conditions and at a prearranged time had concentrated on receiving a picture of the chosen site from the senders, who would then be concentrating upon the transmission of such a picture. The 'receivers' described the picture they had received and made drawings of it. The 'senders' recorded the site selected, and took Polaroid photographs of the scene they had concentrated upon transmitting. They then moved to another site and transmitted their new 'message'. In this way up to four experiments a day were conducted, two in the morning and two in the afternoon. Each experiment had lasted five days, giving thirty attempts in all. A team of three impartial judges, who were unacquainted with either senders or receivers, had then matched drawings to photographs for each day's work. Any pair correctly matched was counted a 'hit'. The experiments had yielded an eighty-per-cent success rate: far above chance expectancy. Costigan posited no explanation of this, but merely described his findings.

There was a short covering note from Horne. All articles in *Natural Science*, he explained, were submitted to referees – at least two, sometimes more. The referees for this particular article might bear investigation.

Taggart pushed the note away with a feeling of having somehow been cheated. From what Horne had said, he had expected something more substantial. He poured himself another cup of tea and loaded a piece of toast with marmalade, wondering what to do next.

The first step was obvious: contact the editor of *Natural Science*. He glanced at the offprint. The article had been published some two years previously. He had no idea whether there had been any change of editor since then. No doubt he would find out quickly enough. Meanwhile it was only nine o'clock, and it would be another hour at least before anyone other than secretaries arrived at the office of any magazine.

He turned back to his daily paper. The Zambian government seemed to be having a difficult time, he noticed; the President's health appeared to be giving way, and there was talk of a possible coup. Taggart noted this with some interest. He had the day before received a letter from Prue Heisenborn. As she had promised, she had been along to Costigan Futures Inc. She had chosen copper as her commodity, since she had a convenient copper bracelet; the sensitive had taken her on a ride to Death Valley, which, as Taggart might know (he did not), is the lowest place on earth. This meant, the sensitive informed her, that copper was going to fall steeply. He judged the date by the distance they had travelled to reach their destination. The day he had given her was in a month's time. Zambia, of course, supplied a large proportion of the world's copper, and the newspaper article noted that prices were already rising in anticipation of trouble and shortages. So much for Death Valley.

He set off for the office. He could just as easily ring *Natural Science* from there. It was a lovely September morning, sunny and fresh. Even Hoxton looked inviting, and the half-hour cycle ride to the office

116

would be a real pleasure. Taggart packed his papers into his panniers and set off. Expertly avoiding death in the whirling maelstrom of morning traffic at the Angel, he was soon in the Euston Road, cycling towards Soho. Choking in the exhaust fumes of the stream of taxis and buses which jammed the stretch of road joining King's Cross, St Pancras and Euston stations, he found it hard to credit the existence of Santa Barbara, that pink-washed paradise. Were Prue and Fred Heisenborn even now lounging beside their pool? Well, no, they weren't; it was the middle of the night for them, of course. But in a mere few hours they would be. Despite the fact that he had seen Fred's office, he couldn't seriously imagine either of them working. He couldn't imagine anyone in California working, though he knew they did, sometimes. Partly a function of weather: work always seemed more probable during the winter, he found. It went on during the summer, but with less vigour. During the summer Taggart's thoughts inclined more readily to sex. With John Betjeman he proclaimed:

> I've often thought that I should like
> To be the saddle of a bike.

Sadly, he reflected as he pedalled down Gower Street, he was not in that happy position, and it was some time since he had been in any position comparably interesting. He found himself thinking of Becky Ryan. Now there was a nice girl, and not married either. There were increasingly few such uncluttered possibilities among his female acquaintance.

On this happy note, he turned into Great James Street, chained his bike firmly to the railings, and braced himself (although the day was increasingly warm) for work.

The editor of *Natural Science* was not yet there. He asked the girl who answered the phone whether or not the editorship had changed within the past three years. It had. Damn. Still, the new editor might be able to help somewhat or, if not, might perhaps put him in touch with the old one. He applied himself to other matters and tried again half an hour later. This time he was lucky.

'Hello? John Roberts? Andrew Taggart here from *New Politics*. It was just a query connected with an investigation I'm doing. Thought you might be able to help. It's about an article you published roughly two years ago, by Jerry Costigan, about Remote Viewing—'

What he was expecting Taggart was not sure. What he was not expecting was the stream of invective which now met his ears. Roberts, it appeared, had no wish to be identified with the magazine which had published egregious rubbish of that nature. It was a disgrace to *Natural Science* and science in general. It was sheer superstition of the kind any responsible journalist should be doing his best to stamp out. Had he been the editor then, the piece would never have seen the light of day. As it was, his inclination would be to call in all copies of that issue and pulp them, but this was impossible. If Taggart was planning to give further publicity to Costigan, then he, Roberts, would not only not help him, he would put every possible obstacle in his way.

Taggart said weakly, 'But I just wanted to contact the referees.'

Roberts snapped that he had no idea about any referees and doubted whether there had been any or, if there had, whether it could possibly be worth talking to them about anything. Then he slammed the phone down.

Well, reflected Taggart, astonished. Something up there, that's for sure. What now? Who did he know who might know about this kind of thing?

Becky, of course.

26

Becky was not in her office. The woman on the switchboard informed him in a distinctly snappish tone that she had no idea when or whether Dr Ryan was likely to be in, nor where she might be found. Taggart was puzzled until he remembered that this was still the long vacation, when all mere workers, such as departmental secretaries and switchboard ladies, doubtless assumed that teaching personnel were off on their annual skive in the sun.

In fact, Becky was merely at home. She was busy designing a new set of experiments, due to start in a few days' time, but she would be glad to see him. She wanted to know more about what had happened in Los Angeles. There was too much they hadn't been able to discuss on the phone. Had there been any new developments?

Yes, quite a lot; and he was hoping she might be able to help him.

So would he like to come and see her? And if so, why not today? The countryside was really lovely just now.

Taggart needed no second bidding. He did not keep a car; he found a bike more useful in London, and taxis could always be charged to expenses. However, Becky's cottage was not easily approached in any other way. Well, the *Sunday Review* wouldn't balk at a little more car rental.

He drove happily up the Edgware Road and zoomed on to the M1. Was there anywhere a more disgusting road? he wondered, racing up its grimy length while enormous trucks did their best to kill him. The Southern California freeways were like paradise compared with this. Soon, however, he turned off into what might have been another country, of small towns basking in the late summer sun and lazy, verdant pastures. By half-past two he was drawing up outside Becky's absurd cottage.

She was sitting outside at a small table in the sun, jotting things down on a large pad and making little sketches. She greeted him rather flatly. Recent events had knocked the bounce out of Becky. The sunlight slanted through the branches of an old walnut tree and sent leaf-shadows dancing across her jotting pad. She should have been perfectly happy, but evidently was not. She loved him, Taggart suddenly thought. Whatever she says, she loved him. Poor kid. He felt a pang of jealousy.

In fact Becky's distraction had other causes. The news about Jasper had indeed been a shock, but it had merely exacerbated more immediate miseries. She glanced at her watch. Joe, her philosopher friend, ought to be phoning about now, if he was around. He worked every morning and always phoned (when he did phone) in mid-afternoon, when the brain (he liked to explain) was numbed by lunch and before impending domesticity began to cast its long shadows at around five o'clock.

One reason she had asked Taggart down with such alacrity was that he provided an escape from the abiding curse of afternoons at home, waiting for the phone. How disproportionate it all was, she thought. Just as bad, in its way, as thinking about poor Jasper –

worse, almost, because she felt guilty. This was not the correct time to be brooding on the pleasures of the flesh. One started an affair with no thought but for the present and (let us not kid ourselves, Dr Ryan) with no depth of feeling. A mere infatuation, an indulgence of the senses, icing on the cake. Then the first unmistakable inklings of that sensation which she always classified to herself as 'paddling through mud': effort and tension where everything had at first been easy and taken for granted. One tried to ignore it, but there it was, the inevitable prelude to afternoons of waiting for the phone, those interminable duels with one's better self. Today, she thought at about eleven o'clock, I shan't think about him and I most certainly won't phone him. Then, as the day wore on, and the phone, lurking there silent and unforgettable, did not ring – or only rang with trivia, a lurch of the heart each time followed by a hollow in the stomach – resolution diminished along with concentration, until by three-thirty the whole thing was unbearable, and why shouldn't she call him, for God's sake? These are enlightened days, are they not? Must the little woman still lurk in her burrow waiting for the call of the masterful male? So she called, and there he was, and of course it was all right – just overlaid with a thin layer of mud.

Taggart interrupted this train of thought by saying, 'Actually what I wanted was to find out more about Jerry Costigan.'

'What sort of thing? I don't know very much about him. He simply pays my salary.'

'Yes, and why d'you think he does that?'

She shrugged. 'Guilt, or something? He did remove Jasper, one way or another.' The phone rang. She started (clearly a call eagerly awaited) and, muttering

'Excuse me', ran into the house. She emerged ten minutes later, looking singularly downcast. 'Sorry about that. Just a student wanting to fix up supervisions for next year.'

'Do you know anything about his *Natural Science* article, was what I wanted to know,' Taggart said as she sat down. At this rate not only would they never reach the point, they would fall out before there was any chance of doing so.

'I've got a copy somewhere. I'll find it, if you want to wait.'

'What, the magazine?'

'Yes, what else?' She stared at him, surprised.

'No, nothing.' Taggart shook his head, and Becky disappeared once more into the house, returning with the magazine a few minutes later.

Taggart took it. It bore, naturally, the name of the editor of that time: Michael Anthony; of course, he should have remembered. It also contained an editorial explaining that *Natural Science* was publishing this piece not because it advocated this approach but simply because it felt its readers might like to be aware of what was going on in this area, about which it felt doubtful and which (it wanted to make very clear) it was not by any means endorsing, but which perhaps should not be ignored. The offprint, needless to say, had omitted this qualifying stricture.

'Do you know anything about this article?' Taggart wanted to know.

'What sort of thing? I know about that work, of course.'

'What d'you think of it?'

'Well . . . *Natural Science* printed it, didn't they?'

'Would it have been refereed?'

'Their articles always are, and I imagine they'd have been especially careful with that one. I don't know who the referees were, though.'

'Ah.'

'Was that what you wanted to know?'

'That's one of the things.'

'Cup of tea?' offered Becky, who did not wish to be left alone with the telephone. 'It'll all be in their files, won't it? At *Natural Science*?'

'The current editor doesn't wish to know anything about it. But I'm sure I can easily find Anthony.'

'If you can't,' said Becky, 'I've got a friend who works on *Natural Science*. We were psychology students together. He could get you the file.'

They sat in the sunlit garden drinking tea. The phone did not ring. Taggart explained to Becky about the Heirs of Washington and filled in some other details. At half-past five he reluctantly excused himself. He must get back; there were some proofs he had to check at *New Politics*. He looked wistfully at Becky.

'Why don't you come back with me?' he hazarded. 'Then when I've done the proofs we could go somewhere. You could stay over if you wanted.'

She glanced at her watch. There would be no phone call now. Joe would have left for home, or elsewhere. She felt a certain sense of triumph. Temptation resisted for today; tomorrow she would feel strong. But she did not feel like an evening alone at home if it could be avoided.

'All right,' she said.

27

As they drove down the grimy reaches of the M1, stage-lit by the evening sun, the news on the car radio confirmed that there had been a military coup in Zambia and that panic on the markets was sending the price of copper soaring.

'Well,' said Taggart, 'Costigan Futures doesn't strike again.'

'They've got some time left,' said Becky defensively.

'You believe in all that, then?'

'I don't disbelieve it out of hand. Would you expect me to? Anyway, why should you? You've seen it work once – you were telling me.'

'Anything can work once. I can put a fiver on a horse and it may win.'

'That's what I object to,' said Becky. 'You simply assume it's all rubbish. That's what's been worrying me about having approached you in the first place. If there's anything to be found out I'm sure you'll find it. But what I'm afraid you'll do is just use it as a stick to beat us all with and make us look like halfwits.' Her voice rose, Taggart noticed, as she beat the psi drum. He had noticed the phenomenon before. The rise in pitch signalled the end of reasoned argument and the beginning of Articles of Belief: Faith, the Leap into the Unknown. He had never had any sympathy with religious feeling, and he did not want to get into a religious argument now.

'I haven't any axe to grind,' he said levelly.

'Then why were you talking to Horne? Don't you know about Horne?'

'Only that he's a very skilful operator.'

'Well, he may be that, but he's also paranoid. Obsessed. His whole stock-in-trade is showing up people like Jasper and Jerry and me and making us look ridiculous. If you tell anyone interested in the paranormal that you've been talking to Horne, I can tell you what will happen. They'll simply refuse to speak to you.'

'Thanks for telling me. I'll be discreet.' They drove

124

on, and Taggart said mildly, 'Excuse my mentioning it, but it seems to me that you're a little edgy this afternoon. Has something happened?'

'Sorry,' said Becky. 'But it's true about Horne.'

They lapsed into silence. When they got to the *New Politics* office, it was half-past seven. Taggart said, 'I must just go and check those proofs. Come on up.'

The office was almost empty. While Taggart worked, Becky wandered around, torn between the desire to nose into the piles of paper which lay everywhere around and an inhibiting sense of shyness.

The proofs did not take long. After he had finished with them, Taggart consulted the book in which he kept uncompromising phone numbers. Included were the home numbers of several scientific journalists with whom he liked to check details. Michael Anthony's was among them. Eight o'clock: he was as likely to be at home now as at any other time. Taggart dialled.

Anthony sounded annoyed. Probably got him in the middle of dinner. 'Oh, it's you. Well, what d'you want? I assume you want something.'

'Yes,' said Taggart. He felt no compunction. Anthony owed him favours; he had tipped him off about more than one good story when he had come across things that seemed too purely scientific for *New Politics*. 'You were still at *Natural Science* when they published that piece of Jerry Costigan's.'

'Was I not!' said Anthony. 'What a hornets' nest. I must have been mad. You're not reopening that one, are you? If that's what you were thinking of, let me strongly advise against.'

'What d'you mean?'

'It's a long story.'

'I've got time.'

'And I was just about to have some dinner. . . . Oh,

well, briefly: Costigan sent me this paper. He'd got these really astounding results – have you read it?'

'Yes.'

'Well, then, you know what I mean. Here people had been trying this sort of thing for years and years and getting excited if they got a just marginally higher-than-chance success rate. And really, even if they had done what they said they had, which was usually unlikely if one looked into it, it didn't seem like much to write home about. But this was different. It seemed to put the whole business on a more substantial footing. Costigan was a respected scientist, a physicist, with a real name in his field – not in the Nobel class, but not so very far off. Then he suddenly gets interested in this. Don't ask me why; that wasn't my business. The important thing was, here was someone who knew how to design experiments and knew what to look out for. And here he came up with sixty-, seventy-, eighty-per-cent success rates. Well, something was happening. How could one just ignore it? Either way it was a story. If he was cheating, that was a story; and if he wasn't, it was even bigger.'

'And he wasn't?'

'You can imagine, we checked.'

'There were referees?'

'There are always referees for articles in *Natural Science*. This time we had three of them.'

'How did you choose them?'

'We didn't exactly go to Costigan and ask him who he might like,' said Anthony stiffly.

'Of course not.'

'On the other hand, we had to use people who knew something about the subject. They were the ones who'd be aware of the problems, after all.'

'What d'you mean?'

'Well . . . ' Anthony sounded slightly embarrassed. Taggart said nothing. Here was the nub, or a nub; he could feel it. 'It was no use bringing in people who'd never had anything to do with this kind of thing before. They wouldn't know what it was about, and half of them would have refused to have anything to do with it anyhow.'

'And the other half?'

'Well . . . ' Anthony was now perhaps deeply regretting this conversation, but Taggart had no intention of letting him off the hook.

'Yes, well?'

'The trouble with this sort of subject', Anthony began again on a different tack, 'is that people simply aren't dispassionate about it, and what you want from a referee is dispassion. You don't want him to be taken in, but it's no good if he's so violently against whatever it is that you're trying to discuss that he can barely talk about it for ten seconds without some deletable expletive. Referees are there to check the work, not to rubbish it.'

'Ah, open-mindedness. Must have people who are open-minded.' Taggart was delighted; he was always pleased to find a connection. 'One of the key words of the paranormal. "You're a filthy sceptic, I am open-minded."'

'Something like that. You can see the problem we had.' Anthony still sounded uncomfortable.

'No one would agree to referee it who anyone would accept as impartial,' Taggart said cheerfully. 'Why didn't you just refuse to publish?'

'I wanted to publish. I've already explained. And we were very careful about putting in that disclaimer in the editorial. It just seemed so . . . well, narrow-minded does seem to me the best way to put it,

127

whatever its connections . . . to turn down something like that out of hand. Of course, if I'd known how Costigan would use it—'

'What d'you mean, exactly?'

'Oh, you know. Making thousands of offprints without the disclaimer. Using the thing as a launch pad for that ludicrous business of his—'

'Which seems to be doing very well.'

'So I understand,' said Anthony.

'I've run a couple of tests on it,' said Taggart.

'And has he done well for you?'

'I don't know whether I ought to tell you this, speaking as a filthy sceptic,' said Taggart, 'but the first one was spot on. I really didn't know whether to be glad or sorry.'

'How about the second?'

'Don't know yet. Doesn't seem too promising so far. But to get back to the subject,' said Taggart inexorably. 'Did you find any referees in the end?'

'Yes, three. I don't recall the exact details; they'd be on file. But I can remember roughly what they did. One was a magician—'

'Not Horne?'

'Not Horne,' said Anthony impatiently. 'One doesn't ask a man's bitterest opponent to referee his work. Horne makes his living out of rubbishing the likes of Costigan.'

'OK.'

'Albert Kotchinsky, I think his name was. Something like that. I took advice from a man I know who's in the Magic Circle. Then there was a physicist who'd also dabbled about in this kind of thing, and one was an SPR nominee. After all, they know about what to look out for in this kind of thing, and they're more anxious than most to stop any cheating going on.'

128

Anthony sounded defensive. 'Why all this interest, anyway?'

'Oh, Costigan figures in an investigation I'm doing.'

'Well, be careful.'

'Why? Think he'll hex me or something?'

'Don't be so cocky,' said Anthony. 'But that isn't what I meant. It's just that I've never known a subject arouse such passions. You wouldn't believe.'

'I don't.'

'In that case,' said Anthony, 'you're the enemy: not mine – theirs. Don't say I didn't warn you.'

28

Taggart put down the receiver. It was only after Anthony, too, had safely disconnected that Becky, who had been listening on an extension, felt safe to do likewise.

'Interesting, wasn't it?' Taggart glanced at his watch. Eight-thirty. 'Shall we go and have something to eat? I think it's about time the *Sunday Review* stood you dinner.'

They made for a modest Italian establishment in New Oxford Street, near the *New Politics* office. Taggart ordered half a carafe of wine for Becky; he would stick to mineral water, as he always did when he might have to drive.

Becky suddenly said, 'This is all very well, but how am I going to get back? It suddenly struck me in the middle of that phone call. Here I am in London, and my car's at the house. Public transport doesn't exactly pass my door.'

'Don't worry about it.'

'I didn't worry about it. In fact, I was in such a state when we left that I didn't even think about it. But I can't help wondering.'

'You can stay at my place, and I'll run you back tomorrow. How's that?'

'I don't want any more entanglements,' said Becky firmly. 'My life at the moment is just one damn thing after another – or not, which is even worse. I don't wish any more.'

'Who even suggested such a thing?'

'Nobody. I just wanted to make things quite clear before we began. I'd be delighted to stay at your place. It's very kind of you, but . . . well, you know what I mean.'

'I know what you mean.'

This conversation was brought safely to an end by the arrival of their tortellini alla panna. After several minutes' concentration, Taggart leaned back with an air of relief and said, 'Well, what did you make of that?'

'Michael Anthony?' Becky took another mouthful and chewed thoughtfully. 'He regrets he ever did it.'

'Obviously. You don't have to read very far between the lines for it to be clear that that's what lost him his job. Not the kind of thing the publishers of *Natural Science* want in their magazine. Now that I come to think of it, I seem to remember vaguely hearing something about it, though it didn't register much then. Not my line, and anyway I was probably in the middle of some story at the time. But you only had to hear the new chap's reaction – what's his name? Roberts – to know that.'

'Good for him,' said Becky stoutly. 'Someone who'll stand by his principles, at least.'

'Stand by *your* principles,' said Taggart rudely. 'But that isn't what I meant.' He waited for a reaction.

130

Becky just went on eating. 'Don't you want to know what I meant?'

'I'm not sure I do.'

'Oh, come on, Becky, it was just a joke. No, but seriously: had it ever struck you', said Taggart, leaning across the table and speaking softly, 'that Costigan may be at the bottom of all this?'

'All what?'

Taggart leaned back and sighed. 'Why are we here?' he asked rhetorically. 'What was it that brought us together in the first place? Your friend Jasper. He disappeared, remember?'

'But what did Jerry Costigan have to do with that? It seems straightforward enough. Jasper went out and got mugged. Jerry offered him a job in America, and people tend to get mugged there. That's the only connection I can see.'

'Yes, looked at that way . . . but let's look at it another way. Costigan offers Jasper a job; Jasper takes it and disappears. Costigan doesn't know this, or pretends he doesn't. OK. The next question is: why did he offer him the job in the first place?'

'Because he didn't get the Cherfassian Chair.'

'So he took pity on him and thought, what this lad needs is a change from that dusty old academic niche? Let's give him a break? I can tell you, when I met him sweet charity wasn't the first quality I should have associated with Jerry Costigan.'

'It could be,' said Becky acidly, 'it could just be that charity had nothing to do with it. Did you ever meet Jasper? No, I thought not. Well, I can tell you, if you ever had you wouldn't think of him as a potential recipient of charity. The reason he was given for being offered the job was that Costigan wanted to open this new office in Los Angeles, and Jasper was just about the best person he could think of to run it. Which I should think was probably true.'

'That's possible. But there could be another reason – which was that Costigan simply wanted to get him out of the way. And the first step towards doing that would be to get him over to Los Angeles.'

Becky digested this new thought in silence for some minutes. Then she said, 'I suppose it's possible. But why would he want to? Why? I simply can't see it.'

At this point the next course appeared: veal for Taggart, who knew what he liked, which wasn't much, and always ate it regardless of monotony; kidneys done with garlic, lemon and parsley for Becky, who was very fond of this dish but (since it left a strong scent of kidneys and garlic on the breath) felt unable to indulge herself with it when any sort of intimacy was to follow. Tonight, however, this was not a problem. More of a problem, she felt, would be the avoidance of it. An ally such as garlic was not to be overlooked.

They ate in silence for a while. The veal was chewy, making conversation hard to conduct through it. The kidneys were delicious, and Becky did not wish to be distracted from them. After a while, though, Taggart laid down his knife and fork. It was not so much that he was defeated as that he couldn't be bothered to continue the fight any longer

'I can think of one very good reason,' he said. 'Your friend knew something that Costigan didn't want known. So he did the obvious thing.'

'You mean he killed him? You've been reading too many detective stories lately,' said Becky crisply. 'That sort of thing doesn't happen in real life.'

'No,' said Taggart. 'What happens in real life is what happened here. You try and get the person on your side, so that if he spills the beans he'll be damaging his own interests as much as yours. You appeal to self-interest. It's much the best way. It usually works, and you don't have to worry about ending up in prison or something.'

'But that doesn't explain why Jasper disappeared.'

'Ah, well,' said Taggart. 'Maybe it didn't work this time, that's all.'

They drank their coffee in silence while pondering the implications of this. The fate of Jasper Hodgkin loomed darkly over them. For the first time Taggart believed what Becky had believed all along: that he really was dead. He might not have convinced her as to the possible reason for this, but he had convinced himself – a not unusual occurrence. Taggart's stock-in-trade was outrageous hypotheses, and he generally found himself pretty convincing. He was also frequently correct, even, or especially, in what at first seemed to be the wilder of his speculations. This was his special value to *New Politics*, a journal otherwise lacking in sensationalism. The value of *New Politics* to him (the reason he stayed there, despite having been offered tempting reasons to move elsewhere more than once during the past few years) was that there was little attempt to edit the substance of what he wanted to say. In journalism, small may not be beautiful, but it is free.

In silence, too, they made their way back to Taggart's car and drove to Hoxton. Not even the clear September night could beautify the environs of the Kingsland Road. Battered, grimy terraces were interspersed with pockets of post-war council housing and enormous gaunt churches. One of these terraces of two-up, two-down houses, rescued just in time from the demolition squad by the new movement for rehabilitation which swept this part of London in the 1960s, was where Taggart lived.

His terrace, like many others in the area, was

divided between the original inhabitants and the incoming middle classes, finding here a relatively central part of London with houses they could more or less afford. Taggart was unique in being middle-class but living like the original inhabitants, in primordial squalor. An indefinable musty smell, based not on food but on sheets long unwashed and cleaning never thought of, let alone begun, reached out to welcome them. Becky was tempted to retreat before it. To Taggart, though, it was the smell of home, barely noticed and fundamentally welcoming. What caught his attention was an envelope on the mat.

It was a telemessage from Santa Barbara and it read: NEW DEVELOPMENTS CONTACT MCKEN-DRICK, followed by a United States telephone number.

29

Taggart's only thought, once he had received this missive, had been to contact McKendrick. Eight hours' time difference; early afternoon in Santa Barbara. The number on the telemessage hadn't answered. He had taken a brief quarter-hour to show Becky where she might sleep – on a divan in his study – to clear some heaps of papers off it on to the floor, to locate a sleeping bag in a cupboard and to point at the bathroom door. Then back to the telephone. She needn't have bothered with the garlic after all. Once Taggart was following a lead he could think of nothing else.

Still no answer the next time. What now?

Becky had gone to the kitchen in search of a cup of coffee and, finding the entire stock of crockery stacked over and around the sink, was now washing up. It seemed as good a way to pass the time as any. Taggart dialled again. No reply. Perhaps British Telecom had got the number wrong. Well, there was one way to find out. He dialled the Heisenborns and got Prue; dragged her away from the pool, no doubt.

'Why, hello,' she'd said. 'Are you back in California? Lucky you got me. I was just on my way to a class.'

'No, I'm in London. Look, Prue, can you do me a favour – do you know Tex McKendrick?'

'Sure.'

'Can you give me his phone number?'

'Home or office?'

'Both.'

It had turned out that the number on the telemessage was not garbled. It was McKendrick's home. He was unlikely to be there during office hours. Taggart thanked Prue and told her he might be seeing her soon. Then he called McKendrick's office. A girl's voice answered. Sure, Tex was there. She would put him through.

While he waited, Taggart had pictured the skate-boarders swirling round the Santa Barbara campus while the surf pounded the beach below. It certainly was a long way from Hoxton.

'McKendrick,' said a voice, interrupting his dream.

'Tex, this is Andrew Taggart. I just got your message.'

'Why, yes. I tried to call you but there was no reply.'

'So what's happened?'

135

'Can't explain over the phone,' McKendrick had replied. 'But I think you'd better come over just as soon as you can.'

After that it had just been a question of making the arrangements. There was a flight to Los Angeles at nine the next morning. Taggart would drive to the airport and get that. Becky would make her way home next day by taxi and train at the *Sunday Review*'s expense. They decided that she, rather than Taggart, should follow up the referees on Costigan's article; there might be something interesting there.

'Anyway,' he said, 'you're in the trade yourself, so it won't seem suspicious. You can say it's something to do with your work.'

'They won't believe that.'

'Does it matter? You'll know what questions to ask, at any rate.'

'I'll do what I can.'

'And if you hear anything about the Heirs of Washington funding anyone in your line,' Taggart added, 'let me know at once. Keep your ears open. If they were interested in Jasper, they may be interested in other people, too.'

Becky, surveying the sleeping bag on the divan in Taggart's study, with the prospect of spending half the next day in trains and taxis, had suddenly been seized by a deep desire to sleep in her own bed. She'd said, 'You know, I think I could just get the last train, if you take me to the station.'

'OK.' Taggart's mind was already focused on other things. They bundled into the car and drove to Euston at a steady sixty through the empty streets of north-east London. Becky caught her train with a minute to spare. She boarded it with a feeling of deep relief, tempered with a consciousness of the first approaches of middle age. When she was nineteen she would never have thought twice about spending the

136

night in a filthy sleeping bag on someone's broken-down divan. These days, home comforts were getting altogether too appealing. And, of course, there was more to it than that. Despite their earlier conversation, she'd had her doubts about whether she would have been allowed to spend the night in solitary splendour, at any rate without a demeaning argument that would have left her with the alternatives of either behaving like a silly fifteen-year-old virgin or else saying something unforgivable (that is, explaining exactly why she did not wish to go to bed with Taggart). Either way would have been deeply unsatisfactory.

Taggart, having dropped Becky, set his alarm clock for six and fell into a dreamless sleep.

And now here he was once again driving through the hot afternoon into the brown Californian hills. Santa Barbara had changed not at all in the two weeks since Taggart had last been there. No reason why it should have, of course. He had noticed this before: the curious dissociation between the fast-moving events of whatever story he happened to be following and the stillness of the places where it unfolded. He felt almost at home as he drove off the expressway and through the town to the Heisenborns' place, where they had arranged to meet. McKendrick had been insistent on that point. No question of his office or his home, wherever that might be. It was all the same to Taggart, and he felt he owed the Heisenborns at the very least the pleasure, doubtful though it might be, of keeping up with events.

The Heisenborns and McKendrick were waiting, inevitably, by the pool. They were drinking whisky sours. Taggart said, 'You've certainly got life taped out here.'

'We've got the weather taped, certainly,' said Fred

Heisenborn genially. He had a remarkable capacity for showing no surprise in any situation, as though he was habitually faced with unknown journalists demanding his help in tracing the contacts of dead British parapsychologists.

'Oh, it's more than that. I've never seen anyone here actually do any work. I mean, the impression is', said Taggart, feeling awkwardly like one who finds himself getting deeper and deeper into a maze but can see no way back, 'that people spend most of their time on the beach, or round the . . . well, the swimming pool.'

'Many of them do,' said Heisenborn. 'Doesn't it strike you as a splendid way to pass the time? Besides, it's possible to work even beside a pool. Hadn't that struck you either? Look at you now. Isn't that just what you're doing?'

'Throw off the guilt complexes of the old world,' Prue put in. 'Look at me. I used to feel bad about being too thin.' She gestured at her bony body. 'Used to stuff chocolate eclairs in secret because being thin *and* intellectual was just too much. Then I came out here, where it's impossible to be too thin, and as for being intellectual, nobody cares because nobody knows. They don't have conversation on the West Coast. And on the East Coast to be intellectual and thin are positive advantages. So I'm able to let myself go and eat health foods even though they're not fattening.'

Taggart declined a whisky sour and aired his white legs by the pool.

McKendrick said, 'Don't you want to hear what I've found out?'

'Why d'you think I came all this way?'

McKendrick lay back on his lounger and said, 'Well.' His Taxas drawl drew the word out to almost

138

unbelievable lengths. Taggart, who always found it hard to adjust to the slow pace of speech anywhere west of New York, could hardly bear the tension of listening to Tex McKendrick and wondering what the next word was going to be. It was almost as suspenseful as waiting for the verb in German. Not that speaking at British speed hastened the pace of life over here, since almost everything had to be repeated in order to be understood.

'Well, I spoke to some friends,' McKendrick said. 'Like, I know a few people there on account of I do a little software for them now and then.'

'NASA, he means,' interjected Heisenborn.

'Sure,' said McKendrick. 'OK. Course, they've been messing with the paranormal for twenty years or more. You knew that.'

'More or less.'

'Well, the word was that they'd dropped all that. Tried it a few times and nothing happened, so they just let it go. Either thoughts don't travel in space or astronauts aren't good subjects, but whatever the hell it was, it didn't work.'

'Weren't the Russians supposed to be trying it?'

'Oh, sure,' McKendrick agreed amiably. 'Which came first, the chicken or the egg? Either they did it because they heard we were or we did it because we heard they were. Can't risk letting the commie clairvoyants get ahead. What if they managed to get inside the heads of the Chiefs of Staff? I guess they thought the same. But after a while when they didn't get anywhere, I guess they thought they had better things to do with astronauts' time or somethin'. Funds aren't totally limitless even at NASA.'

'Or in Moscow.'

there either, I guess, though I don't know

anything about that. But it's a small world, so I asked one or two guys if they knew anything about li'l Cal Baker's new interest.'

'And did they?'

'Well, a lot of people knew about him doing *something*,' drawled Tex, 'but nobody knew just what. Then I ran into this guy, an old colleague of mine, he's at CalTech now, Pasadena way. And guess what? He's into psi – in a specialised kinda way, that is. Been lookin' into fire-walking, matter of fact; found out how you do it.'

'How?' Prue wanted to know.

'Somethin' about walkin' on wet grass first and not stoppin' to take photographs right there in the middle of the fire. Anyhow, he's had his ear to that bit of ground for a while now, as you might say.'

'And what had he heard?' asked Taggart.

'Your friend's name,' said Tex laconically.

'My friend? Which one?'

'Both. The word is, Jerry Costigan met li'l Cal at some kind of psi congress – I don't know exactly – and explained all about how he had this wonderful scheme that would make everyone's fortune, only he needed a little bit up front. So Cal said OK, he'd help out . . . on condition that he got Jasper Hodgkin out here to work for him.'

30

Fred Heisenborn had refreshed everyone's drinks except Taggart's, who found his capacity for alcohol annoyingly limited.

'What I heard', McKendrick went on, 'was that

after Hodgkin published his stuff . . . when was that? Two years ago? Somethin' like that . . .'

'About that,' Taggart agreed.

'He was invited out to the coast a whole lot, right? Just the sort of thing they all want to hear out here. Scientific proof of magic. They've been trying to do it in places like Stanford for years, but the trouble is, the guys that are interested in it don't have the imagination, and the guys with imagination prefer to stick with real-life mysteries at places like CalTech. So here comes Hodgkin with some real theory of how behaviour is affected – that's about it, isn't it? Monkeys or whatever learn how to do something and suddenly monkeys everywhere turn out able to do it.'

'Vitalism,' said Heisenborn. 'The collective unconscious, the vital force: nothing so new there. It's all in Jung.'

'I don't think it's the intellectual aspects that attracted our friends,' said McKendrick drily.

'They presumably contacted Hodgkin on one of his visits here?' said Taggart.

'No, I think they just sampled him, and liked what they saw.'

'Has he done anything with humans, then? Or do they think the Russians are just apes who got above their station?'

'I guess they saw possibilities and wanted to get him over here to develop them.'

'But why would he do it?' asked Heisenborn. 'As far as I've been able to tell, all British academics are on what you would call the centre left; that's what we would call dangerous commie sympathisers over here.'

'Not Jasper Hodgkin,' said Taggart. 'That was one of the things I checked: background and affiliations. Apparently his politics are quite right-wing – part of the current romantic revival, I imagine. There's a

141

certain cult among intellectuals. Delicacy of feeling and Neanderthal politics. I suppose it helps them feel superior to the rest of us.'

'Well, the Heirs didn't know anything about that, or not as far as I know. When they got interested, they decided to work through someone who they knew for sure was on their side.'

'Who?' said Taggart. 'D'you mean Costigan?'

'That's what I heard. He really is on the right, apparently, though he doesn't make a great thing of it.'

'I suppose, if you're a nuclear physicist, you can't be too far right. Politically sound.'

'I wouldn't know,' said McKendrick pleasantly. 'I keep away from politics myself.'

'Well, that explains one thing about Costigan, anyway,' Taggart mused. 'Somehow his outfit doesn't convince me as a sound business enterprise.'

'Not in my experience so far,' murmured Prue.

'So they got him to recruit Jasper?' said Taggart.

'Not even as fast as that. Got him to set him up over here. That way, they could vet him for themselves.'

'So why was he killed?'

McKendrick shrugged. 'Maybe it was just a mistake. Even Cal Baker can't control everything.'

'Very interesting,' said Taggart. 'As far as it goes.'

'Meaning?' McKendrick sounded mildly needled. Since he normally appeared to register no emotions whatever, this indicated considerable annoyance.

'Well, it seems a long way to come for a bit of pool-side gossip and speculation, however well-informed.'

'Oh, I've got a bit more than that,' said Tex happily. He got up and made as if to dive into the pool.

'Spit it out,' said Fred cheerfully. 'This is no time to play games. Look at poor old Andrew there, he's just about to die of frustration.'

'Well, I found out where these experiments are going on, and I thought we might just drive over and take a look.'

'OK,' said Fred. 'So where is it? Is it a walled fortress in the desert or somewhere with a landing strip in the mountains?'

'Neither,' said McKendrick. 'They're down in Baja. Just the other side of Ensenada.'

31

'Baja?' Taggart repeated. 'Where's that?' He knew he was jet-lagged out of his mind, but even so Baja rang no bells.

'Baja California,' Prue explained. 'Mexico. South of San Diego. That's the great thing these days – to have a holiday shack in Baja.'

'The Heirs' place is more than a shack,' said McKendrick.

'But why would they go there?'

'All sorts of reasons,' said Heisenborn. 'Less worries about the law . . . always supposing they wanted to do anything illegal. Privacy. Nice beaches.'

'They think of it as part of the United States anyhow,' said McKendrick. 'It's just mischance that it doesn't belong to us. God was blinkin' or somethin'. Actually, it is rather stupid,' he added. 'If you look at the map.'

'Depends where you're looking from,' said Prue. 'If you were Mexican, you'd think it was stupid that California doesn't belong to Mexico.'

'Or Texas or New Mexico,' drawled McKendrick. 'But they don't, so whaddaya know?'

'So what will you do now?' Fred enquired of Taggart. 'Go down there?'

'Andy and I will drive down together,' said Tex blandly. 'I've got it all set up.'

'Really? How?' Taggart felt unreasonably annoyed. Whose story was this, anyhow? And who was this 'Andy' person?

'Yup,' said Tex happily. 'I have a habit in life,' he explained. 'I never talk about politics. Just let people draw their own conclusions, whatever they may be. And it's really surprising how often they conclude that I agree with them. That's how it is with the Heirs of Washington. They think I just can't wait to meet li'l Cal and be one of them. So I've fixed to do jest that. There's an outfit called Santa Monica Research been doing some work for them, and they want it just as soon as they can get it. So I've arranged to drive it down there myself, seein' as I'm so obligin'. Thought we might go tomorrow.'

'Where are you staying?' Prue asked Taggart.

'Don't know. I came straight from the airport.'

'OK, then you can just leave your stuff here. When d'you want to start?' she asked McKendrick. It seemed to be assumed that he was in charge of this expedition.

It was arranged that they would set out very early the next morning. Taggart would spend the night at the Heisenborns', and McKendrick would call by next morning in his car, equipped with any gear he thought they might need. Taggart felt light-headed, all responsibility lifted from his shoulders. Blissfully, he plunged into the pool.

By 'first thing' McKendrick really did mean first thing, the Heisenborns warned him. At five o'clock he would be there, ready to start and expecting Taggart to be ready as well.

'We will not be around,' Prue assured him. 'We'll lend you an alarm clock.'

When the moment came, however, there was no difficulty about it. In the early morning, jet lag came into its own. At five, when McKendrick's car drew up at the door, he was not only dressed and ready, bag packed and coffee in hand, but even had a cup of coffee ready for his companion. McKendrick accepted it gratefully. He looked reassuringly all-American, Taggart thought. Nothing like blending into the countryside in circumstances like these.

The big Texan looked across his coffee cup at Taggart. 'You know,' he said, 'you could almost pass for a Mexican. Small and dark and, well . . . '

'Scruffy,' said Taggart comfortably. 'Don't worry. It doesn't bother me. If it did, I wouldn't be, would I?'

'You said it,' said Tex. 'You never know, it could be useful.'

Tex's car was a big gold Chrysler. Taggart was faintly surprised by this. Somehow he had assumed that Tex would drive one of the small European models that generally accompany a liberal American conscience. But he was Texan, after all.

The morning was beautiful. Behind the mountains the sky was beginning to pale; to the west the sea glimmered darkly. The roads were almost deserted. They drove south, the sea on their right, the mountains on their left. By six, they were approaching Ventura and more traffic was beginning to appear on the freeway. The sun was just behind the mountains now. At Santa Monica they left the freeway and picked up some breakfast: ham, eggs and hash browns. They agreed that this was the best meal in America. Then back on down to San Diego and the frontier, six lanes by now humming with cars and trucks, music playing on the radio, windows open to the wind, and

145

everywhere visible the playthings of the Pacific coast: dune buggies, cars towing boats and loaded with windsurfers and motor-bikes, the shore lined with apartment buildings, marinas and picnic sites.

Then the frontier, and everything stopped. On one side, white buildings, prosperity and a six-lane freeway; on the other, nothing. A dirt road wound down towards Tijuana. The air was filled with the smell of cheap frying-oil. The cars bouncing over the ruts were ancient wrecks which a hundred yards further north would long ago have been pancaked in some junk yard. On either side of the road, shacks announced in Spanish that they repaired tyres as new.

'Another world, eh?' said Tex.

'Yes,' said Taggart. 'The third.'

They drove on. Tijuana in the morning sun was not beautiful. Its tawdriness was such as to make the memory of Los Angeles almost dignified. The streets were lined with shops selling lacy hammocks, cheap embroideries and flip-flops made from car tyres. All these establishments were filled with Americans. Mexican life went on elsewhere.

They drove on. Now there were fewer cars, and the road was very narrow. Odd shacks were visible on either side of it. They stopped for lunch at one such place, poised on a rocky promontory overlooking the sea. After their fried eggs and beans they wandered down to the beach, the smell of cheap oil hanging in their nostrils. The rocks were covered with mussels. A little further along, a family of Mexicans were eating these with application, forcing them open and scooping the contents happily into their mouths. Taggart, never an adventurous eater, felt no temptation to try for himself. Nor, apparently, did Tex. He shook his head distrustfully. 'Can you imagine the pollution?' he asked. Taggart, as it happened, could not. As far as he could see, the shack where they had just eaten was the only dwelling for miles. Was that enough to cause pollution? Still, there seemed no reason to argue.

Tex gestured towards the car. 'Let's get on,' he said. 'There's some great beaches further south.'

They drove on, the blue Pacific shining on their right, brown hills rising steeply on their left. It was a peaceful scene. Taggart felt himself becoming drowsy. He said, 'Tell me more about these people.'

'The Heirs?' Tex grinned. The road was almost empty, but (Taggart realised with some surprise) he was not driving particularly fast.

Taggart could not imagine himself resisting the temptation to put his foot right down, for once in his life. He had noticed this characteristic of American drivers before, always with surprise. In Europe, a speed limit was there to break; in the States, it was simply accepted. Nevertheless, he was almost shocked at such knee-jerk moderation, especially in one who looked so potentially fierce.

'The Heirs,' Tex repeated reflectively. 'Well, now. I first ran into them when I was working for some defence think-tank around Santa Monica. That place is but full of guys simulating all kinds of wars on computers. It's a nice way to pick up a few thousand bucks between whiles, know what I mean? Add to the confusion a little. Anyway, these guys aren't particular who they work for. Naturally, there aren't that number of takers – I mean, who for Christ's sakes spends their entire life wondering what will happen if the next war goes this way or that way? Defence contractors and the Pentagon, that's about who. And the Russians, I guess, but they aren't going to come to us for that; they've got their own places. That's about it, except for a few private crazies with several millions to spare and an obsession to feed. Cal Baker, the guy

147

that runs the Heirs, is one of those. Comes from Oklahoma . . . found an oil gusher in his back yard one day. Terrified the Russians are going to come and take it away from him, and spends his life trying to make sure they don't.'

'Isn't this rather a long way from Oklahoma?'

'Well, Baker really likes beaches. He came to California and saw the sea for the first time. There aren't many beaches in Oklahoma, that's for sure. But the ones in Southern California are all full up, and the ones up north are covered in fog most of the time, and even when they're not, the water's too cold for swimming. So where else could he go?'

'Where, indeed?'

They drove on. Suddenly they caught a whiff of fish on the breeze.

'Sardines,' said McKendrick. 'Must be getting to Ensenada.'

32

The small town of Ensenada has two sources of income: sardine fishing and Yanqui tourists. There are motels and pizza parlors and a strong smell of fish. When he saw the pizza parlor, Tex sighed with relief.

'Real food,' he said. 'I was beginning to think I'd never see it again.'

They ordered some pizzas and sat down to eat and to work out their plans of campaign. According to Tex, the Baker place was a little way south of there. He pulled out a sheet of directions and compared it with the map. He nodded, took a long pull of Coke and sat back contentedly.

'OK,' he said. 'What now? You're the boss.'

A tall, thin man wandered past outside the window. Taggart felt vaguely that he had seen him before, but could not place him. The world is full of tall, thin men. He glanced at his watch. Three o'clock. The usual mid-afternoon surge of jet-lag exhaustion was beginning to hit him.

'I'm rather tired,' he said. 'Why don't we stop here and go on tomorrow?'

'That's fine by me.'

They found a motel, checked in, then drove out of town for a quick swim unassaulted by the smell of sardines. There was not a lot to do when they returned to Ensenada. After several beers and a hamburger they went to bed, ready to start off early next morning.

Baja California, a long, thin peninsula stretching seven hundred miles south from Tijuana, is nothing if not monotonous. Beach and hills go on and on, apparently indefinitely. After about an hour's drive next morning, however, McKendrick suddenly exclaimed, 'Here it is.'

It was a point where the road, which for most of the way ran along a thin strip of plain between sea and hills, suddenly rose and went a little inland. On their right Tex pointed to a dirt track leading in the direction of the sea. A hundred yards or so away, it reached a high stone wall, pierced by a gate.

'Is there a house in there?'

'That's what they say,' said Tex, reading his directions.

The wall was about eight feet high. The gate was metal, with a bell and a speaking grille let into the wall

149

beside it. The sun blazed down. There was no sign of life except for a lizard sunning itself on a large succulent which grew beside the gate. McKendrick got out and rang the bell. It made no sound that they could hear. He rang again. Again there was no sound, but this time the entryphone crackled.

'*¿Quién es?*'

'It's Tex McKendrick come to bring something for Mr Baker.'

The crackling stopped. Once again there was total silence. The lizard didn't budge. Taggart, who was sweating freely, got out of the car. The phone crackled again. This time the voice was American.

'Who is this?'

'Mr Baker? My name's Tex McKendrick. I've brought the Santa Monica research stuff for you, sir.'

'OK. Bring it in.' There was a click, and the gate swung open. Taggart and McKendrick got back into the car and drove through. The gate clanged shut behind them.

On the other side of the wall, the landscape changed abruptly. Sprinklers played on green lawns; palms and oleanders stood lushly in groups. A gravelled drive led to a low white house set on the edge of a cliff. White chairs stood invitingly around a table in the shade, but nobody was occupying them. As they drew to a halt in front of the house, the door opened. An unsmiling Mexican closed it again behind them. Judging by the expression on his face, he thought little of them, though whether this animosity was directed personally towards them or was a feeling he had about Americans in general it was impossible to say.

The house was built in traditional Spanish style, with tiled floors, few openings to the outside world, and on the inside a colonnade enclosing a patio with trees and fountains. The colonnade formed three sides

150

of a square. The fourth side, overlooking the ocean, was open, the view framed by tall plants, with broad steps down to a swimming pool apparently hanging in space. In fact the pool was set in a terrace that had been made in the cliff, and steps led down steeply from it to the beach below.

Two men were standing by the pool. They were silent, the sort of silence which follows a conversation just interrupted. One was the tall, thin, vaguely familiar figure Taggart had noticed in Ensenada. He stared at them with a curious, impersonal fixity, slightly protuberant blue eyes bulging out of a thin and sallow face. The other man was much shorter. He wore a long white shirt over white shorts and was holding a drink in his hand. This, presumably, was 'Li'l Cal'.

He said, 'You didn't say you brought a f-friend.'

'I told you,' said the tall man. He spoke very slowly, with some indefinable East European accent. Cal Baker shot him a look, partly impressed, partly (it seemed to Taggart) scared. Taggart wondered whether to mention that he had noticed the tall man in Ensenada yesterday (and so, presumably, vice versa) but decided against. No point in making unnecessary enemies, nor in drawing unnecessary attention to oneself.

'Mr Baker?' said Tex smoothly. 'I've really been lookin' forward to meeting you, sir. Your stuff's in here.' He held up a black briefcase. 'Perhaps you'd like to check it before we go, make sure everything's there. And this here's my friend Andy Taggart. When he heard I was coming to see you he really wanted to come along too. We really like what you're doin', and we wanted to meet you. Sure did.'

Taggart grinned ingratiatingly and held out a hand. Baker looked surprised and shook it half-heartedly. His handshake was limp and cold, somehow not what one might have expected from the leader of the Heirs

151

of Washington. In fact Baker, thought Taggart, was altogether unexpected. Not that he had had any fixed expectations; what, if anything, he had envisaged was, he now realised, something more in the nature of a mature Tex McKendrick than what he saw before him. That, surely, was what Oklahoma oilmen would look like. Yet nothing could have been less like Tex than Cal Baker.

Baker was, to begin with, a very small man. Taggart was not tall, but he was taller than Baker, who could have been no more than five feet five at the outside. He was not just short, he was weedy, with round shoulders and a hollow chest. He wore pebble glasses and had a pronounced stammer.

'I like to have some w-w-w-w-warning about things,' he now said reproachfully.

'I'm sorry, Mr Baker,' said Tex heartily. 'Like I said, we're real enthusiasts for what you're tryin' to do, and we hoped we might be able to help you some.'

'How?' said the tall man.

'Well.' Tex gave him a winning smile. 'Any way we can, I guess. I heard you had sometheng really interestin' goin' on here.'

'Where did you hear this?' the tall man asked.

'Well, you know,' said Tex comfortably. 'Word gets around that sometheng's goin' on, even if nobody knows quite what.'

In Baker's face, conflicting emotions fought. Part of him evidently approved of the iron discretion urged by his severe companion. But this was eventually overcome by what seemed a childlike delight at the new toys at his disposal.

'Yeah, we've got s-s-somethin' really amazin' goin' here,' he sputtered enthusiastically. 'Important. We're goin' to change world history, isn't that so?' He turned

152

to his companion, who scowled stubbornly but discreetly and, though with obvious difficulty, said nothing. 'Look!' cried Baker joyfully, pulling a folded page of newspaper out of the pocket of his shorts. This was presumably what had been under discussion before Taggart and McKendrick made their entry.

The newspaper was the *Los Angeles Times*, the previous day's edition. On the front page, circled in purple ink, the lead story revealed that, despite American intransigence, the Russians had announced that they were unilaterally extending the moratorium on nuclear weapons testing which had been in force on their side for the past six months.

Tex and Taggart looked obediently at the paper and then back to Baker. It was hard to know what to say.

'Yup,' said Tex finally. 'I saw that.'

'We're getting there,' said Baker.

'You mean . . . you did this?' Tex, despite himself, sounded doubtful.

'When I s-s-said it's big, it's really big!' Baker burst out. 'Though s-s-s-strictly it's not me that did it. It's Karlis. Did I introduce Mr P-P-P-Padvaiskas?' The tall man inclined his head. 'He's the head of our little t-t-team here. We're going to change w-w-w-world history!' he finished in an excited rush.

Taggart, at the mention of the tall man's name, could not prevent himself looking up involuntarily. It rang a bell, but for the life of him he couldn't think where. However, he had now placed the man himself. He had first seen him on Venice Beach, hanging around outside Hodgkin's apartment that day.

'I see that we have interested Mr Taggart,' said Padvaiskas sardonically. He spoke curiously slowly; all his movements were oddly slow. He was still staring at them fixedly.

153

'Of course!' Taggart tried to make himself sound as ingenuous as it was possible to be. 'It's fascinating! But what exactly is it?'

'It is very hard to explain,' the tall man firmly replied.

'I'd sure be grateful if you'd try, though,' said Tex eagerly. 'You mean you actually had something to do with the Soviets going ahead with the moratorium?'

'Yeah!' cried Baker. He took the paper and waved it in the air. To judge by appearances, he could hardly restrain himself from dancing. 'That's it! We've got inside their heads! We've done it!'

'Gee! That really is something. But how do you do somethin' like that?'

Taggart thought back feverishly over what he could recall of the past couple of weeks' manoeuvring on the moratorium front. Hadn't it been expected that the Russians would make this very move as a propaganda ploy, or a lure to a summit, depending on your view?

'Are you going to do the same thing for everyone?' he enquired.

Baker looked at him incredulously. 'What, get our side to d-d-d-declare a m-m-moratorium?' He sounded genuinely shocked. 'Why would we do that?'

'Well . . .'

'But that's the p-p-point!' Baker was almost incoherent in his vehemence. 'That's it! It's the ultimate w-w-w-weapon! They d-d-disarm themselves! Then we d-d-d-do what we like!'

'Oh, of course!' Taggart tried to make himself inconspicuous. He didn't like the way Padvaiskas was looking at him. He seemed to be trying to bore inside one's skull with those goitrous eyes of his. In fact, that was probably what he *was* trying to do.

'Do you have a team working on this, did you say?' Tex asked. 'I mean, could we join it? Could we help?'

'I am afraid not,' said the tall man coldly, drawing out his words. Lucky the whole world wasn't filled with people like him and Tex, thought Taggart, or everybody would spend so much time waiting for them to get to the end of their sentences that nothing would ever get done. 'One needs very special skills. We have the people here,' he added.

A silence followed. There seemed nothing more to say. A manservant arrived with drinks, and everyone watched while he set down the tray on the table and laid out glasses, bottles, soda water and other paraphernalia. He bowed and disappeared.

'Help yourselves,' said Baker, waving a hand. 'I n-n-never drink in the morning. Bad for the l-l-l-lymph.'

He watched them while they examined the contents of various jugs. There was fresh pineapple juice, fresh lemon juice, ice and a jug containing a colourless liquid which, McKendrick explained, was tequila. Taggart stuck to the pineapple juice.

'Here's to your work,' said Tex, raising his glass.

'Well, we've had some s-s-setbacks,' Baker said seriously. 'I can't pretend we haven't. But I think things are going along now. We're working on it.'

Tex said, 'I guess you can't trust those guys.'

Padvaiskas said, as though unable to contain himself, 'We don't have to trust them any more. We are in control.'

They drained their glasses. Baker was apparently lost in thought. Suddenly he seemed to make up his mind. 'Want to see something?'

'Sure.'

Padvaiskas looked up. Perhaps he knew, or divined, what Baker had in mind: he looked reluctant, even agitated, opening his mouth and then shutting it again. Taggart guessed it would become more difficult

155

to see Cal Baker in the future. Presumably not many visitors arrived unexpectedly in Baja California, and it would not be difficult to weed them out altogether. Even so, exactly what made the tall man so nervous it was hard to say.

Baker got up, and they followed. He trotted, followed by his little procession, past the pool, through the house and out to where a lone white building stood on the edge of the cliff. It had no windows, and the door was closed. Baker produced a key and opened it, shutting it carefully behind them.

Inside, air-conditioning buzzed. Concealed lighting bathed them in artificial daylight. A large enclosure of metal mesh in the centre of the room contained a comfortable chair, at the moment vacant.

'It's the Thinking Room,' Baker confided in awe-struck tones. 'That there's a F-F-F-Faraday cage to prevent electronic i-interference.' He looked around him. 'Can't you feel the aura? There's so much power in this room. I come here sometimes to s-s-s-speak to my mom. She's on the Other Side,' he explained, 'but this here's a bridge.'

Tex turned to Padvaiskas, who had followed them disapprovingly, perhaps engaged on a damage-limitation exercise. 'And is this where you do your work?'

The tall man nodded almost imperceptibly.

Baker said, 'Yup, we'll wipe out the commies from here. Of course it's not j-just Karlis—'

'I think we should leave now. Auras are delicate things,' said Padvaiskas.

'Sure. Let's go now.' Casting a last glance behind him, Baker led the way out and locked the door. They returned through the house and back to the pool-side. The audience was at an end. 'Well, thanks for bringing the stuff. I don't need to say – this is all s-s-secret,' Baker said, nodding to the Mexican manservant who now reappeared, answering some mysterious summons. Perhaps Padvaiskas had imparted some elementary telepathic techniques. Or maybe there was a hidden bell by the pool. Or possibly his instructions were just to appear every fifteen minutes in case he was needed.

Padvaiskas said, 'We shall of course know if you say anything.'

They drove towards the front gate, which opened before them and clanged shut after them. Taggart turned to Tex and opened his mouth, but Tex shook his head and said smoothly, 'Say, Andy, can you get my camera? It's in the front pocket. I just want to check how many exposures I've got left.'

Mystified, Taggart obeyed. Tex took the camera and pressed a small button. A high-pitched whine filled the car. He pressed the button again, and the whine stopped. They were driving south again now. Tex seemed as disinclined to speak as ever. After a short while he pulled off the road and said, 'I sure need a piss. How about you?' They climbed up a low sandy mound and down the other side. Tex said, 'Bugged. I thought they might. That Mexican had plenty of time to do whatever he wanted.'

'Who? Baker? He seems so . . . innocent.'

'Well, he's not. But I guess it's more likely that nasty Latvian he's got there. He has his ways of being clairvoyant.'

'You certainly came prepared.'

'I sure did. Nobody on earth's more paranoid than the far right, except maybe the far left. The combination of that and the occult – it was too much to miss.' He glanced, not without triumph, at Taggart, who had not made this self-evident connection.

'Well, you were right.' Taggart did not begrudge

157

Tex his triumph. He had revelations of his own. 'I've seen Padvaiskas before, actually.'

'Oh, where?'

'A couple of times. He was wandering round Jasper Hodgkin's apartment at Venice Beach when I was there with the cop. I didn't think anything of it, but you know how you take things in, sort of subconsciously. Then I saw him again in Ensenada, going past the window of the pizza parlour. I knew he seemed sort of familiar, but couldn't quite remember why. Then when we saw him again here, it all fitted together.'

'Wow. He's kinda keepin' an eye on us.'

'Keeping an eye on things generally, I should think. We just happen to be it. I must say,' said Taggart thoughtfully, 'I shouldn't be at all surprised if he wasn't the one that bashed poor old Jasper over the head. He looks a nasty piece of work to me.'

'Well, one thing's certain, li'l Cal didn't. It isn't just that he couldn't. He has enough money to pay someone else, and of course he would – if it wasn't just a mugging. And I know you think it wasn't. But why would they do that?' Tex wondered. 'I can't see that any more than I can see why Costigan should want to cover it up.'

'Perhaps he didn't know.' Taggart sat down on top of the mound and looked across the road down to the sea. An ancient truck rattled past, looking as though it was composed of pieces of several different original trucks: perhaps the result of the kind of artistic labour they had seen so enthusiastically advertised around Tijuana.

'You've got to be kidding. He must have known.'

'Not if he wasn't in on it. Say what's his name, Padvaiskas, did it? Why tell Costigan?'

'But they must have known someone would start

worrying about him,' said Tex.

'Perhaps they knew that nobody would, very much. After all, nobody much did, did they? No, what I can't make out is why they would want to knock him off. After having gone to so much trouble and expense to bring him over. It seems pretty clear that this amazing secret weapon has something to do with telepathy, which is presumably why they wanted him in the first place.'

'Perhaps he got insubordinate and wouldn't co-operate. Then of course he'd know too much to be safe loose,' Tex speculated. 'Or maybe it was just dear Karlis taking an independent initiative. Jealousy. He's in control there, and he damn well wants to stay in control.' He glanced at his watch. 'Shall we roll?'

33

As they climbed down towards the car, Tex said, 'I'm going to turn the radio on high. Then it should be OK to talk.' He fiddled with the controls and found a station playing Mexican music, turned it up loud and headed south once again.

'Why are we going this way?' Taggart wanted to know.

'Thought we might do some fishin'. I know a real good place just a little way on from here. As we're here, might as well enjoy it.' Tex drove on a while in silence to the strains of a mariachi band. 'Say, do you believe in this stuff?' he asked.

'Believe in it?' Taggart was startled.

159

'Yeah, you know. Believe in it.'

'Do I believe Karlis is the reason Mr Gorbachev said he'd go on not exploding bombs? Do I believe in fairies? No, I don't.'

'Well, don't sound so surprised. Lots of people do, and not just crazies like Baker.'

'Why, do you?'

Tex shrugged. 'I just don't know. I don't have a knee-jerk reaction one way or the other. I'm surprised you do. You don't strike me as a knee-jerk sort of fellow.'

Taggart considered his feelings. 'I suppose,' he said slowly, 'it's because it's essentially authoritarian. People want to feel they're not responsible, that everything's planned out, the way they used to feel about religion. If you can foretell the future, then it's going to happen anyway, and you're not responsible for it. As for telepathy, I can't imagine anything more vile. It'd be as bad as vision-phones – the end of privacy. I don't know why people imagine you could turn it off just when you didn't want other people inside your head.'

'And you're essentially anti-authoritarian and secretive?'

'Oh, absolutely,' Taggart grinned.

'You don't feel that may leave you rather deficient in imagination, for example?'

'No, only in respect. Why, do you believe it?'

'*Believe*, that's a big word. I preserve an open mind.'

'Oh, I don't,' said Taggart decisively. 'I think I can say without fear of contradiction that I don't have an open mind.'

The road turned towards the sea again, and after a little while McKendrick stopped the car. 'This is the place I was thinking of,' he said.

It was spectacular. A cliff overhung a wonderful beach, mile after mile of uninterrupted white sand. Some dune buggies were tearing up and down the beach, and on top of the cliff a group of boys were practising hang-gliding. As they stopped the car, one soared off over their heads and landed rather heavily on the beach below.

Tex got out, opened the back of the car and began to pull out a bundle which Taggart had vaguely registered as being there beneath their bags but he had taken to be some rubber sheet kept in the car for the mysterious reasons people did keep that sort of thing in their cars. It turned out, however, to be an inflatable dinghy.

Carefully, Tex dragged this on to the beach and removed another large, heavy item from the depths of the car. This proved to be an outboard motor. 'Thought this might be handy,' he said. 'Let's get blowing.' In half an hour, slightly dizzy from deoxygenation, they had a boat. Some fishing rods were fitted together, dried bait was revealed, and they were complete. 'Be prepared,' said Tex.

'I always was a rotten Boy Scout,' said Taggart.

'Look after this lot while I park the car.' Tex disappeared. The hang-gliders continued to soar overhead while the dune buggies roared up and down. Nobody took the slightest notice of Taggart and his boat, just another plaything on the beach. Not a Mexican was in sight. Beach toys held little interest for Mexicans, except in so far as they could be stolen. Taggart hoped Tex would immobilise the car. He seemed to be taking a long time about parking it, so perhaps that was what he was doing. When he reappeared he shrugged and said, 'I've hidden it away

161

as well as I could, and short of taking off all the tyres there's not much else I can do. We'll just have to chance our luck.'

Tex sculled them out into the Pacific. There was hardly any wind, and the sandy ocean-bottom was clearly visible beneath them. Taggart glanced down at his knees, which with all this unaccustomed exposure to a southern sun were becoming pink-tinged. Tex tugged at the engine cord. After a few tries it caught and started.

'I hate those things,' said Taggart. 'Can't bear the suspense.'

They chugged back up the coast in the direction of Baker's place. Soon it appeared: the white house on its terraced cliff face, steps leading down to the beach below, a sandy cove between small rocky promontories, the 'thinking room' a little way further along the cliff.

'Private as you like,' said Tex. 'Only way you can get to that beach is by sea. The water's real deep round these rocks.' He handed a rod to Taggart and threaded bait on to his hook. They began to fish.

It was now two o'clock. Perhaps the inhabitants of the house were eating lunch, or perhaps they were engaged upon their experiments. Either way, not a soul stirred.

Suddenly the scene erupted into life. Gesticulating figures appeared on the cliffs, and at the same time a yacht which had been hovering on the horizon began to make for the shore. Various people were visible on its deck. One man was scanning the scene with field-glasses. They came to rest on Tex and Taggart, crouched in their dinghy. A tall, thin figure – Padvaiskas – was now visible on the cliff, making his way slowly down a steep path. He, too, had field glasses and, possibly following the line of sight of the

162

man on the yacht, also turned them on Tex and Taggart.

'What on earth are they looking for?' Taggart wondered.

'Us, looks like.'

'Can't see why they should be. We haven't done anything.'

'Those guys are naturally suspicious.' Taggart could not help feeling uncomfortable, knowing he was the focus of so much attention. He scratched his knee self-consciously and looked at the sky. Tex, on the other hand, seemed sublimely unworried. All he said was, 'I've got a bite!'

'Do you think they're trying the 'fluence on us?' Taggart said. 'Do you feel an irresistible urge to throw yourself overboard or make for the Baker place? I can't say I do, but maybe I have more resistance than Mr Gorbachev.'

'You know that conversation we were having about believing,' said Tex, carefully playing his fish. 'I think the real question isn't what you or I think, it's what they think. Does Karlis over there really believe he's got us hooked on his will?' The fish threshed about in the water. It was a big one. Then Tex said, 'Damn! It's got away. And I was telepathising it, too. Well, shall we make for shore?' He reeled in his line. Taggart, who had had no bites, did likewise. Slowly and casually, Tex began to turn the boat round.

A dinghy was now lowered from the yacht. It buzzed noisily off round the northern promontory of the little bay.

'They sure are looking for something,' Tex observed. Another dinghy was lowered and began to make in their direction. By now they were chugging steadily southwards, in the direction of the beach where they had left the car.

163

'No need to hurry,' said Tex. 'What have we got to hide, anyway?' But the yacht dinghy was still nowhere near them when they arrived at the beach.

'You be deflating the boat while I get the car,' said Tex, and he showed Taggart how to do it by pulling on the valve. Soon he was back. The dinghy from the yacht was approaching the beach, perhaps fifty yards out.

The car, Taggart noted with relief, seemed to be intact. Tex got out and opened the rear door. 'Just stow it in there,' he said, bundling the dinghy into the back seat and stowing the engine in its box on top of it. Taggart began to see the point of big American cars. As they drove away, they could see two men from the dinghy jump out into the shallows and race on to the sand. They ran shouting after the car, waving their arms. Tex waved airily back and drove on towards the road.

Before they could pull on to it, two cars zoomed past at great speed, heading southwards. They were new and fast, and so had by definition to belong to Americans. 'Must be from Baker's place,' said Tex.

'Looking for us?'

'Could be. If so, they've gone too far.' He started off back north at speed. 'Trouble is, this is the only road. Baja California, a one-road province.' They approached the dirt track leading to the Baker estate, and noticed another vehicle at the junction. As it started to move, Tex put his foot down on to the floor, and their car leapt forward as if something had bitten it. 'It may not look much,' said Tex, 'but it has a customised engine.' The other vehicle tried to intercept them but missed by what looked to Taggart like inches. He felt shaken, not having bargained on kamikaze drivers on their tail, but Tex seemed unperturbed. He looked back. No one was following them. Perhaps.

the intercepting car didn't have their turn of speed and wasn't about to waste time on a hopeless chase.

'Think that's it?' he asked hopefully.

'Looks like it, for the time being,' said Tex. 'I still can't make out what they're after. To think I almost stopped to ask those guys on the beach if I could help them some way.'

They drove on at top speed, their tail-wind almost knocking a decrepit van off the road. Then there was a crack from ahead of them, sounding as if a stone had hit the car, and the windscreen shattered, totally obscuring the view of the road ahead. The car swerved. Tex knocked some glass out, cursing. Taggart finished the job. The road reappeared. They were almost over the edge of the cliff, still going fast. Tex swerved back on to the road and kept on driving. The wind hit them in the face like a hot blanket.

'What was that?' asked Taggart.

'Shotgun. They sure are after something.'

'Think those were Baker's people?'

'If they weren't, that is some coincidence.'

'If they were, it proves that when it comes to it they don't believe in the power of mind.'

They drove on and were soon through Ensenada without any more strange encounters.

It was evening by the time they reached Tijuana and crossed from the world of dirt tracks into that of six-lane highways. Taggart was surprised to find how relieved he was to be back in the alien glitter of California. In Mexico he had the definite sensation that anything could happen and no one would know or care. That, presumably, was part of the attraction for Baker and his strange outfit.

They drove on in silence. Taggart felt himself dozing, and hoped Tex felt more alert. At La Jolla they stopped to get a new windscreen fitted and ate a hamburger while they were waiting. Then they hit the road again.

It was almost midnight by the time they reached the Heisenborn place. The door opened, and Fred and Prue came out to greet them.

Fred said, 'Hi! We hoped it was you. So what happened?'

But before they could answer Prue cried, 'I must tell you! I've got to tell you! The new regime in Zambia announced last night that it's trebling copper production, and this morning the price was right down!'

'Was today the day?' said Taggart, suddenly wide awake.

'Today was the day,' said Fred Heisenborn, 'and Costigan Futures scores again!'

'Oh, and there was another thing,' said Prue. 'A telephone message from a friend of yours, Andrew. Becky Ryan. She said to tell you that the Heirs are funding someone with a very funny name: Padsomething. I've got it written down.'

34

The West Coast is eight hours behind Britain. Staggering down to the kitchen at nine the next morning, Taggart blearily tried to do the sums. It would, he worked out, be five o'clock at East Midlands University.

'What I don't understand', said Prue, 'is why you're so desperate to get this information. What does it matter who's funding someone?'

'I think they tried to kill us yesterday. And I'm pretty sure that they're behind whatever happened to

Jasper Hodgkin. Would you mind if I used your phone?'

'I just made two thousand bucks,' said Prue. 'Use away.'

Five thousand miles away, the phone rang. Becky looked at it furiously. She was just at the key stage of her experiment, had just rung the bell to wake the subject up and had to note down her responses immediately if the whole thing was not to be a waste of time. The sleeper in the cubicle stirred. Becky was testing for out-of-body experiences in sleep. She had tried various methods of inducing her subjects to leave their bodies and fly high above themselves, at least high enough to read the number written on a card and lodged on a shelf near the ceiling of the cubicle. Sensory deprivation, cannabis, lack of sleep, hypnosis: all had been tried and all had failed. So now she was trying the dream state. The phone went on shrilling. It seemed to have been ringing all day, each call more boring than the last. There were only two people she wanted to hear from, Joe and Taggart, and she had given up hope of either of them today. Why didn't the damn thing stop? She decided to give it three more rings. After that she would pick it up. It went on. The sleeper stirred again. Becky lifted her receiver just as Taggart was about to replace his.

'Oh, Andrew, it's you! I've been so worried about you!'

It was true. For the past two nights she had been unable to sleep, plagued by violent yet imprecise imaginings in which Taggart and Jasper whirled round and round, caught on some almighty Big Wheel run out of control. The sleeper sat up. Becky waved goodbye to her afternoon's work.

'I thought you weren't there. I was just about to ring off.'

'Well, here I am.' If only, thought Becky crossly, the power of the mind would be more precise. What she needed was not lurid dreams but some way of knowing whether a phone call was worth taking or not. 'Are you all right?'

'Just about. Listen, what was that you found out about Padvaiskas?'

'Why? Does he tie in?'

'Think he tried to kill us yesterday.'

'So that was it.' Becky's wavering faith in psi was restored, for the moment at least. 'But why him? How does he fit in?'

'I'm not sure, and it's a long story, anyhow. Look, what did you find out?'

'Hang on a sec.' Becky raced to open the door of the cubicle for the now fully awake and bewildered subject. 'Write down anything you dreamed,' she hissed. 'Did you get a number? Be with you in a minute.' She raced back. 'Sorry. Well, it was easy enough. I got a list of posssible funding sources from Openshaw – you know, the new Cherfassian Prof. I thought he'd know what might be available, and he did. It turns out that the Baker Foundation, through the Heirs of Washington, has been a possible source of research funding in the area for the past couple of years. They give an annual Fellowship, and it's been held for two years by the same person.'

'Padvaiskas.'

'That's right.'

'What does he do exactly?'

'In psi?'

'What else. Why, does he have another job?'

'Yes, he works at Bush House for the BBC External Services. The Latvian Section, or something.'

'Outdoor relief for émigrés. Well, that ties in. It means he's very right-wing. And what does he do in psi?'

'Telepathic behaviour modification. Sort of mind over mind. He's been experimenting with cats for years.'

Taggart recalled his last view of Padvaiskas: fixing them with his field-glasses from the cliff-side, no doubt willing them both to jump into the sea. 'It doesn't work,' he assured her.

'The Baker Foundation thinks it might, obviously.'

'Oh yes, they think so all right.'

'Will you be back soon?'

'Yes, I should think so. Don't forget to follow up those references,' said Taggart, casting his mind back what seemed like a thousand years.

He put down the phone feeling somewhat dazed. 'They're mad,' he announced.

Prue poured him a cup of coffee. 'Quite true,' she said comfortingly. 'I'm surprised you hadn't realised it before. Now, tell me the story.'

'Where's Tex?'

'Went as soon as he'd left you here. And Fred's been gone for hours now.'

Slowly, over coffee and orange juice, he told her.

'So what did you do about a windscreen? There seemed to be one this morning.'

'Stopped at a place in La Jolla. They fitted one on the spot.'

Prue shook her head. 'Curiouser and curiouser. And how about this?' She held out a copy of that day's paper. A front-page headline announced: OKLAHOMA BILLIONAIRE TO RUN FOR PRESIDENT. The story read:

Cal Baker, the oil billionaire from Oklahoma who funds the right-wing Heirs of Washington Foundation, today announced his intention of joining the Presidential race. Baker says he will run as an Independent candidate. A retiring figure with a pronounced stammer, Baker is confident that he will win the minds of the voters with his platform of fundamentalism and extreme anti-communism. Asked if he had some unknown factor to aid him in what otherwise seems a hopeless cause, Baker said, 'Maybe that's just what I do have.' He would not, however, explain its nature.

Another headline on the same page announced, US EXPLODES NEVADA BOMB BUT GORBACHEV STANDS FIRM:

The Soviet leader today announced his intention of sticking to his unilateral moratorium on nuclear weapons testing despite the refusal of the United States to join in on its side. He said, 'The future of the world is at stake and we for our part continue to do everything in our power to ensure a safer world. It has become quite clear by whom the safety of the world is threatened.' Administration officials dismissed this as a propaganda move and say that Russia had anyway come to the end of a test series before announcing its moratorium.

Taggart thought of Padvaiskas standing unsmiling beside the pool and announcing, 'It is not a question of trust any more.'

He said, 'I don't know what to think any more.'

35

After speaking to Taggart it became clear to Becky that trying to concentrate on OOB experiments would be simply a waste of time. Her heart wasn't in it, and she might as well get on with the only thing she *was* interested in. So she cancelled the rest of her week's programme and phoned her friend on *Natural Science*. After a short delay and a merciful lack of questions he produced the references she wanted. There were three. One was a Mr Albert Kotchinsky, a magician. One was a Cambridge physicist called Dr Michael Anderson who was known to be interested in parapsychology. The third was a Miss Josephine Tempest-Scott, a member of the Society for Psychical Research.

Copies of the references themselves arrived on her doormat next morning. They were not very long or full, but they varied very much in tone. Miss Tempest-Scott's was fulsome. She thought this work was of the highest importance and ought certainly to be brought to the notice of the readers of *Natural Science*. Dr Anderson was more cautious. He could find no fault with the methodology described, and, that being so, the results were certainly striking and ought to be published. Kotchinsky, the magician, was the least enthusiastic of the three. He found it hard to believe that fraud did not play some part in results such as these, but had to confess that he could not work out how the trick was done. This in itself was hardly enough to damn the work; so the article was published.

The question was, should she write or phone the

referees with her request? Her inclination was to write. For one thing, she didn't like phoning people she didn't know out of the blue, and writing let her off this particular hook. For another, she herself objected to being cornered on the telephone, and assumed others felt similarly. On the other hand, it would be nice to get on with things. People put awkward letters aside and try to forget about them. And they might contact Jerry Costigan to check on her credentials. Well, they might do that anyway; it was a risk she had to take. At least they were less likely to turn her away with a raspberry than if she were Andrew Taggart, a man whose reputation could not endear him to potential subjects for investigation. She decided on a compromise. She would write; and if she did not receive a reply within a week, she would telephone. That way things would not drag on, and she would not be calling out of the blue.

Within two days, somewhat to her surprise, she had had a reply to one of her letters. It was from Miss Tempest-Scott. She would be delighted to see Dr Ryan. Would she care to telephone and make an appointment?

Miss Josephine Tempest-Scott lived in a block of mansion flats near Campden Hill. In the entrance was one of those old-fashioned boards on which the name of each tenant is painted opposite a little sign with a sliding mask to show whether the person in question is IN or OUT. Miss Tempest-Scott was IN. The place was enveloped in tomb-like silence. Outside, the clamour of Kensington Church Street was only a few yards away. Here, beige carpeted stairs wound shallowly upwards. Miss Tempest-Scott lived on the third floor. Becky decided to save her energy and got into the old-fashioned cage-lift. It creaked slowly upwards. When she arrived at the third floor and emerged on to

172

the beige-carpeted landing, a door opened magically to greet her.

'Dr Ryan?' said a spruce, white-haired lady, dressed in a chic black suit, diamonds glittering on her lapel. 'Do come in.'

Becky wondered if this was ESP in action. If it was, it was the first time she personally had experienced it, after so many years of searching.

'I heard the lift stop here and I knew it must be you,' said Miss Tempest-Scott, leading the way into her flat. 'Just on time. I do think that's so important, don't you? An essential element of good manners.'

Once inside the flat, the thick beige carpeting changed to thick dark green, and long green curtains deadened all sound even more completely. Within this green plush world, Miss Tempest-Scott lived amid Sheraton piecrust tables and glass-fronted bookcases containing elegant bindings. There were some large square green plush armchairs, covered to match the curtains, with intricate crocheted antimacassars. The effect was impersonal but comfortable. On one of the piecrust tables was a tray containing a silver teapot and some delicate china cups. 'Tea?' enquired Miss Tempest-Scott. It was just four o'clock. Becky accepted gratefully, and clutching her eggshell cup in terror of somehow breaking it, found herself mesmerised by some watercolour ducks flying over a watercolour marsh on the wall over the fireplace. Miss Tempest-Scott placed another piecrust table tactfully beside her knee. When she put her cup and saucer down, she was mortified to hear them rattle against one another. Why be nervous, after all? Miss Tempest-Scott seemed quite charming and utterly benign.

'I'm so pleased to meet you,' she was saying now. 'I'm so interested in your work. Tell me, have you had any luck recently?'

173

'No, I'm afraid not,' said Becky absently. 'But we keep on trying.' She was wondering how she could broach her subject without seeming too much to impugn the reputation of her current patron. 'I hope you didn't mind my writing. The fact is, there's been a . . . a slight, um, question about Dr Costigan's methodology in the remote-viewing work, and we' (always more reassuring to hide behind the royal 'we') '. . . we wanted just to clear it up.'

'Quite right, my dear. One can't be too careful about things like that,' said Miss Tempest-Scott, upholding the stern principles of the SPR. 'How can I help you?'

'Well, what was the procedure? Can you tell me? Did you look into his methodology? Did you keep any notes? That sort of thing.'

Miss Tempest-Scott shook her head. 'No, no. Nothing like that. What happened was that the editor of the magazine got in touch with the Society and asked them if they could give the name of someone experienced in the field to referee this paper. I am well known in the field of clairvoyance, so they sent it to me. But as you see, I am not an academic like yourself. I don't pretend to great intellect. Simply, I have this gift. So what could I do but apply my usual criteria? I asked myself whether the work felt right, what the vibrations were. And I have to say that it did. Nothing could have been more sympathetic than the vibrations I received – as far as I remember. Well, that must have been so, because I recommended it in the strongest possible terms.'

'I see.' Clear as mud, thought Becky. So much for that one. Suddenly Miss Tempest-Scott leaned across to her.

'My dear, forgive me. But I sense, talking of vibrations, that you're in great distress. Are you

174

worried about someone? Someone close to you?'

Involuntarily, in astonishment, Becky nodded. Miss Tempest-Scott seized her hands. 'I sense . . . a confined space – no movement – perhaps a hospital bed?' she intoned. Becky suddenly pictured, vivid before her eyes, the morgue as Taggart had described it, the drawer containing the body. She shuddered. 'Don't be distressed!' cried Miss Tempest-Scott. 'I can tell you – the confinement will pass! It has passed! Your friend will be free and you will see him . . . it is him, isn't it, my dear? You will see him again! Soon!'

Unable to bear any more, Becky snatched her hands away and rushed out of the flat and into the earthly glitter of Kensington. Silly old trout, she thought as she snivelled her way down Church Street. Well, she could tell her one thing. Devotion extends so far and no further. Jasper might be enjoying the life of the spirit on the Other Side, but Becky had absolutely no intention of rushing to join him there just yet.

36

In the slanting yellow rays of the evening sun, the walnut tree spread its dappled shade on the lawn to greet her. But today even the sight of her cottage, which normally filled Becky with the pleasure of satisfied proprietorship, was not enough to comfort her. Slamming the car door, she stamped unseeingly past the late roses. There was a letter on the mat. She tore it open. It was from Anderson, the physicist who had been the second of the three referees. The note was short, almost curt. He made it a point of principle never to discuss matters of this sort and must therefore decline to see her. Yours sincerely. Sod.

She wondered about Kotchinsky. Two down, one to go. If her present luck held, even supposing there were something to find out, she would not find it. She decided that if no letter arrived in the morning she would telephone Kotchinsky. Then she had a hot bath and took a detective story to bed.

The morning was cloudy. It was the thirteenth of September. Late summer was sliding into autumn. Nothing interesting in the papers; nothing pressing at the university. To pass the time, Becky went out into the garden and began to cut herself a bunch of roses. The postwoman called a cheery 'Good morning!' as she cycled past the gate without stopping. Well, he might have written to the university. Nine o'clock: the department secretary should be there and in half an hour might actually be so. Not that she, Becky, could talk; here she was cutting roses. However, unlike the secretary's, her position was not secure, so she might as well make the most of it while it lasted. Costigan's grant was only for a year, and it seemed highly unlikely that he would renew it if – or when – he got wind of her current activities.

At nine-thirty she phoned the department. There were no letters for her there either.

Kotchinsky, according to the details supplied by her friend Nick, lived in Golders Green. Becky had had several schoolfriends who lived in that part of London; she wondered idly if any of them had known Mr Kotchinsky. Perhaps he had performed at their parties. She had vague memories of children's parties at which depressed-looking men pulled endless strings of knotted silk handkerchiefs out of empty top hats. On second thoughts these were presumably not Kotchinsky, who must be a higher class of magician altogether. She dialled the number. For quite a while no one answered. She was about to hang up when the ringing at the other end ceased and a woman's voice said, suspiciously, 'Hello?'

'Oh, hello,' said Becky. 'I'm trying to contact Mr Kotchinsky. Is that the right number?'

'It's the right number,' said the woman, sounding as if she were about to burst into tears. 'but I'm afraid you can't speak to Mr Kotchinsky. He died three months ago.'

37

'Oh God,' said Becky, 'I'm terribly sorry.' She hesitated. There is little one can say in such circumstances that will not sound crass, intrusive or presumptuous. If you work for the gutter press, that is all in the way of business, but Becky did not work for it, and was (as her mother had often said proudly to her aunts) a Really Nice Girl. On the other hand, she did badly want certain information, although as things stood she might be more likely to get it via Miss Tempest-Scott or one of her friends.

'Are you the young lady who wrote from East Midlands University?' asked the voice on the other end of the phone, presumably that of Mrs Kotchinsky.

'Yes.' Becky wondered how she had been so unerringly identified as young. Perhaps Mrs Kotchinsky, too, had special powers.

'Well, you must get in touch with Mr Horne. Joseph Horne – do you know him? He is in charge of all my husband's papers.'

'Yes, I know Mr Horne. I'm terribly sorry to have

troubled you, Mrs Kotchinsky.'

Horne, thought Becky. Just my luck. She felt a curious reluctance to contact him. Not that he had ever been anything but obliging, on the various occasions they had met. There was nothing she could put her finger on; simply, she couldn't bring herself to trust him. He was too slippery a customer for that.

So: was she or was she not going to pursue this trail any further? Put like that there seemed to be little choice in the matter. She looked up Horne's number and dialled.

'Horne here.'

'Oh, Mr Horne, it's Becky Ryan.'

'Becky, my dear. And what can I do for you?'

'Well . . . I've just been talking to Mrs Kotch-insky.'

'Who referred you to me. So when are you going to come and see me?'

'Oh, I—'

'Hoping to do it all on the phone, were you? I can see that it's a bore dragging down to London. But it's a long story, and I'd rather not tell it on the phone. You'll see what I mean when you hear it.'

'It's just that I was in London yesterday.'

'Oh, dear. Well, no hurry. I'm always here, except when I'm on tour, and that's not for a long while yet.'

Becky thought quickly. There was no question of turning to her work with a clear mind, not with this constantly pricking her conscience. 'I could come down today.'

'Today, fine. When will that be? This afternoon? I have to get to the theatre around six. No matinee today, so that's all right.'

'I'll be along after lunch.'

Euston again. At least she could walk to Horne's place from there. He lived in a block of service flats

178

just down the road, near Great Portland Street.

Setting off into the grey expanses of the Euston Road, she was almost blown off her feet by the gale sweeping around the foot of the Euston Tower. This eased somewhat as she crossed the road, but she hurried nervously past the small street leading to Fitzroy Square. No sign of Costigan. Still, she did not feel at ease until she was safely in the lift ascending to Horne's eyrie on the fifth floor.

Horne's block, unlike Miss Tempest-Scott's, was not stiflingly respectable. Few of the flats seemed to be in private occupation. Several were occupied by firms of accountants, and there were two osteopaths. When Becky arrived on the fifth floor, a depressed-looking Arab woman was letting herself furtively into a door marked 11. Becky, however, was bound for number 10.

Horne opened the door quickly in response to her ring. 'Becky, my dear girl. So nice to see you. You managed to slink past Fitzroy Square without disturbing the lion in his lair?'

'You mean Jerry Costigan?'

'Of course. Don't look so surprised. Eva Kotchinsky sent your letter on to me. Besides, I've been wondering when you or your Mr Taggart would finally get round to this. There you go again. I don't know what you take me for – one of Dr Hodgkin's telepathists, maybe? It's quite simple; isn't it always? It was me that recommended Mr Taggart to look into the question of the referees in the first place. Didn't he tell you?'

'Probably. It must have slipped my memory.'

By now he had led Becky into his sitting room. She had been here before, and it hadn't changed since her last visit. There was still the clutter of posters, programmes and assorted theatrical souvenirs; the glass-fronted bookcase full of books on magic still occupied most of one end wall, and a large armchair still failed entirely to conceal a hole in the red carpet beside the window. A thin layer of dust covered everything.

'Sorry it's such a mess,' her host apologised, his small form busily indicating regret as he ushered her into the armchair. 'My help's given up, and I haven't got round to getting another. You know how it is.'

There was not now, nor ever had there been as far as Becky knew, any sign of a Mrs Horne. The only person figuring in any of the photographs liberally sprinkled around the room was the magician himself, always neat and dapper, the only indication of passing years being a slight receding of the hairline, an increased rigidity in the set of the face and a suggestion of added black on the hairline moustache.

'If you knew all along that we'd need to get in touch with you about Kotchinsky's papers, why didn't you say? It would have saved a lot of trouble,' said Becky crossly.

'Always so straightforward, dear Dr Ryan!' laughed Horne. 'You're in the wrong field, you really are. I must have told you so before.'

'You have.'

'But I, you see, am not straightforward. I like to see how people work. If everything's laid out at once, what room is there for surprises? Besides, what's the rush?'

Becky took a deep breath as she felt the waves of irritation closing over her head. Was it possible that anyone could be so aggravating? Whether because deviousness breeds deviousness or because she simply didn't trust him, she felt unwilling (as Taggart, for similar reasons, had felt unwilling) simply to tell Horne the whole story. She said cagily, 'It's just that I'm afraid there's something wrong.'

'Well, that's true, of course,' said Horne calmly. 'Poor Kotchinsky died. That's why you're here. But he's dead. Saving time won't do anything for him any more.'

'Oh.' Becky let her breath out. 'I meant, someone may have been killed – or may be in danger.'

'Right again. Kotchinsky was.'

'Killed?'

'I think so, very probably. No one else seems to think so, mind you, or at least they haven't said anything.' Horne spoke airily, apparently unconcerned at what he was saying.

'But . . . if that's what you think—'

The magician shrugged. 'Would you like coffee? Tea? No? Well, what I say is, why stir up a hornets' nest? What good would it do? Kotchinsky's dead; it won't do him any good. Perhaps you or Mr Taggart will solve the mystery.'

'But how did he die?'

'Heart attack . . . in his dressing room. He was doing a show in Brighton. They found him when he didn't come out after the show.'

'A heart attack: that seems fairly straightforward.'

Horne shrugged. 'Have a look at the papers. See what you think.'

'That's just what I'm trying to do.'

'Now, then, my dear Becky, don't get cross. The papers. Now, I haven't got them here—'

'You mean you brought me all this way—!'

'They're not far off,' said Horne comfortingly. 'And much safer where they are. It's the easiest thing in the world to break into a private home these days. Happens all the time, especially in the middle of London.'

'So where are they?'

'With all the rest of Kotchinsky's papers,' said Horne. 'In the Harry Price Library.'

38

Becky, like anyone interested in psychical research, knew about Harry Price. His fame extended, and perhaps still extends, well beyond these narrow boundaries. Who has not heard of the Borley Rectory ghost, of which he was the chief publicist and probable begetter? This bizarre episode was entirely character-istic of a career in which perverse motivation was allied to a genius for publicity: a combination which, in the end, did not endear Harry Price to the doyens of psi. The embarrassment he generated was such that it was only with reluctance that London University was persuaded to accept the bequest of his library, an unrivalled collection of materials on magic, psychical studies and other *curiosa*.

'Haven't you been there?' said Horne. 'Well, it's a treat in store. I'll give you an introduction to the librarian. He's there on Wednesdays, or used to be. It's a while since I was there. Today's Wednesday, isn't it? You can walk there from here, if you want. It's not very far.'

The Harry Price collection, he explained, was housed in the squat tower of the Senate House which looms over Bloomsbury. It was, Becky had to agree, nothing if not convenient – almost on her way back to Euston. It hardly constituted a detour.

Armed with Joseph Horne's note of introduction, she made her way thoughtfully through the September streets. Past the Telecom Tower with its mothballed revolving restaurant; past Heal's with its ground-level mirror hypnotically reflecting your feet; past Dillon's – well, no, it wasn't possible simply to pass Dillon's:

all those shiny new books waiting to be bought . . .

She was thumbing through a heap of new novels ten minutes later when a voice said, 'Isn't that Becky? I thought you were searching for truth at East Midland.'

It was Jerry Costigan.

Becky, to her mortification, literally jumped. Her feet almost left the ground, and simultaneously her heart dropped towards her stomach. She must have looked as appalled as she felt. Costigan appeared puzzled and said, 'Are you all right?'

'Yes, of course.'

'You looked as though you'd seen a ghost. I can't see why I should have that effect on you!' he said jocularly.

'I . . . mm.' Becky was lost for words. What can you say to a man whom you suspect of having murdered, or of having been involved in the murder of, your closest friend and colleague? And whose professional bona fides you are currently investigating – *are*, precisely, on the way to investigate?

'What are you doing down here?' asked Costigan.

'Oh, checking out a few things.' She glanced down guiltily at the novel in her hand.

'No need to look like that,' he chaffed her. 'You're allowed to come to London and look at the books once in a while. Why didn't you drop in and say hello? My office is only over the way.'

'I know.' She forced a smile. Silly to feel so scared. What could he possibly do to her here? And why should he want to? As far as he knew she had nothing against him; on the contrary.

'Where were you off to, anyhow?' Costigan went on relentlessly. 'Are you here in the way of work, or is it purely pleasure?'

'Oh, a little of both, you know.' She gave a nervous giggle.

'Got time for a cup of coffee?'

'I don't think so.' Becky glanced firmly at her watch. That would be too much. Anyway, time was getting on. She didn't know how much stuff there'd be to look at once she got to the library. At this thought she blushed. Costigan drew his own conclusions and raised a meaningful eyebrow. 'My dear girl, the last thing I want to do is pry into your private affairs. Anyway, drop in and see me some time. When you've got a bit more time.' He grinned and went upstairs with a wave of the hand. He didn't look like a murderer. As soon as he was safely out of sight, Becky put down her book and hurried off towards the Senate House Library.

Outside, the white concrete tower was imposing. Inside, nothing could have been shabbier. As usual in such places, the stranger's sense of disorientation was enhanced by the feeling that everyone else in the place was not only rushing at top speed but knew where they were rushing to. Ascending by a battered lift to the fourth floor, she was spilled out on to a dirty green landing and directed through a turnstile into the library.

'Harry Price Collection? Did you know which book you wanted?'

It wasn't exactly that she wanted a book, Becky explained. She had a note for the librarian . . .

'Wait a minute. I'll see if he's there.' The duty librarian phoned.

Becky, meanwhile, scanned the long room anxiously. The usual spacious tables, the quiet bustle of a much-used library, book-covered walls, the opening and shutting of catalogue drawers. There was one face, however, that she most definitely did not want to see – though as far as she knew, Costigan was still in Dillon's. He certainly wasn't here. Nevertheless, she felt thoroughly unnerved. What, after all, could be more designed to throw one off one's balance than suddenly coming face to face with the villain whose nefarious doings one is at that moment investigating? She could feel her intentions written in letters of fire upon her forehead. However, he had not appeared to read them.

The librarian put down her phone. 'All right,' she said. 'Mr Hetherington'll meet you up there. It's on the eighth floor. Go up the stairs through that door and turn right.'

The stairs up the tower were winding and narrow. Becky's footsteps echoed on the concrete. No one else was in sight. On the sixth floor she found her way barred by a red rope bearing the sign NO ACCESS PAST THIS POINT. Presumably this message was not meant for her. She ploughed on upwards. On the eighth floor she turned right as instructed through a door leading into the stacks. It was very dark in here: nothing but endless shelves of books which appeared to be about art history, dark green metal shelves on concrete floors with narrow corridors between.

Suddenly a voice shouted, 'Hello, is that Dr Ryan?'

She turned towards the source of the voice. To her right a door stood half-open at the end of a corridor of books. The space beyond was dimly lit, and from it emerged a stocky, white-haired figure, presumably the curator of the collection. She turned thankfully towards him, as a traveller in a blizzard might towards a beacon light.

'Mr Hetherington? I was beginning to think nobody was up here.'

'Not many people are, usually.' He led the way back through the door upon which a dingy card proclaimed: HARRY PRICE COLLECTION.

39

Mr Hetherington shut the door after them. If the stacks had been gloomy, the room in which they now found themselves was gloomier by far. Not that 'room' was really the appropriate word for this space. It was simply a partitioned-off section of the stacks, with a grimy window looking out (if it had been possible to see through it) on to another wall studded with equally opaque windows. So little light was admitted through this window that nothing could be made out within except by artificial light. To this end, two lamps, each containing a sixty-watt bulb, hung far above the head of any readers. Dusty shelves reached to the ceiling, packed with tomes whose titles might, with close study, dimly be discerned. Tottering piles of books and file boxes stood on tables, and along the wall to the right of the door more boxes and folders were precariously arranged.

'Well,' said Mr Hetherington, 'welcome to the Harry Price collection. I'm so pleased to meet you. You are the Dr Ryan who's been doing all that fascinating work on OOB experiences, aren't you?' Becky admitted that she was. 'I see', he went on, scrutinising Horne's note, 'that you want to see the Kotchinsky papers. I'll get them in a moment. But while you're here there's all sorts of other things you might like to have a look at.' He beamed. Amid the murk, his enthusiasm shone with a benign glow.

'Kotchinsky,' Mr Hetherington continued, 'Kotchinsky. Only just come in, actually. Someone was asking about them not long ago, but we hadn't yet received them. Now if you'll bear with me a moment, I know I put them somewhere. We get so much stuff coming in here, and now that I only come in once a week these days it's almost impossible to keep up with it all. We were behind with the cataloguing as it was. Perhaps while I'm sorting them out you'd like to have a look at a few things. I think this would interest you, and this, and this.' He pulled down books as he spoke and handed a small pile to Becky, who perused them dazedly while he rummaged now among piles of boxes on a table.

Mr Hetherington certainly knew his stuff. These were all titles of some relevance to the work she was doing and which, on a more spacious occasion, she would certainly have liked to read. But just at present it was hard to concentrate, especially as one of the boxes on the table fell to the ground with a crash and flew open to reveal a delicate white hand on the end of a sleeve.

'Spirit hand,' Mr Hetherington explained, stuffing it back after a quick check for damage. 'Victorian.' He replaced the box and turned his attention to a pile of manila folders. Edging up to take a closer look at the 'spirit hand', Becky caught a glimpse of the labels on some of them: 'Houdini Letters 1'; 'Spirit photographs'; 'Fire-walking 2' . . .

'Ah!' cried Mr Hetherington triumphantly. 'Here they are.' He turned to Becky, balancing a pile of box files under one arm. 'Did you know Kotchinsky?'

'No, I never met him.'

'Awfully nice man. Tragedy that he died. Very sudden, I believe. Wasn't obsessed like some of these magicians. Know what I mean?'

'You mean like Joseph Horne?' said Becky, naming the only magician she knew.

'Joe Horne, yes, he's a case in point. Can only think of one thing.'

'What's that?'

'Exposures, of course. Showing up fraud. I can never make out whether it's because he would have liked to believe but could always see through, if you know what I mean, so it made him a bit funny that way. That was the case with Houdini. Took it too far if you ask me. Of course, he was quite right, but one has to see both sides of the thing.' Mr Hetherington had, it seemed, never experienced a moment's difficulty when it came to seeing both sides of anything. If he carried anything to the point of obsession, it was fairness.

'Well, a fraud's a fraud,' said Becky, faintly surprised to hear herself taking this side in the argument.

'Yes, but it seems a bit strange to approach the subject on the assumption that everyone's a fraud. That was what Houdini did. Now with Horne it may be a little different. If you ask me, a lot of its professional jealousy.'

'And what about Kotchinsky?'

'Ah, now, Kotch, that was different. He was interested, but not obsessed. Always took an interest, but it was a benign interest. What exactly was it you wanted to see? Anything particular?'

'I believe he refereed a paper.'

'Oh yes, the Costigan piece.' Mr Hetherington, despite his happy-go-lucky style, put his finger once more unerringly on the spot. 'Well, I expect you'll find the stuff in there. I haven't had time to have a look at it, myself.' He glanced at his watch. 'If there isn't anything else you want, then I think it's about time for me to be going. Look, here's the key. Lock the door when you leave, would you, and give the key to the

188

librarian downstairs. I'll tell them it's OK. If you want to come back when I'm not around, just tell them I said it's all right and they'll let you have the key.'

'You've been very kind,' said Becky.

'That's my job, isn't it?' Mr Hetherington bustled around for a few minutes checking various items, then said goodbye and left.

Becky sat at a small table, the box files heaped around her. No sound was to be heard. In the twilight of the book-stacks nothing moved. On the shelf directly in front of her were a selection of ancient-looking leather-bound books. She opened some of them at random. There were eighteenth-century treatises on optical illusions, a sixteenth-century manual of magic and various sexual *curiosa*. A draught moved the light, making the shadows swing. With a guilty start, Becky replaced the books on the shelf. Nobody was around, but she couldn't help feeling the presence of the spirit hand lurking in its box. What else might not be concealed in the innocent-looking boxes piled dustily in the gloom behind her? Intrigued, she got up and tried one or two, revealing a set of glass lantern slides which threatened to cascade out and smash on the floor at her feet. Narrowly averting this catastrophe, she bundled the slides back into their boxes and returned, chastened, to her seat. Clearly the spirits, whoever they might be, intended her to concentrate on the work in hand. She opened the first of Kotchinsky's box files.

It quickly emerged that most of the large mass of papers now confronting her were of no interest – or at any rate, not relevant to the matter in hand. Box after box was filled with correspondence between Kotchinsky and other persons she had not heard of, and some she had, discussing various arcane topics. There were records of engagements and payments, and old

189

playbills detailing performances up and down the country. After a while the unending procession of trivia began to take its toll. Whereas at first she had tended to scan every piece of paper for fear of missing something vital, her inclination as time wore on was to skip through entire boxes at speed. She came to realise that this was a result not only of boredom but of hunger and fatigue. She glanced at her watch. Seven o'clock: the library, she knew, shut at eight. She could either plough on or leave it for tonight and come back another day.

She decided to look at one more file before she left. Somehow she didn't relish the notion of another day in the Harry Price Library. Mr Hetherington had remarked in his jovial, open-air way that people sometimes asked him if he didn't get worried by ghosts and things in here. Becky found it hard to dismiss the notion as easily as she would have liked. Here she was searching through a dead man's archives for the piece of paper that (if Horne was to be believed, which was quite a big if) might have led to his death. Why shouldn't it lead to her death? If Costigan had been so desperate to stop whatever it was getting out then, wouldn't he be just as desperate now? Suppose he'd followed her up here. Suppose he was on his way up those stairs now, lurking, ready to jump out at her in those dark stacks . . . Nobody, she realised, had been up on this floor since she'd been sitting here. They would be quite undisturbed. The dim light above her head flickered, and a draught played round her ankles. She shivered, and not just from the cold. She was on the point of shutting the file and giving up – for the day, or more probably indefinitely – when something caught her eye. She had been idly turning over the papers in the file, not really concentrating on them, when she came to a thickish folder and, glancing down, saw that it was marked BRIGHTON EXPERIMENTS 1983 – REMOTE VIEWING.

She swallowed and then gulped with relief and excitement. This was it. This must be what she was looking for.

What now? Even if she had time to read it thoroughly, she would never be able to concentrate up here. Better copy the whole thing and take it home with her to peruse at leisure. She picked up the folder and went downstairs. No sign of Costigan. The photocopying room was closed for the night, but the librarian directed her to a change machine. There was a small queue of people waiting at the photocopiers, but it was still only seven-thirty. She should just make it.

By eight o'clock she was leaving the library with the satisfying sense of a job well done and a substantial sheaf of papers in her briefcase.

40

The distance from Malet Street to Euston Station is very short but to Becky, clutching her trophies, it seemed endless. This was Costigan's territory. She knew he was in the area, and what would she do if she ran into him now or, worse, if he made a point of running into her, having followed her movements all afternoon without her knowledge? Her footsteps echoed hollowly as she made her way through the almost deserted darkening streets of Bloomsbury. It was with relief that she came to the bleak and traffic-bound expanse of the Euston Road. At least there were lots of people here, and even more milling around the station concourse. The next train in her direction was not due to leave for another hour. She made for the bar and ordered a double brandy. At such times a girl needed fortifying. She sank gratefully into the impersonal crowd downing its drinks all around her. No sign of Costigan, and no sign of him again as she climbed into the train. Not many people at this time of night, and none of them seemed at all interested in her. She wondered whether to look at the papers now but decided against it. She would never be able to concentrate, and there were a lot of them. In fact, she was exhausted. She leant back in her seat and instantly fell asleep, not waking up until the stop before her own.

She was still in a sort of daze as she got out, gave her ticket in and went to find her car. It was hard to think of any place more depressing than a station car park. As usual, when she had arrived the place had been almost full and she had had to park at the very furthest corner. Now it was almost empty. She wondered idly if her car would still be there; not many got left overnight, and the place was an easy target for thieves, open and not overlooked. But yes, there it was in its corner, a red Mini with (she noticed with annoyance) a rear light broken. Damn. She knew she had parked too close to the one next door. He might have been more careful. She hoped that his rear light was broken, too. She got in, carefully deposited her briefcase on the seat beside her and started out. The hedges of the country lanes closed around her, the headlights ploughing ahead like pioneers blazing the trail. Her cottage was at the far end of the village, standing almost by itself up a small lane. Here was the village at last, and here was the lane.

She was about to turn into the driveway when her

blood ran cold. There was a light on in the cottage.

Without thinking she drove past the driveway and some way up the road before pulling into the side. Not that that was much of a precaution: in the silent country night, cars could be heard for miles, and if anyone was listening they would have heard her stop. Still, she had to stop somewhere.

She ran over the possibilities in her mind. Who had the key? There was Mrs Tidmarsh, her cleaning lady, but she only came in the mornings, and this wasn't one of her days. She certainly wouldn't have left the light on, since she would have had no cause to put it on in the first place. Joe didn't have a key, and even if he had, she couldn't picture him sitting there in her absence, waiting. In fact, nobody else had one. She began to tremble. There were only two possibilities left. Someone had broken in, and it was either burglars or Costigan. Costigan more likely; he knew she was in London and had rushed to his car and blitzed up the motorway to find . . . what? The letters from Miss Tempest-Scott and Dr Anderson, to name but two. The game of innocence was up.

Well, nothing to be done. She would have to go and face him. She hadn't had the cottage very long, and had no particular friends in the village she could call on. Still, no need to be foolhardy. She hadn't noticed if the curtains were drawn in the kitchen, which was where the light was, but even if they were, she ought to be able to see inside, since they were thin and didn't meet in the middle; they had come with the house and she hadn't got round to making new ones. She left the briefcase in the car and locked it carefully. No need to take more incriminating evidence into the trap. Walking on the grass verges, she made her way back to the cottage.

The road here was well below the level of the house.

193

She saw that there was a car parked on the steep gravelled incline leading to the garage. If it was burglars, they were being remarkably open about it. Avoiding the gravel, she climbed the low front garden wall and crept across flower beds and lawn until she could see in the kitchen window.

The curtains were drawn, but quite a lot could be made out through the gap. From where she was standing she could see one side of the long kitchen table and the central-heating boiler in its recess behind it. The place didn't look as if it had been ransacked, or indeed disturbed in any way, and no one was visible. Must be on the other side of the table, if there was indeed someone there. Cautiously, she shifted her angle of vision, so that she was looking towards the side with the upright piano against the wall. Yes, there was someone there. She craned a bit further – he was sitting in the corner right by the window, underneath the standard lamp. He moved slightly, and she could make out his face.

It was Andrew Taggart.

41

'God,' said Becky, letting herself in the back door, 'you didn't half give me a fright.'

'Sorry,' said Taggart. He was eating some bread and cheese and reading a detective story. 'I just got back, and the secretary of your department said you were around, so I thought I'd wait.'

'How did you get in?'

'Easy.' He waved a plastic credit card in the air. 'You really ought to get a new lock. This one wouldn't keep out a child of four.' He looked at her. 'Why were you so frightened, anyway? Who could it have been?'

'How was I to know? I thought it was either burglars or Jerry Costigan.'

'Costigan?'

'I met him today. In fact – look, why don't we have a drink and I'll tell you the whole story.' She fetched a bottle of wine, poured a couple of glasses and told him about her adventures of the past few days.

'You mean you've got the stuff here?'

'In the car. If it was Costigan, I thought I'd be better without it.'

She went to retrieve the Mini and when she got back spread the papers out on the kitchen table. There were a lot of them, because she had copied them without really taking in what they contained. Looked at now, they seemed to fall into three groups. One consisted of the correspondence between *Natural Science* and Kotchinsky, including a copy of the Costigan article and a request from the then editor for an evaluation of it. Kotchinsky, as she already knew, had not been especially enthusiastic about the piece, but had been unable to make any specific criticisms of the material to hand. Was the editor able to supply any more detail? Unfortunately he was not, and it seemed to him unreasonable (he wrote) to ask for more detail than would be required for any other scientific report. The demand of parapsychologists was always that their science be taken seriously and treated like any other science. That was what he was doing. Costigan was well respected for his work as a physicist; the same criteria should be, and were, applied to his work as a parapsychologist. What, on those terms, did Kotchinsky think? On those terms, the magician replied, why was he one of the referees? One would hardly ask a magician to referee a physics paper; and if he was included among the referees for a paper of this sort, was this not because fraud might be suspected? No satisfactory reply to this seemed to have been forthcoming. Soon after, the paper was published. It seemed that Michael Anthony had been keener to give this piece of work space in his magazine than he had cared to admit.

This was followed by another set of correspondence, of more recent date, between Kotchinsky and a fellow magician named James Hotwell. The two had apparently met at a Magic Circle conference during which it had emerged that Hotwell had worked with Costigan on the famous set of remote-viewing experiments. After this meeting, Kotchinsky had sent Hotwell a long letter. He was still troubled, he wrote, about the Costigan paper, upon which so much store had been set and which had established (in certain eyes) both Costigan and his subject. Kotchinsky did not want to seem narrow-minded, but he was not convinced. In his opinion not enough enquiry had been made into how these extraordinary results had been obtained. An eighty-per-cent success rate was phenomenal and, if it had been obtained by parapsychological means alone, revolutionary. Could Hotwell shed more light on the subject?

James Hotwell, it seemed, was happy to oblige. As far as he was aware, no trickery had been used.

Costigan's procedure for his remote-viewing experiments had been fairly simple. During each series he worked with an experimental partner and a subject. The subjects were persons who had previously shown an aptitude for this kind of work; the partners were fellow parapsychologists. In each case, as he had described in the article, Costigan and his partner had selected a series of sites to be visited. Then one of them had gone off on site visits, perhaps two or three a day, while the subject had remained at the laboratory with the other partner. It was arranged that the travelling partner would be at one or another of the sites at prearranged times and would then, for a quarter of an hour or so, 'transmit' a picture of the site to the subject, who would record what he or she received, verbally or by drawing or both. Several series of these experiments had been carried out. They had, on the face of it, seemed very successful; at any rate, Costigan and his partner appeared satisfied that the subjects' descriptions frequently matched the places. But that was only the beginning.

After the laboratory experiments were over, the next stage was to test whether or not the descriptions of the different places could be matched by a third party to the targets they purported to describe. A list of the targets, with photographs, together with the subjects' descriptions and any drawings they had made, had been sent to Hotwell, who was an old friend of Costigan's and interested in this type of work. He had then matched transcripts and targets. It was on his success or failure that the experiment stood or fell. In the event, the success was amazing. He had matched the subject's description to the correct target in eighty per cent of cases, so apparently proving the reality of remote-viewing abilities. His letters to Kotchinsky indicated that the disinterested nature of his own involvement in this work could not possibly be called into question. There it was, and here were the transcripts. He added a note to the effect that other judges had been as successful as himself.

There was now an interval, during which Kotchinsky had thought about this. The first thing he had done was try to match transcripts with the target lists himself. He had found, to his surprise, that he, too, achieved considerable success. He then set about trying to analyse why this should be so.

Comparing the descriptions and drawings with each other, the success seemed almost inexplicable. They were, when it came down to it, singularly undifferentiated. They brought to mind in their universal applicability the famous personality analysis which, when presented to a class by a psychology teacher, seemed to every single member of the class a uniquely accurate description of his or her own personality. So how had Kotchinsky and Hotwell achieved their success?

After he had studied the transcripts for some time, Kotchinsky came (so he thought) to see how this had been done. For in the transcripts were not only descriptions, but various clues identifying the order in which they had been made. The first experiment, for instance, was characterised by nervousness on the subject's part. There was a reference to 'the second place of the day', which was the second target. Another reference was to 'yesterday's two targets'; this was the third target. Costigan congratulated the subject on having 'three successes behind you'; this was the fourth target, and so on. It was also noticeable that, as the series went on, the descriptions became less wordy. All these clues, taken in almost subconsciously by the reader, led inexorably to the correct order. Kotchinsky, having worked this out, then wrote to Hotwell, asking if he had been sent the list of targets in the order in which they were visited. Yes, replied Hotwell; he had. This was the same list he had sent Kotchinsky.

'Excuse my stupidity,' said Taggart when they reached this point, 'but I can't see why all this is so significant. I'm not versed in the arcana of parapsychology.'

'That's got nothing para about it,' said Becky. 'It's pure psychology. The experiment can only be valid if there's nothing there apart from the date to indicate what order things should go in. The first part of the experiment isn't really objective. The person doing the remote viewing—'

'Guessing.'

'Whatever you like to call it. The person sits there in the lab with Costigan or his partner. The other experimenter goes out to look at whatever's been selected. The subject, the guesser, describes whatever it is he thinks the experimenter's looking at. Then when everyone's back together again in the lab they decide whether the description really does fit the place or object, or not. Of course there must be times when it obviously doesn't, and times when it obviously does. OK so far?'

'Yes.'

'But then there'll be a lot of other times when it isn't so apparent. It might be, or it might not; depends what you read into it. A round object may be a bandstand or a pond or a coin on the ground or a dome – you can imagine. There's always the danger that the experimenter, who obviously wants the thing to work, will be carried away and score too many hits. Allow it as a correct guess, that's what we call a hit. So the really important part of the experiment is the double blind, when the set of targets and the set of descriptions are all sent to an outside judge, and he has to match them. It's perfectly clear what ought to happen. There should be a number of targets and the same number of descriptions, transcripts of what was said in the lab. No order for either set. But in this case what happened was that the outside judge was sent the list of targets in the order they were actually viewed, so that all he had to do was fit the correct descriptions to them. Well, that would still be all right if it wasn't quite clear from things that were said in the transcripts

199

what order the transcripts came in. So all the outside judge had to do was fit the transcripts to the targets in the right order.'

'But why didn't he realise that at once?'

'I suppose because you tend to see what you're looking for, and presumably the descriptions were ambiguous enough to fit. The internal clues were the kind of thing you could easily take in without realising.'

'Do you think Costigan realised?'

'That's the question, isn't it?' said Becky sadly.

The same question had evidently occurred to Kotchinsky and when he read about the establishment of Costigan Futures Ltd he had decided to have it out with Costigan. After all, this was not necessarily fraud aforethought; it might well be sheer experimental carelessness. Costigan, being a physicist, not a psychologist, had perhaps not been as sure as he ought to have been of the techniques for constructing a psychologically valid experiment. But people would be hazarding their money on the strength of the reputation his work had established. He had written to Costigan from Brighton where he was appearing, setting out his findings. What did Costigan think?

A week after writing this letter (the carbon neatly preserved in the file along with the rest of the material) he had suffered his fatal heart attack. There had been, it appeared, no reply from Costigan – at least, not on paper.

Becky and Taggart stared at each other across the pile of papers.

'So much for Jerry Costigan,' said Taggart. 'D'you think he did him in, somehow?'

'That's what Joe Horne thinks.'

'But do you?'

Becky said nothing. She felt thoroughly miserable. Six months ago, she reflected, she had been quite happy, pursuing a line of research which fascinated her alongside a colleague who was also an old friend and a world authority, conducting her life as she thought fit and having a lot of fun. And now the old friend had gone, brutally murdered, possibly by the same person who had just hammered the final nail into the coffin of her faith in her work – who also happened to be her present employer. And, a mere bagatelle but not without its significance for her mental state, her love-life was in tatters as well.

She shrugged. 'Why not?'

Taggart glanced at her sharply. 'Is that what you think of him?' When she failed to reply he went on, 'Cheating's utterly reprehensible, and all that, but would it really drive someone to murder?'

'It would be the end of his reputation . . . and his livelihood. Costigan Futures is built on that piece, really.'

'And on results – which it seems to produce . . . Anyway, I don't think Costigan Futures lives on its business income. It's a front for Cal Baker; one of his many, I guess. But you're right, he wouldn't be interested in someone who'd been exposed as a fraud.'

'What would he do?'

Taggart recalled the bizarre set-up near Ensenada: fish-eyed Padvaiskas and the unpleasant Mexican servant, and the body he had seen in the morgue. 'Have his head bashed in and dump him, I wouldn't be surprised. Drop him, anyway. I expect his mommy would instruct him to. Did you know Baker is running for President?'

'I think I did hear something in the news. I haven't been concentrating on current affairs just recently. If he did kill him,' said Becky, pursuing her own train of thought, 'how did he do it? Kotchinsky had a heart attack. They must have had a doctor in who said that. Wouldn't there have been an inquest?'

'Yes, there would. It's just the timing, isn't it? It's too convenient, too pat. Of course, there are ways of inducing heart attacks,' Taggart mused. 'I mean, if someone has a bad heart in the first place, all you need to do is give them a really awful fright. Or you can inject air into a vein, or administer a poison that's very hard to detect. . . . In the end, everyone's death's due to heart failure. The doctor can't be wrong if that's what he puts on the certificate. And if there wasn't any suspicion of dirty work, and if Kotchinsky had a weak heart anyway (we can check that; I expect Horne would know, or Mrs Kotchinsky certainly would), then no one would look much further. Why should they?'

'Suppose we can prove that Costigan was visiting Brighton when Kotchinsky died?'

'Suppose pigs flew. For one thing, if he really did knock the old boy off, he'd have been careful to make sure nobody knew he was there – and certainly that nobody saw him at the theatre. And supposing he was in Brighton? He used to work there, didn't he? I'm sure he's got lots of perfectly good reasons for being there. No, I should think it would be more or less impossible to actually prove anything at this distance. We'd just be laying ourselves open to libel.'

'We could publish the stuff. At least that would destroy his reputation.'

'How long have you been in this game?' said Taggart. 'You must know by now, surely. Once someone's established as a guru, nothing can destroy his reputation. Look at Uri Geller. Think of all the scepticism about him. Has it stopped him making millions? The fact is,' he concluded, 'people want to

202

believe, and nothing's going to stop them, certainly not boring old reason. No, we'll have to think of something a bit better than that, and one thing's clear: we're not going to think of it tonight.'

Becky, meanwhile, had been idly opening some letters that Taggart had found on the mat when he broke in and had thoughtfully stacked on the end of the table. She hadn't noticed them before. They didn't look interesting. Most of the envelopes were brown, with windows. There was one with a University of London seal on it. She saved it till last. It was a letter from Openshaw. 'Dear Dr Ryan,' it opened formally:

> I believe I mentioned that the Baker Foundation – which, as you will remember from our recent discussions, is interested in our field – is sponsoring a conference on Recent Developments in Parapsychology, to be held in Santa Barbara in October. As one of the organisers, I should like to invite you to give a paper.

'Anything interesting?'
Becky held out the letter.
Taggart perused it and his eyes widened. 'D'you think Costigan'll be there?'
'Almost certainly, I imagine.'
'Well, then, I think I see a way!'

42

The eve-of-conference party was held at the Santa Barbara Faculty Club, an elegant and luxurious setting which filled the British delegates with envy. There were a great many guests. The conference was the kind of thing that attracted a lot of publicity in this part of the world. In addition to such stars of the psi firmament as Openshaw, Charlie Cakebread (the Lamarckian who had had his own effect, the Cakebread Shift, named after him), Jerry Costigan (who had achieved enough certainty to start a profitable business based upon stock-market prediction), Karlis Padvaiskas (who, although not a full-time academic, had achieved such remarkable effects with cats), Ermintrud Schmeel (the flying-saucer expert from Syracuse) and many more, there were representatives of the press from all over the States – and not just interested in the parapsychology. The conference, after all, was part of what was intended to be a Presidential bandwagon which would roll Cal Baker all the way to the White House. It was the official opening of his campaign. He had already given a press conference in the Hollywood Hilton when he had hinted at the powers that would be available to him and which no previous incumbent had been able to tap. The conference, he assured everyone, would provide a foretaste of things to come.

'Any idea exactly what he has in mind?' Andrew Taggart, representing the British *Sunday Review* and *New Politics*, asked Tex McKendrick, a staff member of the Institute for an Ideal World, under whose auspices and in whose premises the conference was being held.

'I don't, exactly, but I do know there sure are going to be one or two surprises,' said Tex. He looked across with an inscrutable smile in the direction of a group of people gathered round the Presidential candidate.

'How on earth did you swing it?'

'Swing what?'

'Getting the circus set up over here.'

'Well, we're interested in this sort of thing. You knew that. I'm a member of the Heirs of Washington;

204

you knew that, too. The boss's wife is a great enthusiast—'

'Has she tried it again?'

'As a matter of fact I believe she did, and as I haven't heard any more about it I guess maybe it didn't work quite so well the second time. Still, she struck good once.'

'We may have some surprises of our own.'

'So I understood. I was talking with Dr Ryan. She's quite somethin', isn't she?'

'Maybe you'll have more luck than I did there,' said Taggart gloomily, remembering the extremely uncomfortable night he had spent on Becky's old sofa.

A tall figure detached itself from the crowd and began to wander slowly around the garden. 'I sure am looking forward to seeing Karlis doing his stuff with cats,' said Tex. 'Do you think he can read our minds this moment?'

'He wouldn't need to read minds to hear what we're saying,' said Taggart pedantically. 'Just exceptionally good hearing. In the jargon I believe it's called hyperaesthesia. But anyway, that isn't his bag. That was the late Jasper. He's the behaviour modification specialist.'

'Let's hope the rest of li'l Cal's campaign is as effective as his attempts to modify our behaviour, then,' Tex murmured.

43

Cal Baker stood at the podium surveying the audience. His stammer, so marked in ordinary conversation, was much more controlled in a situation like this. He had been taking expensive lessons, and all that could be detected was a certain hesitation, a sort of hiccup, at the start of some words. Nevertheless, he still failed to cut an impressive figure. The expensive suit and the aura of money and ambition only emphasised the puniness of the personage on the podium, the lights flashing on the pebble lenses of his spectacles.

'He must be nearly blind,' Taggart whispered to Tex.

'With that much cash he could be quadraplegic and still be up there,' came the whispered reply.

'It gives me great pleasure to open this conference,' Baker was saying. 'I believe it will mark a new start on many different levels. The human mind is capable of more than has yet been realised, and I believe we are on the brink of finding out how to tap some of this potential.'

'Like oil,' Taggart commented.

'I expect that's how he sees it. Except it won't run out.'

'The people who first achieve this will have great power,' Baker went on. 'And if, as I believe, those people are right here in this hall now, then we can be sure the power will be safe in their hands, to be used rightly and justly in the interests of the free world. My mommy always said to me – and still does, for she's able to talk with me almost as freely in death as she did

in life – "Cal, never hurt a fly . . . unless you have to."
Well, I reckon that's a fine philosophy, and I intend to
stick with that. And with your help that will be the
philosophy of the next President of the US of A.' He
looked up and glanced round, waiting for the round of
applause which ought to have greeted this line.
However, this being an academic rather than a
political meeting, consisting, moreover, largely of
non-Americans, it was not forthcoming. After a
moment he moved smoothly on to the peroration.
'And I can tell you that in that case, and as of now,
your work will have no greater friend than me, and
any help I can give you I surely will.' He sat down, and
now the applause rang out as the scent of cash sweetly
permeated the hall.

Nodding his thanks, Baker left the podium. His
place was taken by the chairman, who announced that
after a coffee break the conference proper would begin
with the first paper, in which Mr Karlis Padvaiskas
would discuss his work with remote behaviour modification in cats.

Over coffee Taggart asked Becky, 'Is he that
important? Would he usually open a conference of this
sort?'

She shook her head. 'I believe it was a special
request from the Baker Foundation.'

The hall was noticeably emptier for the first two
papers, given respectively by Padvaiskas and Openshaw. Padvaiskas described what was obviously old
stuff, with blurred film of cats moving in various
directions; his relentlessly snail-paced delivery did
nothing to enliven the occasion. Taggart sat through
it, waiting for any reference to what had been going on
at the Baker place, but there was no mention of it. For
the moment, it seemed, the secret weapon was to
remain a secret. Tex and Becky were off somewhere

else, and when Openshaw got up to take the podium Taggart decided to join them. The Cherfassian Professor's several carefully polite references to the preceding paper made it clear that he felt he should have been invited to open the conference, but when he began on his own work (the guessing of random numbers) it became apparent that, as openings went, this one would have been no more stirring. There wasn't even any film of cats.

Becky wasn't on until the following day. Her paper, on out-of-body experiences, would follow Costigan's; which would describe the work of Costigan Futures. That was for the next afternoon.

Filled with health-giving cottage cheese and fruit, the delegates assembled for their second afternoon. The morning had been largely taken up with a demonstration of fire-walking in which one person, who had (against all advice) stopped in the middle of the trench of coals to take a photograph, had got badly burned. The new and special powers referred to by the Presidential candidate had not yet manifested themselves; but since Costigan was well known and was talking about a proven business enterprise, a large audience assembled to hear him.

He began with a brief description of the remote viewing experiments which had convinced him that it was now becoming possible to control certain powers of mind systematically. Then he moved on to the work of Costigan Futures. He described its theory and procedures, and then went on to cite various outstanding successes it had achieved, including those involving Stallybrass and Mrs Heisenborn, who he believed was in the audience today (Prue, blushing, stood up and nodded). There was a statistical analysis of successes achieved, and then his time was up and questions were invited.

A smallish man with a head of wavy silver hair stood up. He spoke British English with a slight cockney twang and was clean-shaven with sideburns. Costigan stared at him as though he couldn't believe his eyes. The man wanted to know if certain queries regarding the original remote viewing work had ever been made public. If not, could he enlarge on them, and maybe Dr Costigan could deal with them here and now?

'What is your name, sir?' the chairman asked. 'Perhaps you'd like to make your point as briefly as possible.'

'Kotchinsky is my name,' said the silver-haired man, adding, turning back towards the speaker, 'I believe we last met in Brighton.' But when the chairman turned to Costigan, it became clear that he had been taken ill. He had turned very white and fallen back in his chair.

The chairman stood up. 'Ladies and gentlemen, I'm very sorry, but something seems to have happened to our speaker,' he announced anxiously. 'Is there perhaps a doctor in the audience . . .?'

Evidently that would be the end of Costigan's presentation. The audience milled about, buzzing with excitement. What was this query referred to by . . . Kotchinsky, was that the name? People looked to see if they could find him. Perhaps he would enlighten them further. But he had disappeared – absolutely vanished.

Tex turned to Taggart and Becky. They had been sitting together at the back of the hall. 'Was that your surprise?' he asked. When they nodded, he commented, 'Well, if you don't mind my saying so, it fell a little flat.'

'Flat?' said Taggart.

'Well, if only you two know what the hell was going on! Aren't you going to share the secret with the rest of us?'

'Us and Costigan,' said Taggart. 'Don't forget that. Boy, was he surprised!'

Becky said, 'It's me next. I must go and get ready.'

'This should be interesting', said Tex.'

'Don't you believe it,' said Taggart. 'Don't let your feelings for the dishy Dr Ryan blind you to the essential dullness of the work she does. None of your mysterious powers there, as far as I can make out.'

The audience was now reassembling, and after a short while Becky walked out on to the platform. She stepped confidently on to the rostrum and looked around. Her blonde hair, done up neatly in a French roll, shone under the lights, but even this most respectable of hairstyles failed to make her look very academic.

'Before I begin I want to make an announcement,' she stated. 'I am proposing to change the subject of my paper, and I hope you won't mind too much. I want to talk about survival of bodily death.'

Taggart looked at Tex, but he was giving nothing away.

'I want to start,' said Becky, 'by recalling the beginnings of our special area of interest. You will remember that this was all to do with the question of survival after death. That was the interest of the Fox sisters, who began the craze for spirit-rapping here in the United States in the 1850s; and that, although expressed in a rather more scholarly tone, was the interest of the founders of the Society for Psychical Research in London. And, of course,' she added, surveying the audience, 'that is still the great interest of a lot of us even here today. Mr Baker, for instance, talked about communicating with his dead mother.'

There was a pause, during which the audience, somewhat embarrassed, fiddled with its programmes and note pads. This was all very well but was it scholarship? Research into the paranormal at the end of the twentieth century had come a long way from those rather naïve and embarrassing beginnings.

'I personally was never particularly attracted by this aspect of our subject,' Becky went on, 'but it does have a certain undeniable fascination, especially when one experiences it oneself – as I have done recently.'

Taggart sat up. He couldn't imagine what Becky was up to. Tex remained impassive.

'It isn't given to many of us to actually meet ghosts,' continued the speaker, referring to her notes, 'but I hope you won't think I'm having you on when I assure you that this has happened to me twice recently. Twice I've met, spoken to and, well, touched people I know for a fact to be dead.'

There was complete silence. Everyone was listening now.

'The first occasion, or perhaps I should say the first ghost, you've all recently met as well.'

There was a crackle as everyone sat forward, wondering what on earth she meant. Pencils and papers fell to the floor unheeded.

'You may have noticed the devastating effect Mr Kotchinsky's question had on the last speaker. This is because Mr Kotchinsky, as the speaker knew for a fact, is dead!'

Now there was a buzz of excited chatter as everyone looked round for a sign of either Kotchinsky or Costigan, but neither was visible. Kotchinsky had presumably melted back into thin air, and Costigan had not yet recovered from the effects of meeting him again so unexpectedly. Becky, however, did not linger over this revelation, but went steadily on.

'But he isn't the only ghost I've met walking about recently. The second one will be known to a great many of you. You all read his obituary not so long ago. Now here he is to tell us about life beyond the grave. Dr Jasper Hodgkin!'

211

44

It took about ten seconds for the body of the hall to clear. Such press as had remained to cover the second day of what had seemed to be a notably uneventful conference rushed for the phones. The rest made for the platform. It is not often that one gets the opportunity to meet a ghost. And, if this was not a ghost, it is not often that one meets an old friend (for the parapsychological world is a small one, and almost everyone in it knew Jasper) apparently risen from the grave.

Which was he: a revenant or merely a case of mistaken identity? This was the first question on everyone's lips. One couldn't tell simply by looking, but he seemed solid enough – tall and suntanned, his dark, curly hair and tentative smile all exactly as before. He assured everyone that he was very well, none the worse for his curious adventures (his own phrase) and delighted to be back among them.

The press, having phoned their stories through, now returned to bombard him with questions. Flash-bulbs popped like silver rain. Meanwhile, virtually unnoticed, a small, silver-haired man hovered on the outskirts of the mob. It was the second ghost: Kotchinsky.

At this point Tex appeared, shouldering through the mob authoritatively. He put one arm around Jasper and another around Becky and yelled above the din, 'I'm sorry. Dr Hodgkin and Dr Ryan have been instructed not to talk to anybody. If you will excuse us now.'

He then nodded – a signal to some helper up in the gallery somewhere – and, in the best pantomime traditions, a trap-door opened beneath their feet, and they sank gracefully beneath the stage. They made it to the side door, where Taggart was waiting at the wheel of Tex's car. Kotchinsky was also waiting in the car. They piled in and roared away just as the mob, realising what was happening, arrived at the door in their turn, to be rewarded by a sight of the vanishing car.

'Well!' said Tex. 'That was great, really great. Did you see their faces? Oh, wow! How are you, ghosts?'

Kotchinsky, in the act of peeling off his silver hair, said with quiet satisfaction, 'I think we made our mark.' Joseph Horne's shiny black coiffure made its appearance. He shook his head with relief. 'Oof, that was hot.'

Jasper smiled.

Taggart, who was looking distinctly unwell, glanced back at him. 'Sorry, Tex,' he said. 'I don't feel too good. Could you take over?' He pulled the car to the side of the road and slid out. Tex took his place, and Taggart got in the back beside Becky.

'What's wrong?' she asked.

'Sorry,' he said again, shaking his head. 'I just wasn't prepared. You didn't tell me what was going to happen, and the last time I saw . . .' He nodded in the direction of Jasper and said no more. He hadn't enjoyed his visit to the morgue.

They drove on in silence, sobered somewhat by the memory that someone actually had been killed – two people, if Horne's suspicions of Costigan were correct. Tex turned into the dirt track leading to the Heisenborn place.

Taggart said, 'Are they expecting us?'

'Yup. I thought we'd better let Prue and Fred in on

213

it. It's his Institute, after all.'

A short while later they were sitting in the sun outside the Heisenborns' kitchen, clutching whisky sours and martinis. Nobody spoke, nobody knowing quite where to begin.

Taggart, sipping his whisky with unaccustomed relish, said, 'Well, of course I'm all for melodrama, but can you tell me quite what was the point of the last bit? I do as I'm told, no one can say I don't, but it isn't as if they were thieves or criminals or something. Isn't it the others who should be making the quick getaway?'

Tex glanced at Becky and said, 'I should have thought you'd appreciate it if anyone would.'

'Me? Why?'

'Why, we've just made you a present of the sole rights to the world's biggest scoop!'

45

'As a matter of fact,' said Jasper urbanely, 'I don't believe we've met.' He smiled his charming, rather fey smile across at Taggart, who was sitting staring at him and juggling the picture of the undoubtedly living Jasper with the indelible image of the bashed-in corpse he had seen at the morgue.

'It was Andy who identified your body,' said Tex, who was clearly enjoying the situation. 'Or brought it to the attention of those who could.'

'What did it look like?' Jasper was understandably curious.

'Well . . . like you – a bit. The face was smashed in. But hair, build . . .' Taggart gestured helplessly.

'Wonder who it was,' said Fred Heisenborn. 'I

214

guess they'll have to reopen the case.'

'I thought they were going to arrest me at one time, for want of anyone better,' said Taggart, recalling the dour Sergeant Shilling. 'At least this gives them something to get their teeth into. Especially as the finger points straight at Cal Baker. I assume he picked some poor bugger just because he looked like Jasper. Presidential candidate on murder charge . . .' He pictured the headlines, not without relish. 'Though I still can't work out why he did it.'

'I told you it was the biggest,' said Tex. 'As for the corpse, we'll come to that later.'

'So what happened?' asked Fred. 'One moment you're the late lamented and now here you are all over again. Tell us the story.'

Jasper and Tex looked at each other and burst out laughing.

Taggart said, rather huffily, 'I'm glad you think it's so funny. This has put some of us to considerable trouble and unpleasantness.'

The immediate effect of this was to make them laugh even more. Then Jasper collected himself, saying, 'Sorry. But I promise you that if it hadn't been for you I certainly wouldn't be sitting here now. You know that after the Cherfassian Chair interviews, Jerry Costigan offered me this job. Obviously I wasn't going to refuse. I was a bit bored with East Midlands' – he looked apologetically at Becky – 'and even if I hadn't been, it was a big anticlimax, I was all keyed up to do something new and bigger, you know how it is. So I probably would have accepted almost anything. But this wasn't just anything. It sounded rather interesting. And Costigan had already done some remarkable work.'

'Huh!' snorted Becky. 'We know how he did that now.'

'Well, not having access to privileged information, I

215

accepted it, like the rest of the world. And as for the new thing, it seemed to be working, too. Everything looked very prosperous, and business pays on results – unlike academia.'

Fred said, 'It certainly did work sometimes, but then I guess so does everything. It's the usual thing in that sort of line. People are so keen for it to work that they discount the times when it doesn't. It worked often enough for people to have plenty to talk about. That didn't have to be so very often.' Prue studied her fingernails.

'But when I got here,' Jasper went on, 'I saw that there was nothing really for me to do. I was just a figurehead, the name that drew people in. So after a while I got a bit bored with this and told Jerry I'd like to do some more work of my own. He didn't seem to mind at all, perhaps he'd been expecting it; and the next time he was over he introduced me to Karlis Padvaiskas.'

'Had you met him before?' asked Taggart.

'I knew his name, of course, and I'd met him once – at the Cherfassian Chair interview.'

'Sounds to me as if that was a selection board for more than one job,' mused Fred.

'I suppose it might have been,' Jasper agreed. 'Anyway, Karlis told me about these very interesting experiments that were going on down the coast, so of course I jumped at the chance. Jerry didn't mind. Probably as far as he was concerned, I'd done my job just by being nominally in charge.'

'We thought he was probably part of the Baker set-up anyway,' said Tex. 'My guess is, Baker financed the whole Costigan enterprise. He liked the idea of it, and it was a good way of recruiting people. That would explain a lot about Costigan's behaviour. He wasn't worried about Jasper because he knew where he was. But he couldn't say, because it was all secret. Boy, does li'l Cal like a secret. Takes the place of ideas. He only has two of those; he's for life after death and the paranormal, and against communism in all its forms, including liberalism or any kind of democracy.'

'And where's Padvaiskas in all this?' Taggart wanted to know. 'If you ask me, he bumped off that poor fellow, just hung around till he found someone suitable. He's a great one for hanging around. Though that's something else I don't see – why he did it.'

'I suppose in case people started getting worried. They wanted to have the option of keeping me as long as they liked, no questions asked. They live in this dream world,' said Jasper. 'Tex is right. Two ideas to be indulged at any cost, and Karlis is in charge of one of them. I believe they first met at some conference the Baker Foundation sponsored a few years ago, before the Heirs of Washington and that whole political side were even thought of. Karlis is an astute fellow; he must have realised he was on to a potential good thing and followed it up.'

'How political is he?' asked Taggart.

'I don't know. I couldn't make up my mind. He certainly believes in what's going on down there, but then I suppose he has to, or has to seem to.'

'What is it, exactly?'

'Oh, telepathy generally.' Jasper spoke as if this were the most normal thing in the world. 'It'd be particularly useful in communicating with submarines deep under water. That's the military application. At the moment they have to surface every time they want to make contact. It's most unsatisfactory. And long-range behaviour modification, of course: you get into their minds.'

'Whose?'

'Well, in this case, the Russians. And then you try to control what's there. It's not unconnected with what I was doing before. I was more interested in the techniques than the politics. Of course, Karlis isn't there full-time . . . or he hadn't been until recently. He had some job in the BBC, Latvian language broadcasts or something like that, so I imagine he's pretty paranoid, like most émigrés. Though I suppose', he reflected, 'it would be an ideal cover. He might just as easily be the KGB. Only he knows the messages he's sending.'

'You sound as though you believe he really is sending them!' Taggart could not keep an insubordinate note of disbelief from his voice.

Jasper looked affronted. 'I see no reason to dismiss the possibility. After all, in the case of my own work the results are certainly there,' he said stiffly.

Taggart was contrite. 'Sorry. So there you all were, happy as sandboys, working for the cause in Baja. What happened?'

Jasper took a pull at his whisky sour. 'Well, it was all right for a while. But there's a limit to what you can do without any contact with the outside world. In my work, for instance, I have to be able to check what's happening with other people in different places. Becky will understand. Actually, it took a while to sink in. We were quite busy, and life was very pleasant, but there was something peculiar, and I began to realise what it was. The place was completely self-absorbed. The outside world was simply discounted. Once I realised this, that there was virtually no outside contact with anyone except a few selected Heirs of Washington who came to visit on yachts from time to time, I began to want to get out, at least for a time.'

'And they wouldn't let you.'

'No. At first, the line was, why did I want to?

Wasn't there everything I could want there? It wasn't as if I was married or had any particular attachments to the outside world. But then it became clear that it wasn't a question of what I might like. There I was and there I was going to stay. I just knew too much about what was going on, for one thing, and I might not come back, for another.'

'Did Padvaiskas come and go?'

'Yes. I suppose the same queries didn't apply to him. So then I really started to get worried. I decided I'd leave on my own, whatever Cal might say, though obviously it wouldn't be easy. But when I went to look I found that my passport and all my credit cards had been quietly removed – I don't even know when – and of course I hadn't a bean. You don't need cash at the Baker place.'

'So what happened?'

Jasper glanced towards a slim, dark girl who had wandered out of the house and joined the circle. Taggart had assumed that she was some relative of the Heisenborns. But apparently not. 'That', said Jasper, 'was when I met Cara.'

46

Everybody turned to look at the dark girl. Jasper was gazing at her affectionately. Becky, Taggart noticed, looked singularly unenthusiastic. Evidently Cara was news to her, unwelcome news at that.

'Are you a friend of Cal Baker's?' he asked.

'I knew him,' said the girl demurely. 'I went around with that crowd at one point.' With her swinging, glossy hair and designer jeans she represented the ur-Californian girl, someone who would blend instantly and seamlessly into any crowd west of the Sierra Nevada. So why not the Heirs of Washington, a crowd like any other – so long as you didn't listen to what they were saying? 'We used to fish off Cal's place in Baja,' Cara went on. 'It was a great place. They have this yacht—'

'Was that the one we saw?'

Tex nodded. 'That's the one.'

'I never really used to listen to what they were all saying,' continued Cara. 'Then I heard Jasper's name, and I thought: wow! Unreal! Jasper's always been a hero of mine. I guess I must have been to hear him every time he's spoken here in California. I'm into auras,' she explained, 'and he has this wonderful aura . . . green – you can see it now . . .'

Everybody looked, but no one could see a green aura. There was an embarrassed silence.

'What Cara hasn't said', Tex put in, 'is just who mentioned Jasper's name to her in the first place.' He paused, then answered his own question. 'Me.'

'You!' The response was all Tex could have hoped for. Becky stared incredulously. Taggart and Prue burst out laughing. Fred Heisenborn seemed unsurprised; perhaps he had been in the secret all along.

'You knew I knew them,' Tex reminded them. 'How else did I get to be the errand boy? After I saw Andy the first time, I met Cara at that place in Santa Monica, and she mentioned this yacht that went fishing off the Baker place. So I said I'd heard a rumour that Jasper Hodgkin was mixed up with them – did she know anything about that? I was just fishing, of course.'

'So then next time we were in Baja, I just asked Cal,' said Cara. 'And he said, sure, Jasper was there, and

220

would I like to meet him? So I did, and we kind of got to know each other.'

'Karlis must have been cross,' said Taggart.

'Yeah, I really think he was,' Cara agreed. 'I guess he wanted to keep Jasper a secret. He kind of took me to one side and said I mustn't tell anybody. So of course I said I wouldn't. And I didn't,' she added virtuously. 'Tex knew already.'

'In the end it's Baker who pays, after all,' said Jasper. 'I think he thought he would reconcile me to my fate by providing every possible comfort. Within the bounds of what he conceives to be possibility, of course, which narrows the parameters somewhat. . . . So anyway, there was Cara, and she seemed friendly enough, and I had to talk to somebody. So one day, when we were swimming, I told her what was happening, that as far as I could see they were just going to keep me there indefinitely as a sort of secret weapon.'

'I just couldn't believe it,' said Cara. 'But then I began to see it was true enough. So we began to work something out. Next time I was in Santa Monica I called Tex and told him, here's Jasper, no cash, no passport, we've gotta do something. And he said he was going to deliver some work down to Baja, and it turned out that that was when I was going to be there on the yacht. So fine, Jasper and I often went swimming – well, no one's going to escape by swimming all the way up to California, they didn't worry about that, and it's kind of hard to disappear on a yacht where everyone knows you and wants to talk with you all the time. So Tex told me when he was going to be there and where he was going to put the car. That was easy. I knew that beach. So we swam round the promontory and there it was, and there was

221

this little boat with Tex and you,' she nodded to Taggart, 'so I knew that part was OK. And we found the car where Tex said it would be, this great big Chrysler with a big trunk. So Jasper got in the trunk—'

'It was very thoughtfully arranged,' said Jasper. 'Towels and dry clothes, cushions and a couple of air holes. But I can't say it was comfortable. I was more or less comatose by the time I got out.'

'And what about you?' said Taggart to Cara. 'Didn't they give you a hard time when you got back without him?'

'No, no.' She smiled sweetly at him. 'I rode with you as well. I was on the floor at the back. Under the boat.'

Taggart shook his head. He wasn't sure what he thought about being part of someone else's story.

'The way we figured it was this,' said Tex. 'If you didn't know, then you wouldn't have to pretend you didn't know. You'd act real natural because it *was* natural. We couldn't let Cara go back, and we couldn't let them see there were more than two people in the car. If they'd done anything more than just wave at us through at the frontier, Cara had her passport, and she could pretend she'd just been asleep. But there's never any trouble there – not if you're white. People just go back and forth all the time.'

'After Ensenada, I kind of came out from under the boat,' said Cara. 'But you were asleep most of the way.'

Taggart shook his head. 'And you mean you were both there, hidden away, all the time? Wasn't that rather unnecessary, once we were across the border?'

'Sure,' said Cara. 'We got out at La Jolla, while the windscreen was being fixed and you guys were having a hamburger. Remember? My folks are from La Jolla. We just went to their place.'

'And here we are!' Jasper concluded. 'Large as life and much more than twice as natural. I can't tell you how glad I am to come out of limbo!'

At this point Prue left the room and returned with several large pizzas and some six-packs of beer. Everyone realised that they were very hungry except Becky, who had been getting more and more red-faced as Jasper and Cara's recital progressed, and who now left the room, closely followed by Tex.

The phone rang. Fred picked it up, listened and said, 'Really? Gee, I'm sorry I missed that. No, I haven't heard a thing. Nobody's here. I guess they've headed off somewhere. Sorry I can't help you. You're welcome.' He put the phone down and said, '*LA Times*. I guess it can't be long before the pack gets on our tail. And before it does, there are one or two things we have to decide.' He turned to Jasper. 'First off, what about you? You're not safe. You should get out of the country. Cal Baker is a nasty and dangerous piece of work, and he won't leave you alone while there's still a chance of shutting you up. I'm being serious. Have you got a passport?'

'Yes, I went to the consul and explained I'd lost mine.'

'Wasn't he rather surprised to see you? You were supposed to be dead.'

'He didn't know anything about that. This was in Philadelphia. I guess Angeleno corpses don't make it into the *Inquirer*. They've got enough of their own. I left Cara's almost at once; we have some family friends in Philadelphia, and I thought her place might not be safe.'

223

'It wasn't,' she said. 'Karlis came to call just after you went. I'd warned my mom someone might, and she told him I wasn't there and she hadn't seen me. I was hiding in a closet at the time.'

'He didn't telepathise you?' said Taggart.

'Seems not,' she replied seriously. 'He was hanging around the place for a while (I guess that would be about a month ago now?), but then he gave up. I just stayed inside.'

'What I don't understand', said Fred, 'is why you didn't just go to the police straight away and tell them they'd made a mistake after all and you weren't dead. Then you'd have been OK; they wouldn't have been able to do a thing to you.'

'Well, for the first few days I was so tired. You can't imagine. What with all the effort, and that journey and then having to get out of Cara's – I just slept for about two days. Then Tex called and told me about this conference, and I was beginning to wonder whether it wouldn't be rather fun to confront them all in public.'

'Rather fun!' scoffed Fred. 'Gee, you guys can be so childish. You simply don't realise . . .' He gave up with a shrug.

'And then Becky called and told Tex they were going to confront Costigan with a ghost, and Tex told me. So I thought, what a good idea! I simply couldn't resist it, and nor could Tex.'

'The first thing you have got to do', said Fred in the tone of voice of a mother reminding her infant for the fiftieth time that he must put his shoes on before he goes out, 'is get out of the country. Out. Now. You and I are going to the airport and you are getting the first flight out to Britain.'

'I haven't any money. Costigan Futures stopped paying me, and I discovered they're still deducting rent from my bank account. Apparently being official-

224

ly dead doesn't release you from a leasehold. Anyhow, I'm not dead, I'm alive.'

'Write a book,' advised Taggart. 'You'll make a million.'

'No problem,' said Fred crisply. 'Charge it to the Institute. You're welcome. It's the least we can do.' He got to his feet. 'Do you have everything you need? Where are you staying? With Tex? OK, we'll pass by there and you can pack a bag. And then we shall go to the airport by way of the police station. You're not leaving this country without letting everybody know you are officially alive. You'd better come, too, Andy.'

47

Sergeant Shilling did not look pleased to see them.

'Mr Taggart,' he said. 'Yup, I remember. What is it this time? You got another body for me? If so I'll thank you to give me the name of the murderer, too, or else I've a mind to take you in for false information.'

'I haven't, not exactly,' said Taggart. 'I thought you'd like to meet Dr Jasper Hodgkin.'

Shilling rocked his chair back on its back legs. 'Excuse me?'

'Dr Jasper Hodgkin.'

'I thought that's what you said. Well, Dr Hodgkin, I sure am mighty pleased to meet you. Wasn't that your body I was dealing with just six weeks or so ago?'

'It wasn't mine,' said Jasper.

'No.' Shilling stared at him. 'Now, how do I know that? You got proof of identity?'

Jasper pulled out his passport and chequebook.

Shilling studied them for a long time, then handed them back. 'Well, I suppose I gotta believe you. All these folk think you're Jasper Hodgkin? OK. Who's the other guy, then?'

'I'm afraid I can't tell you that,' said Jasper politely. 'But I've reason to believe that you were supposed to think it was me.'

'So who killed him?'

'I think probably a man called Padvaiskas.'

'Pad-who? What makes you think that, Dr Hodgkin?'

'It's a long story.'

'Sit down. I've got all evening.'

Jasper told his tale. At the end of it, Shilling rocked back and forth on his chair. For a while he said nothing. Then, pleasantly, as if to an invalid, he said, 'You are asking me to believe that Mr Baker, the Presidential candidate and I believe a well-respected fellow, kept you prisoner down in Baja to work on thought-controlling the Russians while his friend Mr Padvaiskas went out and killed your look-alike and tied your scarf around his neck so that they'd have something to point to if anyone came looking for you?'

'That's about it,' Jasper agreed. 'Put like that, it does sound rather unlikely,'

'Rather unlikely,' Shilling echoed him absently. 'Yup. And what am I supposed to do?'

'I don't know. Arrest Padvaiskas?' Jasper offered diffidently.

'What for? What evidence have I got? You say they kept you prisoner. But you're here, aren't you? You haven't been hurt. It's your word against theirs. Even if you're telling me the truth – and I'm not saying you're not, you may be, why would anyone make up a story like that, for Chrissakes? – all they have to do is say, "Excuse me, officer, what are you talking about?

Sure the fellow came and stayed with us, but he was free to go any time he wanted. All he had to do was ask. As for this body, it's nothing to do with us." And what could I say? It was wearing his scarf. The world's a big place, Dr Hodgkin. Are you really sure that was the only scarf in the whole world like that?'

'Well, if you put it that way—'

'I sure do. Just like any lawyer would. No, Dr Hodgkin, I'm sorry. If I wanted to make damn sure I never got promoted and that I'd be the laughing-stock of the entire precinct, I'd do just what you suggest. As it is, I'll cross your name off my books and that'll be one more body nobody's identified. It happens all the time. Have a good flight.'

Some hours later, Fred and Taggart returned to the Heisenborn house. Taggart had almost decided to return to Britain with Jasper and Cara (who had decided to accompany him to Britain, whether with his active consent was unclear) – but Fred had dissuaded him.

'For one thing,' he said, 'you'll be able to file your story quicker from here. Why waste fifteen hours? At the moment you have this incredible story that you know more about than anyone else. Better get it in quick. Then you can go home, if you still want to.'

Taggart allowed himself to be convinced by this reasoning, and also by the fact that he owed a certain duty to Joe Horne, who was alone with Prue (unless Becky and Tex had reappeared) at Santa Barbara. Sure enough, when they returned they found just the two of them.

'Tex and Becky must have gone off somewhere,' said Prue. 'I got the distinct impression that she was rather upset by Cara.'

'Yes, I think she was.' Taggart did not enlarge on this. He suddenly felt very tired.

'Shall we have the news?' Prue pressed the button on the television. Taggart dozed gently until he felt Prue shaking him. 'Hey, Andy, listen to this!'

It was the local news. Against the background of the conference hall, a breezy young man was speaking to the camera. 'A conference of investigators into the paranormal at the Institute for an Ideal World here at Santa Barbara today featured two people supposedly returned from the dead,' he informed them. 'The conference was sponsored by the Baker Foundation, run by Cal Baker, the Independent candidate for President, and Mr Baker himself opened the proceedings yesterday. Mr Baker is a firm believer in life after death. Neither of the "ghosts"' (the young man spoke the parentheses with emphasis) 'could be found for comment after their appearance, so we don't know how real, or unreal, they are, but one of them was, or seemed to be, the well-known parapsychologist Jasper Hodgkin. Hodgkin came to work here in Los Angeles this summer, and his body was supposedly found and identified in Venice Beach at the end of August. Los Angeles police department say that they saw Hodgkin this evening, and he seemed pretty solid to them. The body that was found remains unidentified.'

'Better get your copy in quick,' said Fred to Taggart. 'I wonder when they'll make it here.'

'Oh, I forgot to tell you, they did. A whole mob of them wheeled up just after you'd all left, but there was nobody here except Joe, who they didn't recognise without his wig, and me. So we just told them we couldn't help them, and they all whistled off again in search of something or other.'

'Not that it would have meant anything to them if they had recognised me,' said Horne. 'That was more of a private affair. Strictly between Costigan and me. I haven't got anything on him, you understand – nothing definite. Kotchinsky was about to blow the

228

gaffe, and he knew it. Kotch died in Brighton, and Costigan was in Brighton that evening; that much I do know. Someone saw him at the show. But more than that . . .' He shrugged.

'What d'you think happened?' asked Prue.

'Who knows? Now, if I were clairvoyant . . . What do I think? I think Costigan went round to the dressing room after the show and—'

'And?'

'Perhaps he had some, what's it called, ricin on the end of his umbrella, like the KGB man who wiped out that Bulgarian in the middle of the rush hour,' offered Taggart. 'Puncture the skin and, bam! that's it.'

'He wouldn't have needed it. All he needed to do was pretend he had something like that. Kotchinsky had a heart condition; he'd had several heart attacks. He knew that what he'd found out destroyed the whole basis of all Costigan's claims about remote viewing. Suddenly the dressing room door opened and in came, of all people, Costigan himself, threatening who knows what if he breathed a word to a soul. It was quite enough to make poor old Kotch drop down dead on the spot. Heart failure, just like the doctor said.'

'The point is,' said Taggart, 'we know he'd decided to face Costigan with all this. He wrote him a letter – we found the carbon in his files. And a week later he was dead. That was the whole point of this charade. It gives us something really sensational to pin on Costigan. In the normal way of things, it's the kind of thing that nobody wants to know. Real clairvoyance gets the customers in; boring academic explanations of how it's all done are a complete turn-off. But the guilty party fainting away when faced by the avenging spirit of the man who spotted the fraud – that really should grab 'em. So excuse me while I go and write it. Could I borrow a typewriter?'

48

Fate, 15 October:

MONKEY TELEPATHY MAN RETURNS FROM DEAD

Dr Jasper Hodgkin, whose name will be known to all our readers, featured in an astonishing scene at the conference on Recent Developments in Parapsychology at Santa Barbara last Saturday. Hodgkin, who had recently been working for Jerry Costigan's Costigan Futures enterprise (see our May 10 issue) and for Cal Baker, whose interest in psi is a byword and whose Heirs of Washington Foundation sponsored the conference, had been reported dead. His body was discovered at Venice Beach and identified by friends and members of the Costigan office. But Saturday's audience saw an apparently quite solid Dr Hodgkin mount the podium to announce that either he had risen from the dead or he had never been over to visit on the 'other side'. . . . Despite their predilections, conference members preferred the latter explanation. Dr Hodgkin and a woman friend then took an early flight to London, where he is reputedly working on a book about his astonishing experiences.

Sunday Review, 20 October:

THE CANDIDATE'S SECRETS – MY ASTONISHING EXPERIENCES AT CAL BAKER'S SECRET HIDE-OUT – HOW JASPER

HODGKIN RETURNED FROM THE DEAD
– by Andrew Taggart

As all Americans and most Britons by now know, Cal Baker, far-right candidate in the coming Presidential elections, likes to announce that he has a secret weapon which will ensure his election. I am now in a position to reveal the nature of this weapon, and how Baker tried to force Dr Jasper Hodgkin, a British parapsychologist, to help him develop it. After a visit to Baker's luxurious hide-out in Baja California, Mexico, a friend and I were able to rescue Dr Hodgkin – we drove him out of Mexico hidden in the boot of our car. But before Hodgkin turned up in Mexico we had thought he was dead. I personally had helped identify his body in a Los Angeles morgue. The identity of this body, who killed it and why are still unanswered questions – though I have some ideas on the subject. But the extraordinary story of Cal Baker, his Heirs of Washington Foundation and his obsession with parapsychology and the supernatural can now be revealed for the first time.

Jasper Hodgkin's first – and unknowing – contact with Baker's people took place at the selection board for the Cherfassian Chair in Parapsychology. . . .

Santa Barbara, 7 February:

Dear Andrew,

I've been meaning to write to you for ages. I felt really bad about never having said goodbye when you went back to London, but I felt so awful at the time – I'm sure you understood. It was silly, but people are silly.

Anyway, I decided to stay on here for a bit, as everyone was so kind and I couldn't bear to go back to East Midlands, what with being paid by Costigan, which seemed somehow obscene, and also Jasper decided to go back to his house there for the moment and write his book, which I expect will make him a million. In the end Cara didn't go with him, I understand she thought East Midlands was a poor exchange for California, which is understandable. She was expecting him to marry her, and the combination of EMU and not being married after all was too much for her. I could have told her he wouldn't. She's published her version of it all in the *Ladies Home Journal*, and I expect you know already that Jasper sold the rights of his book to *Millennium* for half a million – dollars, not pounds, but there isn't much difference these days, is there? One good result of all this is that it's finally broken me of my irrational addiction to Jasper, which has lasted ever since I was a student and made it quite impossible to consider anyone else or any other topic seriously. My belief that there had to be something in OOBs and psi went at about the same time. I don't know whether to be glad or sorry. It's a write-off of so many years. I'm not the only one to be quitting parapsychology. I hear that Costigan Futures has packed up. There was a lot of publicity here. *Nova* did a TV programme about it all, as well as your pieces being published in the *LA Times* and lots of stuff about the unknown body, etc. I know everyone says that any publicity is good publicity, but I don't think anyone much wanted to use Jerry's services after all that. They were afraid they might get bumped off, I expect (there was quite a lot of garbled stuff about the identity of the second revenant at the conference, etc., etc.). And I don't expect there was any more backing from Baker – Jerry's no use to him now. Baker as you know is ploughing on, but nobody expects him to survive the primaries. If he does, it really will be a triumph for those secret powers he keeps talking about. As for Jerry, he seems to have sunk without trace. I heard he wanted to go back to CERN, but they wouldn't have him. And of course his name is mud in psi circles. Poor old Kotchinsky. I still can't make up my mind about all that. One part of me thinks, or would like to, that Jerry really did believe he was on to something world-shattering, and that Kotchinsky dying was just a coincidence. The alternative's so awful, and it isn't as if Jerry's barmy like that appalling Baker, who I can imagine ordering someone to be killed quite easily. But I suppose one has to face facts, or probabilities. My guess is that things just went further than he intended. I expect that accounts for an awful lot of murders (if that's what it was). He's probably teaching physics in some Midwestern college somewhere, and knowing Jerry, he'd think that was punishment enough for anything he'd ever done, though I don't expect Mrs Kotchinsky would agree with him, for one. As far as I know, the other body, the one that wasn't Jasper, is still unidentified. I expect he was some rent-boy or druggie or something. It's awfully easy to get lost out here. I don't know if Padvaiskas really did have anything to do with that, but if he did the police certainly haven't been able to pin it on him. I noticed he was billed to talk about his cats at a psi seminar only the other day.

Well, I don't suppose we'll ever really know about that. Anyhow, what I really wanted to say was that Tex and I are going to get married, and we'd really like you to come if you can. I've got a job in the Institute and we'll live in Santa Barbara. I thought it was about time I settled down, and Tex is such a sweetie . . .

At this point Taggart threw this letter aside in disgust and went down to the kitchen, where he smashed four cups and three plates that were in the sink waiting to be washed. After that he felt slightly better. He wondered what one had to do to qualify as a sweetie.